S0-CFT-941

"If you let me, Courtney, I will be your friend...."

His head lowered until his lips lightly brushed hers. "And more."

How long had she wondered about this man and dreamed about his touch, his kiss? Now, finally, she had the chance to relive that moment aboard ship when he had held her and kissed her until the very breath had left her lungs. She had replayed that scene in her mind for so long, she was certain she had magnified it beyond reality. Right now, this moment, Rory MacLaren was here. He was no longer just a dream; he was real, and warm, and inviting.

Rory wrapped his arms around her and drew her into his embrace.

"Much more than a mere friend," he whispered as his mouth covered hers.

Annie's Book Stop
Roak Mall
229 Center Street
Auburn, Maine 04210

ACE PAPERBACK EXCHANGE

Market Place Mall - 675 Main St.
Lewiston, Maine 04240
786-4505

Dear Reader:

You are about to become part of an exciting new venture from Harlequin—*historical romances*.

Each month you'll find two new historical romances written by bestselling authors as well as some talented and award-winning newcomers.

Whether you're looking for an adventure, suspense, intrigue or simply the fulfilling passions of day-to-day living, you'll find it in these compelling, sensual love stories. From the American West to the courts of kings, Harlequin's historical romances make the past come alive.

We hope you enjoy our books and we need your input to assure that they're the best they can possibly be. Please send your comments and suggestions to me at the address below.

Karen Solem
Editorial Director
Harlequin Historical Romances
P.O. Box 7372
Grand Central Station
New York, N.Y. 10017

Mistress of the Seas

Ruth Langan

Harlequin Books

TORONTO • NEW YORK • LONDON
AMSTERDAM • PARIS • SYDNEY • HAMBURG
STOCKHOLM • ATHENS • TOKYO • MILAN

Harlequin Historical first edition November 1988

ISBN 0-373-28610-4

RUTH LANGAN

traces her ancestry to Scotland and Ireland. It is no surprise then that she feels a kinship with the characters in her historical novels.

Married to her childhood sweetheart, she has raised five children and lives in Michigan, the state where she was born and raised.

*To Elly,
for nagging me*

Prologue

1610 The Irish Sea

The deck of His Majesty's Ship *Admiralty*, ran red with blood. Though the sailors fought bravely, they were no match for the skill of the men who continued to pour across the rails from the pirate ship *Hawk*.

Below deck, the frightened young woman listened with growing horror to the sounds of the battle. The shrieks and wails of dying sailors drove her to the edge of hysteria.

The captain of the *Admiralty* had warned that theirs was a perilous mission. The presence of the two flagships alongside had given her a false sense of security. But the first ship had been badly damaged in a storm on their first day out and had limped back toward a distant speck of land. Yesterday their second protector had disappeared mysteriously during the fog-shrouded night. That event had caused great alarm among the crew of the now-helpless frigate. All morning the men aboard had been tense, edgy. Had they suspected that their vulnerability would invite an attack by pirates in these dangerous waters? Or, worse, had they guessed that the flagship had been deliberately lured away by pirates determined to strike?

At the sound of heavy footsteps, the young woman swallowed back the fear that clogged her throat and glanced at the child who had been given over to her care during this voyage.

"You must not make a sound, do you hear? Not a sound."

The child blinked, then nodded.

The young woman threw open a wardrobe and thrust the child inside, then arranged a heavy cloak in such a way that there was no trace of the human form beneath.

"No matter what happens, no matter what you hear, you must not allow them to find you. Is that understood?"

The child nodded, and the heavy cloak sagged with the movement. The young woman pressed herself against the door and stood, waiting. Within seconds the door to the cabin burst open. Swarthy faces stared at her in surprise before moving menacingly closer. Behind them, a tall, dark figure loomed in the doorway.

"English wench," one of them said with a laugh. Catching her roughly by the arm, he drew her close.

She flinched at the sting of his hot breath against her cheek.

"Not pretty, but a warm, soft body nonetheless."

The young woman bit her lip to keep from crying out. The child mustn't sense the terror that gripped her.

Lady Montieth had been warned about the fate of women taken by pirates. A woman of gentle birth whose family had served royalty for generations, she knew what she must do. There was no other choice.

As the pirate tossed her toward the waiting arms of the second, she took the dagger from her pocket and plunged it in with all her strength. It found her heart.

The men fell back, shocked. They had seen death in a hundred different ways. They were immune to it. But the thought that a delicate Englishwoman would take her own life rather than allow herself to be touched by them was unfathomable. The sight of her blood spilling from the bodice of her pale pink gown left them stunned and reeling.

The tall, dark-haired man strode forward, taking charge. Kneeling, he touched a finger to the feeble pulse at her throat. He stared at her for a long moment, then stood.

When he spoke, his voice was that of a cultured English nobleman. "The wound is mortal. She dies even as we watch. Boney." He turned toward a shriveled sailor whose arms and legs were as thin as a young girl's. Every one of the old man's ribs could be counted through the fabric of his striped shirt. "Remove these men, then find her a pallet, so she may die in dignity."

"Aye, cap'n." The man pushed and shoved the others from the room, then shuffled back within minutes with a folded blanket. As he bent toward the woman's form, he stiffened and drew back.

"Death has already claimed her, cap'n."

"Wrap her. We will see she has a proper burial."

The skinny little man rolled the figure in the blanket and staggered under the deadweight as he carried his burden to the deck.

The captain of the pirate ship moved restlessly around the cabin before settling himself at the desk and opening the ship's log. Seeing the king's seal upon the first page, he spat a torrent of oaths. Though English by birth, he'd been stripped of all land and titles by that same monarch. Seeking refuge at the French court, he had proven himself a shrewd and brilliant sea captain. It was with the unspoken blessing of the French that he sailed these waters, protecting French vessels and those of their allies and plundering any ships flying the English flag.

"Cap'n Thornhill, the ship is listing. The men are anxious."

Thornhill glanced up. "According to these papers, this ship carries no cargo. Yet they had the protection of two flagships. What think you, Boney?"

The old man scratched his head. "The men searched the hold. There was little worth salvaging."

"No gold? Silver? Arms?"

"Nothing more than a hundred or so bolts of fabric and some barrels of fine salt pork. Do I have your permission to allow the men to return to the *Hawk* with their bounty?"

The captain nodded absently and continued to read the ship's log. When the old man returned minutes later, he found the captain, a glass of whiskey in his hand, still poring over the ship's papers.

"Begging your pardon, cap'n. Do I have your permission to take the rest of the whiskey back to the *Hawk*?"

Thornhill glanced up in irritation. "Take anything you wish, Boney. I will follow in a few minutes."

The old man shuffled around the cabin, looking for treasures to loot. Finding a trunk, he opened it, glanced at the array of exceedingly small feminine fashions. Then, with a snort of disgust, he moved to the wardrobe. Spying the heavy cloak, he snatched it up, then stood staring as if he couldn't believe his eyes.

"Will you look what I found, cap'n!"

Annoyed by the further interruption, Thornhill turned. His eyes widened. Pushing back the chair, he stormed toward the wardrobe, then stood, hands on hips, legs far apart, staring down at the tiny figure. Bending down, he plucked her from the cramped quarters and placed her atop the desk.

She was the most beautiful little girl he'd ever seen. He guessed her age to be four or five. Her hair was neither red nor brown but a rich, dark sable that fell in soft curls to her waist. Her features were perfectly formed, with a small, upturned nose and high cheekbones. Her chin was firm, her brow wide. But it was her eyes that held him. They were a curious shade of amber, with just a hint of green in their depths. At the moment they were observing him as carefully as he was observing her.

Because of her restless nature, the child had always been a handful for Lady Montieth. Once again she had disobeyed that gentle lady's orders. She should not have let these men find her. But, she reasoned with a wisdom far beyond her years, there was nowhere to go. The door to the cabin was closed, and this man before her was as big as a giant.

"What is your name, girl?"

She continued to stare at him, and he thought her head lifted just a fraction. Defiance at such a tender age?

"God's blood, girl. Out with it. Too afraid to speak?"

"I do not fear you."

If her voice trembled just a bit, there was no hint of fear in her eyes. Yes, defiance. He'd knock it out of her, and quickly.

"You had best tremble in fear of me, girl," Thornhill said scornfully. "I hold your fate in my hands."

He saw her glance shift to his hands, and he realized that she had no idea what fate was.

But he did.

His gaze rested on the tiny gold medallion that hung on a chain around her neck. He lifted it and read the inscription, then read it again before throwing back his head and letting out a roar of laughter.

Hearing him, Boney took a step closer, peering at him as if he'd lost his mind.

"What be funny, cap'n?"

"This." He removed the chain from her neck and placed it around his own, letting the medallion drop down the front of his ruffled shirt. Then he turned toward the child's trunk. Lifting a sheaf of papers, he read quickly, then turned once more toward the little girl.

"Oh, this is heaven-sent. A sweeter revenge I could never find." Sauntering back to the desk, he stared into the child's intelligent, watchful eyes and gave her a chilling smile. "Your name is given as Anne Courtney Elizabeth. Which do you prefer?"

"Courtney," the child said without hesitation.

"Courtney it is." Turning to the old man, he boomed, "Boney, take Courtney to the *Hawk*. Have her trunk put in my cabin."

"Yours?" The old man stared at him as if he'd gone mad.

"Have you forgotten who gives the orders here?" Turning, Thornhill fixed his gaze on the little girl, who stood quietly watching him. Why did she not cry like other females? he wondered. Why had she not dissolved into a whimpering heap? No matter. "She is mine now. I claim her as my own. When I have finished teaching her, she will be the best pirate ever to sail these seas."

"Cap'n..."

"Leave me. Take her now. Do as I say."

Turning, Thornhill picked up the papers and continued reading. When the old man and the little girl had gone, he rolled the documents and carefully tied them before tucking them into his waistband beside his dagger.

Strolling to the deck, he stood a moment, feeling the ship shudder beneath the onslaught of the waves that would soon devour it. As he glanced at the activity aboard the *Hawk*, a smile curled his lips, making his dark features almost handsome. The child was standing between two sailors, watching him. He swung over the side of the ship, then stood by the rail until the *Admiralty* sank beneath the waves. But he wasn't really seeing it. He was seeing his future.

What an amazing treasure he'd just discovered. What sweet revenge was within his grasp. The daughter of his bitterest enemy would now be molded in the image of

Thornhill himself. And the best part of all was, she would never know. She was so young, he could erase her past. In time it would all become only a dim memory.

Chapter One

1624

The *Hawk* cut a sleek path through the shimmering waters of the Atlantic.

The prisoners, dulled by pain and hampered by the chains at their ankles, were led slowly on deck of the pirate ship. Some had been captured when their boats had been engaged in battle by the *Hawk*. Others had been obtained by Thornhill from French prisons. They came from every part of the world: Africa, Persia, Corsica. They understood very little of the words being hurled at them by the French pirates, but they understood the lash. Whenever they failed to move quickly enough to obey orders, they felt the cruel barbs of the whip being wielded by one of the crew. Some were taken below deck and chained to oars, where they would stay until they dropped. Then they would be replaced by the remaining slaves, who for now were handed rags and buckets of foul-smelling liquid and ordered to kneel.

Rory MacLaren knelt with the others, scrubbing the deck beneath the blazing sun. The chains tore viciously at his ankles, leaving them raw and festering. He clenched his teeth and willed himself to rise above the throbbing pain.

At least here on deck he could see the sky and fill his lungs with the familiar salt air.

Unlike some of the prisoners brought aboard the *Hawk* during its last stopover in France, he never doubted that he would survive. Though he had spent more than a month in a French prison, as a spy and was now considered a permanent slave aboard the *Hawk*, he knew in his heart that one day he would return to his beloved Scotland. It was that thought, and that alone, that allowed him to endure.

A blur of color high in the rigging caught his attention. Wiping his brow with his ragged sleeve, he watched as the captain's daughter moved high above the sails with the grace of a dancer.

From his first day aboard the *Hawk*, Rory MacLaren had watched Thornhill's daughter with riveting fascination. He had first seen her at court, in Paris, where she had been arrayed like royalty in a gown of green satin, with lace inserts at bodice and hem and cuffs of rich ermine. Her thick sable hair had been coiled primly around her head in the latest fashion, and there had been diamonds and emeralds at her throat and ears. The fops at court had preened and strutted like peacocks, vying for her attention. But she had seemed much more interested in affairs of state than in affairs of the heart. A most unusual woman.

Here aboard the *Hawk* she bore no resemblance to the woman he had seen at court. Here she was like some wild creature, with her fiery hair streaming down her back in a riot of curls. She was garbed in a crimson shirt with wide sleeves, with a colorful sash tied around the waist of the tight breeches she wore tucked into tall black boots. Unlike most of the women Rory knew, she had sun-kissed hair and skin, a distinctly unfeminine trait, but the figure beneath the flamboyant clothing was definitely womanly, with high, firm breasts and waist narrow enough for his hands to span. The thought caused Rory's lips to curl into a near-smile for one brief moment. Then he bent once more to his task, lifting his head occasionally to watch her.

"By the gods, she truly does exist. She is not merely the ramblings of a score of madmen."

Rory turned toward the slave beside him. "What are you babbling about?"

"The wench." The swarthy slave raised his head a fraction. "What think you, Scotsman? Is she not the famed Mistress of the Seas?"

Rory's hand clenched tightly around the filthy rag. Stunned, he lifted his gaze once more. Of course. How could he not have guessed? The notorious Mistress of the Seas. For years rumors had been carried by sailors fortunate enough to have survived an attack by a pirate ship. They told of a stunningly beautiful female pirate who did not fear to leap into battle with men twice her size and strength. A woman who could handle a sword and dagger with the skill of a man.

Bending to his task once more, Rory watched her surreptitiously. Thornhill's daughter, the Mistress of the Seas? Was it not obvious that she could do anything the men could do aboard ship, only better? It was she who fearlessly climbed the rigging, hanging high above the deck, oblivious to wind or rain. She obviously knew how to read the stars and was trusted to chart ocean currents. Often she stood by the helmsman at the wheel when the captain went below deck.

From his first day aboard the *Hawk*, Rory MacLaren had had many opportunities to observe the lady. And what he saw only intrigued him more. She laughed and chatted easily with the men aboard the ship, conversing in fluent French and Spanish, as well as English. She had learned enough foreign dialects to get along anywhere in the world. The men told bawdy stories as they worked shirtless beside her and treated her in every respect like one of the crew.

There was a camaraderie in every way, Rory had noted, except one. No one ever touched her. No one. The sailors aboard the *Hawk* took great pains to avoid even standing too close to her. No one ever took her arm or brushed her sleeve. Odd. As if, Rory thought, narrowing his eyes, she wore the mark of a leper.

He turned, squinting into the sun, and studied the tall, dark figure of the captain, who stood beside the helmsman. Thornhill's gaze was fixed on the girl, and as usual he was scowling, giving his features the dark look of the devil himself. It wasn't only the captain's hair and eyes that were black, Rory thought. It was his soul, as well. It was obvious to all who looked upon him. He was a man who enjoyed engaging ships in battle. What was more, he seemed to savor killing. Rory studied the captain, wondering what black deed had closed the man's heart and darkened his soul?

"Back into the hold with you, English dog." One of the crew cracked his whip across Rory's back as the string of slaves was herded across the glistening deck.

Courtney, descending the rigging, heard the sound and winced. Though she had spent more than ten years of her life aboard this ship, she had never grown accustomed to the cruelty. The men, confined to the ship for such long periods of time, often took out their anger and frustration on each other or on the slaves, who bore the brunt of such fury.

She watched as the tall, broad-shouldered slave seemed to draw into himself in order to bear the pain in silence. From the day he'd come aboard with the others she had noticed something about him. He was tall, taller even than Thornhill. But that was not what set him apart. Despite his prison pallor, there was a sense of strength and vitality about the man. Power, she thought with sudden clarity. Though he was a slave in tattered prison garb with chains around his ankles, he had about him an aura of power. Of command. She studied him more closely. Some might have considered him handsome. His shoulders were broad, his back and arms corded with muscles. His hair, though matted and dirty, showed an occasional russet glint. And the beard that darkened his chin was red. His blue eyes, she noted, were in shocking contrast to his skin. A deeper blue than the ocean. A clearer blue than the heavens. And it was his eyes that held her whenever she found him looking at her. Eyes that seemed to see clear through to her soul.

This attraction to a man, and a slave at that, surprised her. She had crossed the oceans of the world. She had tasted the spices of India, the ripe, sweet fruits of darkest Africa. She wore silks from China and had walked along the perfumed shores of mysterious islands in the Caribbean. She had watched the sun rise like a brilliant orange globe from the Indian Ocean and had sailed beneath a canopy of stars in a black-velvet Mediterranean sky. And along the way she had grown into a beautiful, educated woman, completely at ease in a man's world. Never once had she been remotely attracted to a man.

Courtney suddenly realized that she'd been staring shamelessly. She flushed and looked away in confusion. When she turned back, the slave was still studying her in that narrow, watchful way of his. He continued to stare until she thought she couldn't bear his look another minute. Tossing her head, she flounced past the line of prisoners and headed for the galley, where she would spend a pleasant hour with her only friend, Boney.

The skinny little man called Boney moved among the slaves, handing out gobs of ointment that smelled worse than the stench in the hold and burned the flesh until a man thought he might welcome hell itself. It was Boney's own concoction, and though it was vile, it worked. Sores closed over and scabbed. Raw flesh healed.

It wasn't a generous spirit that sent the gnarled old man among the prisoners, it was simple necessity—or so he told himself. He was, after all, a pirate by choice. He had freely chosen to follow Thornhill into exile. Though he knew every cruel act the man had ever committed, his devotion to Thornhill was absolute. He had been with him since Thornhill's childhood. He would never abandon him. And so he justified the little kindnesses by telling himself they were necessary.

It had been necessary to befriend the little girl who had been hurled into this strange, harsh world. Necessary, he told himself, for her survival. And though he turned a gruff face to the others, with Courtney Boney could never be anything but gentle. He doted on her. He had become not only friend but mentor and grandfather, as well. And no one, not even the captain, was fooled.

It was the same with this ritual. It was not that he was kind. Boney knew in his heart that this medicine was necessary. Without humane treatment there would be no slaves to keep the ship functioning. And so, each night, when the slaves were returned to the hold and chained to the wall, he moved among them.

"Old man."

Boney turned at the low tone of command, squinting in the dim light of the ship's hold, and found himself looking into the blue eyes of the Scot. The old man had often marveled at the Scot's ability to endure pain. The powerful back and shoulders were crisscrossed with scars from beatings he'd been given in the French prison, and his wrists and ankles would forever bear the marks of the chains. But the Scot had the bearing of one born to royalty. He showed compassion toward his fellow slaves, often taking a beating one of them deserved and caring for those too ill to care for themselves.

"Aye?"

"Tell me about the female."

Boney glowered at him before dipping his hand into the bucket of ointment and smearing it in the Scot's hand. "Mind your tongue. I would never speak of Courtney in this heathen company."

"Courtney." Rory tried out the name and found it suited her. "Why does Thornhill not leave her at the court of his king? Life would surely be gentler there than aboard this crude ship."

"What the cap'n does is not my affair." Boney moved on, handing out his precious ointment. When all had received their share, he stepped over the sprawled bodies and stopped once more beside the Scot. "Courtney is the finest sailor aboard this vessel."

"Aye." Rory saw the look of pride on the old man's face and knew he was softening. "She had a fine teacher, I would wager."

Pleased, Boney nodded and handed the Scot a second generous helping of ointment. While Rory slathered it on his wounds, the old man continued, "I've been with the cap'n since he was a lad. He's a hard man. But the lass is tough enough to stand up to him. Probably the only one who has ever stood up to him and lived to speak of it."

Boney knew he was saying far too much to this stranger, but he seldom had the chance to boast about the girl who was such a source of pride to him. The two had formed a bond since the day of her arrival aboard the *Hawk*. "I watched her scrub decks until her hands were bloody and raw. But she never complained." His eyes twinkled at the memory. "And she has never dissolved into tears like most females." His voice lowered, and he glanced around to make certain that those around them were asleep. "Only once."

"When was that?" Many times Rory had thought about breaking his chains and using the old man as a hostage to escape. But he had given up all thought of it. Even his fierce strength couldn't break these chains. And he had ascertained the first night aboard ship that Boney never carried any keys on his person. But the old man was useful just the same. He had knowledge to share. Rory gave him his undivided attention.

"The night her young friend, Ian Horn, saved her from being swept overboard during a storm."

Something in the old man's tone of voice caused Rory to become more alert. "Why would that make her cry?"

"Because the cap'n had issued stern orders that no man was ever to touch Courtney. For any reason." Boney stooped down so that his voice wouldn't carry to anyone who might be listening. "She and the lad had become good friends, though it was all very innocent, she being only eight or nine and he about ten year and three. When the storm struck, she was near the rail and would have been swept overboard if Ian had not reached out and caught her. When the cap'n saw it he ordered young Horn to stretch out his hand on the rail. That very minute, in front of Courtney and the entire crew, Thornhill cut off the lad's hand with his own sword."

Rory swallowed the bile that rose to his throat. What sort of man would reward his own daughter's savior in such a manner? How many other brutal things had the girl been forced to witness?

He fought to keep his tone even. "A hard man, your captain."

"Aye." Boney stood, instantly regretting the fact that he had taken this Scot into his confidence. The captain would have his head if he knew. "And a man as good as his word. No man has ever dared to touch her again."

When the old man climbed the ladder and the door to the hold was slammed shut, Rory MacLaren lay in the darkness and contemplated what he had just heard. Courtney. A name as beautiful as the woman who bore it. But she had witnessed horror, as well as beauty. A most unusual story. A most unusual woman.

* * *

The *Hawk* had been at sea for months. This latest voyage had been a long and profitable one. The crew of the *Hawk* had sailed from the placid waters of the Isthmus to the stormy, often turbulent waters off the coast of Wales. They had encountered ships flying flags from as far away as Persia and Turkey, the seat of the Ottoman Empire. Except for those under the protection of France, all had been engaged in battle. And all had fallen to defeat at the hands of Thornhill and his skilled pirates.

The crew was edgy, eager to set foot on solid ground once more. Courtney did not share their enthusiasm. Although it was always exciting to return to Paris and the gossip and political intrigue at court, Courtney was happiest at sea. Though she'd been forced to spend prolonged periods of time on land, getting a proper education, as Thornhill called it, she was at home only aboard the *Hawk*. She was accustomed to the screech of sea birds, the shouting of the crew. Even late at night, as she lay on her bunk, there were familiar sounds—the creaking of the rigging as the *Hawk* sliced neatly through the water, the slap of the waves against the hull. A life away from the *Hawk* would be unthinkable.

Courtney stood by the rail, watching a spectacular sunset. The sails had been lowered, the anchors dropped. The ship bobbed on the waves in a soothing, rhythmic motion. From below she heard the rattle of chains as the slaves were released from their oars and returned to the ship's hold. Soon the sounds of life would fade as everyone aboard the *Hawk* fell into an exhausted slumber.

This was Courtney's favorite time. She was free to spend a few moments in the galley with Boney before retiring to her cabin, where she could study her precious maps or read from her meager supply of books.

When she walked into the galley she was stunned to see the tall, red-bearded slave standing beside the gnarled old man. The slave's eyes narrowed at the sight of her.

Boney barely glanced up as she entered. "Hold this," he said, handing her a bucket.

Motioning for the slave to turn, Boney began slathering his ointment on the slave's back. The slave let out a hiss of pain, then straightened his shoulders and curled his hands into fists at his sides.

The slave's back had been laid open by the whip. The flesh hung in jagged strips. His tattered shirt was soaked with blood. Seeing it, Courtney caught her breath. Then, in an attempt to hide what she considered a weakness, she said in an icy tone, "He must be a very disobedient slave to deserve such punishment."

"Aye. Or a fool," the old man said, putting a generous amount of the ointment on his other wounds. At Courtney's arched look he added, "He took a beating for another, knowing the man was too weak to survive."

Courtney felt an unexpected mist spring to her eyes and blinked it away.

The old man took the bucket from her hands and placed it on a scarred wooden table. As he was about to usher the slave from the room, a voice shouted, "Boney. Quickly. One of the crew is spitting up blood."

The old man seemed torn between going to the aid of a crewman and staying to watch the slave.

Seeing his dilemma, Courtney pulled a dagger from her waist. "I will guard the prisoner, Boney. See to our man."

"Aye." The old man squinted up at the towering figure. "See you mind what the lady says. Those men who were foolish enough to doubt her strength lie at the bottom of the sea."

Rory watched as the old man hurried away. If ever he was to escape this hell, now was the time. He measured the distance between the girl and the crewmen milling around near the rail of the ship. There might be a chance. He studied the dagger in her hand. He had faced deadlier weapons in the hands of men twice the size of this slender creature. He willed himself to be patient. If there was a way to escape, he would find it.

Turning his back, he said softly, "The old man neglected several wounds. Will you be good enough to administer his ointment?"

Courtney stared at the bloody back and glanced away quickly. "I cannot."

Rory turned toward her. "The old man said you were a kind and compassionate woman. Was it said in jest?"

She swallowed, avoiding his steady gaze. "I cannot touch you."

"Cannot?" His eyes narrowed. "Or will not?"

As he took a step toward her, she backed away. Reaching a hand toward her, Rory was surprised to see her cringe before lifting the dagger.

"Do not touch me."

"And if I do? Will you run your dagger through my heart?"

"It is not my dagger you will have to fear. It is my father's wrath."

Rory smiled a cold, dangerous smile and took another menacing step. "I know of Captain Thornhill's orders. The old man, Boney, told me. I also know of your friend's fate when those orders were disobeyed." His tone lowered. "But I am not a cabin boy." His chilling smile grew. "And you are no longer a child."

His gaze swept over her, lingering for a moment on the swell of her breasts, visible beneath the crimson silk shirt. Then he lifted his eyes once more to her face and noted the flush that stained her cheeks.

In one quick movement his hand grasped her wrist, and the dagger clattered to the floor. Her eyes widened in surprise.

No one, no one since the story of Ian Horn had been told and retold, had ever dared touch her. But this man was like no other man she had ever met. His fingers were strong.

Strong enough to snap her bones like twigs. Yet even as that thought flashed through her mind, his grip relaxed and his touch gentled.

"You must not—"

"Shhh." Still holding her wrist, he lifted his other hand, pressing a finger to her lips to silence her. He took a step closer and stared into her eyes. Such unusual eyes. Pale amber, with little flecks of green. In them he could read all the emotions that flickered through her. Surprise. Shock. Anger. Fear.

Fool! he berated himself. He must run while there was still time. It would be a great risk to attempt to make it to the rail before one of the crew spotted him. He could hear their voices just beyond the galley. But was not his freedom worth the risk? Still he did not move. Instead, he found himself mesmerized by this strange woman. Her lips were so soft against his callused fingers. As he continued to hold her by the wrist, he could feel her pulse racing. His own was none too steady.

Courtney felt the heat where his fingers rested upon her flesh. Her sensitive lips pursed against his fingers, then drew back. The hand at her wrist sent tiny flames spreading along her arm and shoulder until her entire body seemed consumed by fire. He was holding her so gently that she could easily pull away, and yet she was unable to move. The hypnotic blue of his eyes held her, tugged at her, until she could no longer think.

She wanted to feel. For just one moment longer, she wanted to feel his fingers, warm on her flesh. What would it feel like to be held in those powerful arms? To be pressed to his chest? To be kissed by those tempting lips? God in heaven, where had such thoughts come from?

She took a deep, shuddering breath and pulled away, breaking contact.

"Never touch me again." Why was it so difficult to speak? Her throat was dry; her words were barely more than a whisper.

"Are you afraid of what will happen to me if I do?" Rory's lips curved into a smile that sent icy needles along her spine. "Or are you afraid for yourself?"

Because his taunt was too close to the truth, she ignored him and bent toward the fallen dagger. As she straightened, she saw two of the crew entering the galley.

Striving for a tone of authority, she said, "You, Simpson. Return this man to the hold."

When she reached the rail, she took in great gulps of night air, then turned. The slave was watching her, while behind him one of the crew held aloft a sword.

For long moments Courtney's gaze locked on the slave's. Was it possible that he could still touch her from so great a distance? Could a simple touch from a dirty, ragged slave leave her so unnerved? Had the man bewitched her?

Lifting her chin, she strode toward the privacy of her cabin to sort out her thoughts.

Chapter Two

With new determination, Courtney threw herself into her chores. There was much to be done aboard the *Hawk*. Thornhill assigned daily tasks to all his crew, and Courtney was expected to work alongside the men. Because of her education and her unique position as captain's daughter, there were additional duties, as well. The navigation of the ship was her responsibility. There were new routes to be studied, weather to be charted. And since, from her earliest days, she had sought the companionship of Boney in the galley, it was now taken for granted that when she had finished all her other chores she would assist the old man.

With all that, it should have been easy for Courtney to avoid the slave. It should have been, but it was not.

He was there in the early-morning mist, dragging his chains across the deck with the other prisoners. As she rounded the corner of the galley, she nearly collided with him. She found herself staring into startling blue eyes, and she would have sworn that beneath the cool gaze a hint of laughter lurked. For one shocking moment she stiffened. Then she drew back until the line of slaves had passed.

He was there in the scorching afternoon sun, bent to his menial task of scrubbing the deck. As she climbed the rigging she could feel his gaze on her, cool and penetrating. When she had reached the very top of the rigging, she looked down from her perch and found his head lifted, his eyes narrowed and searching. When a gust of wind caught her hair, she turned her face toward the sun and felt a ripple of laughter spring from her lips. With the slave watching her, she felt... she felt beautiful. Color suffused her cheeks. What was happening to her? Many times through the years she had felt the stares of curious crew members or slaves. Always she had ignored them or even considered them mildly offensive. Why, then, did this man's narrowed gaze make her feel different? He was touching her, she realized with a shock. Though he was held fast by chains and forced to watch from afar, he was touching her. Touching her in a way that made her flesh oddly warm, her heartbeat oddly erratic. Was it possible for a man to touch her from so great a distance?

Tossing her head, Courtney wound her arm through the rigging and pulled out her spyglass. Scanning the horizon, she suddenly frowned. Land. By day's end they would be passing very near enemy land. They would have to alter their course and stay far from shore. Perhaps, if they were fortunate, they could slip past the land under cover of darkness, thus avoiding detection.

When she came down from the rigging and passed the line of prisoners, Courtney noted that the slave was no longer watching her. His gaze was riveted on the horizon. In his eyes she could read a naked hunger.

Courtney leaned on the rail and watched as the sun slowly disappeared beneath the water, turning the waves into a spectacular sea of fire.

At the sound of voices, she turned. Boney, holding a torch aloft, led the way as a tall figure in chains struggled to carry a heavy burden. She recognized the muscular figure immediately. The slave. The one who watched her. The one who touched her. As he turned she could see that the burden in his arms was another prisoner, obviously unconscious.

She began to run toward them as they disappeared into the galley.

"Set him here." Boney indicated the scarred wooden table.

MacLaren did as he was told, then moved aside to allow the old man to examine the prisoner.

"It will not be ointment this one will be needing." With quick, strained movements, Boney forcefully removed a knife from the prisoner's chest and placed several folded rags to sponge the flow of blood.

"How did this happen?" Courtney looked from the pale, unmoving figure on the table to the slave who stood silently beside him.

"Simpson plunged his knife into the prisoner when he refused to pick up his oar." Boney lifted one of the man's hands, emitted an oath, then dropped the hand and watched it fall heavily to the man's side.

Courtney gasped. The man's hand was bloodied beyond recognition. It would have been impossible for him to handle an oar. One look should have told the first mate that this man had been worked beyond his abilities. But Simpson, like the others aboard ship, was growing increasingly weary and frustrated by the *Hawk*'s extended time at sea.

What sort of brutality were the slaves forced to endure below deck? Courtney had always managed to avoid knowing. But she had heard the cries and moans, had seen the bloodied limbs, the scarred flesh.

She glanced toward the tall slave, who stood regarding her in stony silence. "And what of this one?"

"He was the only one strong enough to carry the other above deck." Boney watched as the color slowly drained from the dying prisoner's face. The man had lost too much blood to survive.

With his back to Courtney the old man added, "Take the slave on deck until someone can take him below and chain him with the others."

Courtney felt a tiny thread of alarm begin to curl itself around her midsection. Did the old man know what he was asking of her? Did he have any idea what danger this slave posed? Not physical danger, for the man was unarmed and in heavy chains. Her dagger would find its mark before he could ever overpower her. If he was foolish enough to jump overboard, he would sink to the bottom of the ocean. But he was a danger nonetheless. With one look from him she became like a weak and trembling leaf. With one touch of his hands she was rendered incapable of movement.

"And if you think to overpower the female," Boney added without taking his gaze from the man on the table, "know that you will forfeit your life if any harm should come to her."

In the light of the torch she saw the slave's lips curl in a smile.

"The lady has nothing to fear from me."

The simple sound of his deep voice had her trembling. Resolutely taking out her dagger, Courtney followed the slave from the galley. Hampered by the chains at his feet and hands, his walk was slow and labored.

Except for the helmsman at the wheel, and Thornhill, who was taking a reading of the stars beside him, the deck was deserted. Neither man took any notice of the two shadowy figures.

The slave lifted his head to the soft breeze, then crossed the deck to the rail, where he breathed deeply. Her dagger in her hand, Courtney paused beside him. She saw the slave's gaze drift to the rugged coastline in the distance. The hunger was still evident in his eyes.

"You know that land?" she asked.

"Aye." His voice was low, choked with emotion. "It is Scotland."

Though from the tone of his voice she knew the answer, still she asked, "Your homeland?"

He nodded.

"Is your family there still?"

There was a barely perceptible nod of his head.

"Tell me about them."

He turned, and in the lengthening shadows she saw the haunted look in his eyes. "My brother, Malcolm, is older than I by two years. When our father died, he became the MacLaren."

"MacLaren. That is your name?"

"That is our clan. MacLaren. And the acknowledged head of the clan becomes the MacLaren."

"Do you mind that your brother is now your leader?"

He smiled, and she thought how handsome he was. The growing darkness hid the dirt that caked his hair and clothing and masked the scars of numerous beatings. All she could see was the outline of his powerful frame. His blue eyes burned with intensity, and his lips, nearly hidden beneath the thick red beard, though proud and firm, seemed touched with a seductive softness.

"Mind? Nay. It freed me to pursue my love of the sea."

"I knew you were a man of the sea," Courtney whispered. "By the way you plant your feet on the deck, the way you fill your lungs with the sea breeze." Why did that fact make her heart soar?

"Aye. I love the sea," he admitted. "As I can see you love it."

Oh, how she loved it. Especially on a clear night, with the sky dripping stars. "Tell me about your land."

His voice, when he finally spoke, trembled with emotion. "Scotland is the great love of my life. Greater even than my love of the sea. It is a rugged land, with high, rocky crags and great, sprawling forests." His voice softened. "But it is much more than a harsh, rugged place. It is beautiful, too. A green land, with clear lakes and meadows in summer that bloom with heather as far as the eye can see."

Her tone grew wistful. "It must be wonderful to have a land such as that."

"Tell me about your land, your home."

She hesitated, then said, "The *Hawk* is my home."

His smile widened. "What land do you call home?"

"I have no land. Only the *Hawk*."

He studied her closely. "A pity. Everyone should have a homeland, a place to which they belong. What of Thornhill?"

Courtney cast a quick glance toward the helmsman. Thornhill was nowhere to be seen. He had retired to his cabin for the night. "He calls France his home."

"But the man is an Englishman. His manner of speech confirms that."

"Do not let Thornhill hear you say that. He swears allegiance to Louis of France. He has vowed vengeance on every English dog who dares to cross his path."

Rory grew silent for a moment, deep in thought. No matter how vehemently Thornhill protested, it was clear that he was English born and bred. What punishment had the captain endured in England to harbor such resentment? And if he had been punished, did that not suggest a crime? Of what crime was Thornhill guilty?

"Regardless of his oath of vengeance, the man is English. As his daughter, does that not make you English, as well?"

Courtney laughed, and Rory felt a little thrill at the husky sound of her laughter. It was rare indeed to hear joyous sounds aboard this dark pirate vessel. "Thornhill declared me a French citizen."

"Citizen, perhaps," Rory said thoughtfully, "but I have seen enough dark-eyed French women to know that you are not one of them." Her hair, a rich, fiery auburn, and her eyes, the color of a stormy sea, suggested she was Irish or

English. The porcelain skin for which the English were famous had been darkened, but life aboard ship would turn any cool beauty into a sun-kissed goddess.

"Courtney," he said, touching a hand to her hair. Soft. It was as soft as a foal's coat of fine down. He had an almost overpowering desire to plunge both hands into her hair.

She had never, never heard her name spoken like that. He made it sound reverent, like a prayer.

She took a step back, brandishing her dagger. "How is it you know my name?"

"The old man told me."

"Boney?" She studied him for a moment, straining to see his eyes in the growing darkness.

"Aye."

"And why would he tell you my name?"

"I wanted to know by what name the Mistress of the Seas was known."

At the mention of her title, she smiled ruefully. "So that is how I am known among sailors."

"Aye." He took a step closer and felt her stiffen.

She refused to back away, choosing instead to hold her ground. Her hand tightened around the handle of her dagger.

"It is not right that you know my name and I know not yours."

"Rory," he said, watching her through hooded eyes. "Rory MacLaren."

"Rory MacLaren." She said it slowly, carefully, rolling it around on her tongue to see if it fit the man. "It is a fine, proud name."

He went very still, shaken by the emotions that surged through him at the sound of his name on her lips.

They heard voices below deck and knew that someone would soon be coming to return him to his prison. Without taking time to weigh his actions, Rory moved a step closer, until they were almost touching.

Lifting the heavy chains, he touched a hand to either side of her face. She flinched and began to draw away, but his big hands tightened their hold, and she was pinned, unable to move away or even to turn her head.

"You must not do this. I order you to stop."

"Is it Thornhill's wrath you fear? Or is it really my touch, Courtney?"

She froze, afraid to move, afraid even to breathe. The feel of his rough hands on her skin sent ripples of pleasure pulsing through her veins.

"I do not wish anyone to suffer as my friend Ian Horn suffered because of me. Not even a slave, Rory Mac-Laren."

"It was not because of you that he lost his hand." Rory's voice lowered until it was a mere whisper. "It was because of Thornhill's cruelty. From what I heard, the lad had just saved your life."

"But he had to touch me to save me. And in so doing he paid a very dear price."

"Aye." Rory lifted her face for his slow, lingering scrutiny.

As Courtney's cheeks grew hot, he added, "Perhaps, for one as beautiful as you, the price was not as high as you think."

Tears sprang to her eyes, and she quickly blinked them away.

"Have my words made you weep?"

"I am not some weak, whimpering female who cries when she is wounded," she said, echoing Thornhill's oft-repeated words while wiping furiously at her eyes.

His voice was warm with unspoken laughter. "Indeed you are not. You are not like any female I have ever encountered. But," he added tenderly, "tears are not a sign of weakness. I saw my father weep, when we buried my mother. And the MacLaren was the strongest man alive. There are times when we are overcome with emotion. At such times, tears should be shared with those we love.''

For a moment she relaxed against him, fighting an almost overwhelming desire to cry. What in the world had come over her? Why did this man's kind words and simple touch make her want to weep? A choked little sob escaped her lips before she swallowed it down and blinked away the tears that sprang to her eyes.

Courtney could not believe what was happening to her. Never, never had she cried. Not when her young life had been forever altered, nor when she had been forced to accept the cruel life of a pirate. And certainly not when she had felt the sting of Thornhill's lash whenever she broke one of his rules. She had wept only once. When Ian Horn's hand had been cut off as punishment for touching her. She had cried as though her heart would break. And now, with this stranger's gentle words and touch, she was embarrassing herself again by crying.

With the heavy chains binding his wrists, Rory clumsily cradled her head against his chest. Her hair swirled forward, covering his hands with a silken cloud. How long it had been since he had felt a woman's soft body pressed to his. He savored the touch of her hair and inhaled the soft, womanly scent of her.

Lifting his hands over her head, Rory drew her firmly against him. She was caught, not only within his arms but with his chains, as well.

For one shocking moment she stiffened, determined to push her way free. She brought her dagger to his throat and jerked her head upward, prepared to do battle.

The face looking down at her held no anger, no threat. His eyes, those piercing blue eyes, caught and held her with a look so burning, so intense, that she had to force herself to look away. His mouth hovered mere inches from hers.

She felt his breath warm against her cheek and was drawn to it.

"You need only draw your blade across my throat and you will be free."

"Do not tempt me, Rory MacLaren."

He brought his face closer, and her hand tightened its grip on the dagger. She stared, transfixed, at his mouth, mesmerized by the thought of those lips on hers.

"I would pay any price," he murmured, bending toward her, "to touch you." His lips brushed hers, and he growled against her mouth, "To kiss you."

At the first touch of his lips, she was lost, lost in a blur of sensations that left her reeling. His lips were warm and firm, and the mere feel of them against her mouth sent icy needles dancing along her spine. As he took the kiss deeper, the ice became heat, the heat became fire, until she found herself clinging to him as a drowning man would cling to a lifeline.

How different his body was from hers. He was tall, so tall she had to stand on tiptoe to reach his lips. The arms encircling her were corded with muscles. The callused hands pressing into the small of her back were strong enough to break her bones without any effort. Yet they held her as carefully as if she were a fragile treasure. His chest was hard and muscled, as well, and she felt the imprint of his body on hers. But it was his lips that held her enthralled. Those clever, agile lips. As his mouth moved over hers, she forgot to breathe. Her heart forgot to beat. She gave herself up completely to the pleasure of his kiss.

As her lips warmed and softened under his, Rory lost himself in her. There was fire in this woman, a fire he had anticipated. She was a wild, untamed creature who would never be content to be a passive lover. But as he continued to hold her, to kiss her, he discovered something more. Something completely unexpected. There was about this woman a sweetness, an innocence, that left him stunned and reeling.

What he was doing was madness. If he was caught he would not forfeit a mere limb. For plucking this forbidden fruit, Thornhill would exact his life. Yet, even knowing that, Rory was loath to draw away. One more taste of her lips, he thought, covering her mouth with his.

He drew her so firmly against him that he could feel the imprint of her breasts on his flesh, could feel the wild rhythm of her heartbeat inside his own chest.

The blood roared in Courtney's temples until she thought she would go mad from the sound. Never had she felt such pleasure. Never had she known such need. What had this MacLaren done to her?

With one last ounce of sanity, she pushed against his chest. As he lifted his head, they both turned toward the sound of footsteps in the darkness.

Instantly Rory brought his hands upward, releasing her from the prison of his chains and his embrace.

Courtney took a step backward. Then, regaining her senses, she lifted the dagger toward his throat in a threatening gesture.

Two brawny crewmen approached. One of them held aloft a torch.

"Boney sent us to return the slave to the hold."

"Aye." Courtney avoided their stern faces, fearful that in the light what had just transpired would be evident in her eyes. But her confusion was not lost on Rory. With a half smile touching the corners of his lips, he gave her a last lingering look before turning away.

Courtney watched as they led him across the darkened deck. Even after they disappeared below, she strained to hear the sound of his chains being dragged across the lower deck.

Turning toward the rail, she lifted her gaze to the heavens. So that was what it felt like to be held by a man. And that was the pleasure to be derived from a kiss. Oh, what sweet torment. She could have gone on forever, locked in his embrace, feeling the pressure of his lips on hers.

She shivered violently. Just moments ago she had been on fire. And now, without MacLaren's arms around her, she was cold. So cold.

The slave, Rory MacLaren, had just done what no other man would ever have dared. He had not only defied Thornhill, he had introduced her to a pleasure beyond imagination, as well.

She turned away, muttering one of Boney's favorite curses. Rory MacLaren would surely haunt her dreams this night.

Chapter Three

Dawn's cold pink light was just beginning to color the horizon. A biting wind whipped the sails in a frantic dance. The dark waters of the Atlantic were rough and choppy. Storms were frequent visitors to this lonely stretch of ocean.

Courtney stirred restlessly. The night had been a long one, with periods of fitful sleep, disturbed often by feelings that alternately soothed and agitated.

She rolled over, determined to keep Rory MacLaren out of her thoughts. A shout from the lookout high in the rigging brought her scrambling to her feet.

"Ship approaching."

Courtney dressed quickly in her crimson silk shirt and narrow, tight-fitting men's trousers. Pulling on high black boots, she strapped a scabbard and sword at her waist and concealed a dagger beneath her bright yellow sash. She joined the crew on deck, prepared to welcome friend or foe. Though her pulse was racing, she was outwardly calm. As she had a hundred times before, she took her place beside Thornhill.

The captain cupped his hands around his mouth and shouted, "What flag does she fly?"

From high above came the lookout's voice. "English, cap'n."

A murmur of excitement rippled through the crowd of sailors. It was rare for a ship to attack a pirate vessel. This was an English warship, sent out specifically to rid the seas of pirates. The decks became a blur of frantic activity. Long before the English came alongside the *Hawk*, the crew was prepared for battle.

"Boney." Thornhill tossed the old man a heavy brass key. "See that the prisoners are secured in the hold until we have finished with these English dogs." To Courtney, the captain added, "It will be your responsibility to see that no one gets below deck."

Courtney felt a sense of pride at the captain's command. The sailor entrusted with the safety of the hold was really being entrusted with the vessel's treasures. Besides the worth of the slaves, the hold contained all the bounty collected during the voyage. There were chests of gold and silver, as well as precious jewels, rich silks, exotic spices and rare goods from the farthest corners of the earth. Drawing her sword, she followed Boney toward the rear of the ship. At that same moment she became aware of the scuffling of feet as the first English sailors clambered over the sides of their ship and boarded the *Hawk*.

While the old man chained the slaves in the hold, Courtney paced beside him, alert for any attempt on the part of the prisoners to escape. Above them could be heard the sounds of fierce battle. There were cries, shouts and the clash of dueling swords, as well as an occasional pistol shot.

When the slaves were secure, Courtney raced toward the open portal, eager to join the fray. Before she could climb the ladder, two swarthy sailors leaped into the hold, each holding aloft a sword.

"Is there no one but this girl?" Both sailors laughed and lifted their weapons menacingly.

While old Boney and the prisoners watched in stunned silence, Courtney faced the first swordsman and ran him through. When she heard a gurgling sound come from his lips, she turned to face her second adversary. This man, quicker and lighter of foot, danced aside as her blade whistled through the air, missing him by mere inches.

"Is there no one but this puny English dog?" she said contemptuously, mocking his earlier words.

The man threw back his head in a roar of laughter, eager to best his small, slender opponent. He darted forward, thrusting his sword skillfully. Equally skillful, Courtney dodged his blade. Then, with three quick steps, she had him backed into a corner. As he brought his sword down, she ducked, then plunged her blade into his chest, piercing his heart.

For one long moment he appeared stunned beyond words. Then, dropping his weapon, he reached both hands to the blade in his chest. Before he could clench his hands, Courtney jerked her arm back, pulling the blade free. With a gasp he fell forward and lay in a great pool of his own blood.

Rory MacLaren felt his muscles strain against the chains that held him fast against the cold wall of the ship's hold. His hands clenched into fists at his sides. These sailors, though not countrymen, were allies. If they were successful in this battle, it could mean freedom. His loyalty to the English king was unquestionable. Yet, with each move Courtney made, he felt himself yearn to move with her. By the gods, she was magnificent. The sailors she fought were twice her size, yet she outmoved them, outwitted them and, in the end, outfought them.

Like all the men of his clan, he had been trained from his earliest years to be a skilled swordsman. He prided himself on his skill. But this woman was nearly his equal.

When the second man fell at her feet, Rory saw her shoulders sag slightly. The two swordsmen had sorely tested her strength. Just then he glanced up and saw a shadow pass over the entrance to the hold. With her head lowered,

Courtney was unaware that a third sailor was about to attack.

"Above you," Rory shouted.

Courtney's head snapped up. For one fleeting moment her gaze met Rory's and held. Turning, she found the pointed end of a sword aimed at her chest. Instinctively she moved aside and thrust her sword upward, catching the sailor in the throat. Blood oozing from his wound, he charged at her, knocking her off her feet.

Rory and the others were forced to watch in helpless silence as Courtney and the sailor rolled around on the floor in a frantic struggle. The sailor managed to roll on top of her, pinning her beneath him. Clutching both her wrists in one hand, he stretched out his other hand toward his fallen sword. With all the strength she could muster, Courtney brought her knee up to his groin. With a grunt of pain, the sailor released her hands. In the blink of an eye she pulled her dagger from beneath the sash and plunged it into his chest. As he fell forward, she scrambled from beneath him. Standing over him, she watched as he writhed in pain.

Courtney was breathless, shaken, her chest rising and falling as she struggled for air. Seeing her distress, old Boney caught her by the arm and began steering her toward the ladder that would take her on deck. But as she stood poised on the first rung, Boney looked up and jerked her aside. A glittering object hurtled to the floor of the hold, missing her by inches.

"Torch." Frantically the old man began beating at the flames that skittered and danced across the wooden flooring.

Courtney watched in dismay as the fire licked at a barrel containing precious spices. A brightly colored bolt of silk smoldered, then burst into flames.

"Climb to safety," the old man shouted.

"Release the prisoners," Courtney called above the din.

"Have you gone mad?" Boney caught her elbow, propelling her toward the ladder.

She pulled herself free and faced him. "Free the slaves. Do it now."

Rory and the others watched as the old man agonized, torn between his loyalty to Thornhill and his sense of fairness. Before he could argue with her logic, three more sailors leaped down into the hold, their swords glinting in the light of the fire. While Courtney faced her opponents, the old man turned the key in the lock, then pulled free the chain holding the prisoners. Rory MacLaren stood very still as, with cries and muttered oaths, the freed men scrambled up the ladder behind old Boney, eager for safety. Not one of them took notice of the fact that the one responsible for their freedom was now outnumbered.

Once again, Rory thought, he was being forced to choose between his own freedom and the need to be with this damnable woman. Had he gone mad? Had she bewitched him?

Picking up one of the fallen swords, Rory instantly made his choice. With the skill born of a lifetime of battle, he leaped to her side and faced the first swordsman. Beside him, he heard the clash of blades as she dueled with a man almost twice her size. Within minutes, Rory had run his blade through his opponent. At Courtney's cry of anguish, he turned. Courtney's dueling partner had skillfully knocked her sword from her hand. With a sneer, the man lifted his blade, prepared to end the battle and her life.

"Courtney!" At the sound of her name, she turned.

Rory tossed her his sword. Twisting, she caught it, dodged her opponent's blade and brought her own through his rough tunic, where it found his heart. With a cry of pain, the sailor joined his dead comrades on the littered floor of the hold.

As she turned with a triumphant smile, she saw another swordsman lift his blade above Rory's head. Her smile vanished.

"Behind you!"

He turned, jumped aside, then bent to a fallen sailor and retrieved a bloody sword. As the swordsman lunged for another attack, Rory brought the blade straight up. The swordsman, impaled on the blade, gave a cry of pain before stumbling backward.

Their battle was still not over. Although there were no more swordsmen to fight, there was an even greater enemy. Fire. Flames licked along the wooden floor and, fed by the bolts of cloth stored along one wall, were quickly consuming everything in their path.

Prying the lid off a wooden barrel, Courtney scooped up their precious supply of salt and tossed it on the flames, smothering them.

Following her lead, Rory pried the lid from another barrel and tossed the entire contents on what was left of the flames. Herring and pickling spices hissed as the last of the fire was extinguished.

While she struggled for breath, Courtney listened to the eerie silence. Even on deck there was no longer any hint of battle. There was no clash of swords, no echo of pistol fire, no sound at all but an occasional moan.

"You are a fine swordsman, my lady." Rory's hand still clutching the bloody sword, rested at his side. "You would make the MacLaren clan proud."

"And you," she said, taking a step closer, "are a strange man."

"How so?" He watched her move, feeling a surge of heat that had nothing to do with the battle just won.

"You could have chosen freedom, as the others did. Yet you chose to stay and fight." When she was almost touching him, she paused and stared up into his face. "You saved my life."

"And someday, perhaps, I shall ask for payment." He stared into her eyes, feeling the heat grow until it was an inferno. "But for now, my lady, this shall be payment enough."

Without warning, he caught her chin and bent to her. His mouth covered hers in a savage kiss.

Stunned, Courtney went very still as fire and ice collided along her spine. Her breath seemed to catch in her throat. She could not breathe, could not move. She was captured, held by a need greater than anything she had ever before experienced.

"Girl. Come quick." Boney's voice above them shattered the spell. "The cap'n's been wounded."

With a little cry she pulled away and headed for the ladder. At the bottom step she paused and turned. Despite the torn rags and bloody sword, Rory MacLaren looked finer to her than any of the noblemen who surrounded the king at court.

"I shall never forget what you did for me, Rory MacLaren. And when he is stronger, I shall speak to my father about setting you free."

With narrowed eyes he watched as she climbed the ladder. Her crimson shirt clung damply, displaying the lush swell of her breasts. The bright sash drew his attention to her tiny waist. Then his gaze moved lower. In the tight breeches, every movement she made along the ladder caused a dryness in his throat.

"I shall never forget you, either, my beautiful Mistress of the Seas."

Courtney stared at the carnage on deck. The English ship, ablaze with dozens of fires, foundered off the port bow. There was no sign of life aboard. The crew of the *Hawk*, though victorious, was milling around in pain and confusion. They had fought dozens of battles, with swordsmen from as many countries. But never had they suffered so many casualties. And never before had they seen their captain seriously wounded.

Quickly assessing the situation, Courtney took charge.

"Boney. Have Thornhill taken to his cabin at once."

"You there," the old man shouted, pointing at two crew members who appeared unharmed. "Carry the cap'n to his cabin."

"Where is Simpson?" Courtney peered at the dead and wounded littering the deck.

"Wounded," one of the crew yelled. "The first mate is losing much blood."

"See to him," Courtney ordered a lanky youth who was leaning weakly against the rail. "All who are able to stand will assist the wounded," she added. "When their wounds have been tended, I want the dead sewn into cloth for burial. You there," she shouted, pointing at a pirate who for all the years she had known him had worn a patch over a missing eye, "collect all the weapons and take them to the hold."

"Aye, captain," he said.

His words were greeted with stunned silence. At the salutation that had always been given to Thornhill alone, several of the crew stared at Courtney in suspicion and alarm. Though she was the captain's daughter and had proven herself a capable sailor, she was a woman.

Courtney became instantly alert to the subtle change in the crew. They were watching her through narrowed eyes.

"How will we make port?" one of the crew called. "The slaves have gone over the side."

"Where they will no doubt drown," Courtney snapped. Then, seeing the questioning looks of the crew, she added firmly, "We have wind to fill our sails. And the sweat of every man aboard. We may be wounded, but we live still."

As she strode away, the crew watched her with growing admiration.

"You heard the captain," Simpson croaked, holding a blood-soaked rag to his side.

Behind her, the crew of the *Hawk* straightened their shoulders and bent to their tasks. If a mere woman could survive, so could they.

It was long past dark when Courtney finally left Thornhill's cabin. Though he was badly wounded and had lost much blood, he would survive. Leaving him in Boney's capable hands, she crossed the deck and paused at the rail.

Though a member of the crew had searched the ship from stem to stern, he'd reported back to her that the slave Rory MacLaren was nowhere to be found. Gone. The slave was gone. And the man beneath the slave's rags was still a mystery to her.

She stared at the dark outline of the land on the now-distant horizon. Scotland. Rory's homeland.

Lifting her face to the sky, she tracked the path of a shooting star across the black-velvet heavens. She would feel the sting of Thornhill's lash when he discovered that she was the one responsible for the slaves' escape from their chains. But even that thought could not discourage her this night. The rough seas would claim many of them. Many more would be found and captured by passing vessels, always in need of slave labor. But some would make it to shore. And one, she thought, would make it home.

Swim, Rory MacLaren, she whispered fiercely. Reach the shore. Find your home, your freedom. Join your clan. And return to your greatest love, your land.

Chapter Four

For weeks, as the *Hawk* slowly limped toward France, Courtney found her thoughts dwelling on the fascinating Rory MacLaren. While she commanded the crew, working alongside them, struggling to keep their spirits up, she thought about the slave who had humbly bent to the deck in the broiling sun.

When Thornhill ordered her publicly lashed as punishment for freeing the slaves, she thought about Rory's strength in the face of humiliation. That thought kept her from crying out. Clenching her teeth, she endured the sting of the whip. Later, in her cabin, she lay in stoic silence while old Boney applied his precious ointment to the wounds.

"It is the fever," Boney muttered, wincing at the sight of the welts that marred her tender flesh. "The fever has addled his brain. When he realizes what he has done, the cap'n will be contrite."

She said nothing. Though it was not in her nature to bear a grudge, she was beginning to believe in her heart that this time Thornhill had gone too far. Had she not fought as bravely as the others? Had she not risked her life to save his precious cargo? Cargo. She went very still. The slaves had been part of the ship's bounty. And she had been entrusted with preserving them. Instead, she had freed them. Her concern for their lives had cost Thornhill a fortune.

"It is my father's right," she whispered.

"Right?" The old man's hand paused in midair. "To have you lashed in the company of the entire crew?"

"It was I who ordered the slaves freed. I mistakenly put myself in their place and decided that I would rather risk drowning than death by fire. I have the skills," she said, sitting up suddenly and drawing her shirt around her. "But I lack the heart for this. I shall never earn the right to be captain of the *Hawk*. I will never make my father proud."

"You listen to me, girl." Boney set down his bucket of ointment and caught her by the shoulders. His eyes burned with a fire rarely glimpsed on his weather-beaten countenance. "It takes a rare courage to put the lives of others ahead of your own." His voice lowered. "I was proud of what you did in the hold."

Tears sprang to her eyes. Annoyed at her weakness, she brushed the back of her hand furiously across her eyes and turned away. What did it matter if she pleased her old friend if she could not please her father?

With her back to him, she said, "Thank you for your ministrations. I am needed on deck."

Boney watched as she buttoned her shirt and strode away. He loved her as fiercely as any grandfather loved his grandchild. But there was nothing he could do for her. Thornhill had molded her into a mirror image of himself—skilled sailor, swordsman and pirate. But it had not been possible for the captain of the *Hawk* to erase her fine breeding. Goodness and nobility were deeply ingrained in Courtney. And one more thing, the old man thought with a weary shake of his head. He had seen the way she had looked at the Scotsman when she had ordered the slaves freed. Though she tried to deny it, locked inside her were a woman's feelings, a woman's compassion, a woman's needs. And in that area he was as helpless as any babe. He had no advice for a woman caught in the throes of first love.

That night, Courtney fell wearily into her bunk. As he had every night since his escape, Rory MacLaren invaded her dreams. Surrounded by flames, he stood beside her, fierce and proud, engaging one swordsman after another. As he had in every dream, he won the battle and then claimed her as his prize. Just as he enfolded her in his arms, she awoke, damp and trembling.

Berating herself for indulging in such fantasies, she rolled from her bunk and crossed to the small, round window. She stared at the moon and wrapped her arms around herself to calm the tremors. In the distance she could see the outline of mountains.

Where was the slave now? Did he ever think of her? Or had she already become just a dim memory?

The *Hawk*'s homecoming was less than festive. Two of the finest ships in the French fleet had not returned to port. The rumors were that they had been engaged by an English vessel. To make matters worse, the English were said to be seeking closer ties with Spain. An alliance between the two countries would further weaken France's position in Europe.

The only good news to greet the crew of the *Hawk* was that the hated King James I of England had taken ill. This was greeted with cheers by the ailing Thornhill. But the news that his son, the Prince of Wales, had sent emissaries to France to inquire about Henrietta Maria, the sister of Louis XIII, left the captain in a distinctly surly mood.

It was being whispered at court that King Louis XIII was considering offering his sister to the Prince of Wales as a bride in order to stop the fighting and strengthen relations between England and France. When Thornhill heard this, he flew into such a rage that he took to his bed for days.

Courtney paced the luxuriously appointed sitting room of their Paris chambers, feeling like a caged bird. At court she was surrounded by silly women in elegant gowns of the latest fashion. They wore full, flowing dresses with low-cut, jewel-encrusted bodices that emphasized the swell of their breasts. Their long hair was twisted into ornate coronets atop their heads or, for the more daring, pulled into ringlets that streamed across their bare shoulders. They neither knew nor cared about the world beyond Paris. Their only concern was the number of conquests they made and the bits of gossip they managed to glean.

The men at court were no better, preening like peacocks whenever they were not consulting with the king's council. Many of them expressed interest in the beautiful young woman, who was obviously different in dozens of ways from all the other women at court. But Courtney ignored their advances whenever possible and became almost insulting to those who dared to press for her favors.

If Courtney felt confined at court, this suite of rooms was even more of a prison. Except for the faithful Boney, the captain refused to see anyone but her. Thornhill complained if she left him for more than an hour. He was peevish, demanding and surly.

Thornhill, though he was slowly recovering from his wounds, was still plagued with fever and weakness. The king's own physician had suggested he forsake the sea and spend a year or more in the luxury of the French court while he regained his health.

To Courtney, the thought of a year in this teeming city was unbearable. Though they had been here only a few short weeks, she found her heart yearning for the freedom of the sea, for the familiar creaking of the planks in the *Hawk*'s deck. The air in Paris was stifling. She preferred the tang of salty sea air. The noisy carts and vendors, the dizzying din of humanity, made her ache for the screech of seabirds and the camaraderie of her fellow sailors.

As the days passed slowly, Courtney was forced to call upon every ounce of her patience. Endure. Even if she were unable to act, she could endure. As she had aboard the

Hawk when she was but a child. As she had when the slave, Rory MacLaren, had left an aching void in her life. Endure.

Thornhill's eyes glittered with a feverish light as his visitor sat beside his bed, speaking in low, urgent tones.

"You have served your king well, captain. Through the years you have sent ten times ten English ships to a watery grave. The wailing of English widows has risen to a chorus that bodes well for all of France."

"I did what I could."

"But there is more, captain. Much more you can do for your king."

Seized by a fit of coughing, Thornhill lifted a handkerchief to his mouth. When the moment had passed, he lay back against the pillows. "I am ill. There is nothing more I can do."

"You can give me the girl. Did you not once confide to me that she was to be the instrument of your revenge?"

Thornhill's eyes glazed over with pain. "I have waited too long. The hated King James will escape my revenge in death before I can put a plan into motion. It is too late to seek my revenge."

"It is never too late, old friend." Thornhill's visitor leaned closer, peering intently into his eyes. "His progeny, the Prince of Wales, is even now arranging for a union with Henrietta Maria."

"That son of a snake." In his fury, Thornhill sat bolt upright, clutching the man's sleeve. "You must use your influence to stop such an alliance."

His visitor gave a chilling imitation of a smile. "And why would I do such a foolish thing?" At Thornhill's look of surprise, he went on smoothly, "How better to wreak havoc on England than to have our French princess within the circle of the royal family of England?"

Thornhill fell back weakly against the cushions. "But how can you be certain Henrietta Maria will cooperate? She is young and, from what I have heard, headstrong."

"She is a devout Catholic. If her orders come directly from her clergy, she will have no choice but to obey."

"You would order your own priests to spy for France?"

The visitor's eyebrows drew together in a frown. His eyes narrowed, and he stared at Thornhill with such intensity that Thornhill flinched and looked away. In a voice trembling with emotion, he intoned, "I will do anything necessary to ensure the safety of my king and country. Anything. And if that means commanding the clergy to spy, it shall be done. I intend to employ every means at my disposal. And I expect you to do the same."

"I?"

"I want the girl."

"Why? What possible use can she be to you?"

His visitor folded his hands in his lap. "She speaks both French and English fluently. She has demonstrated her strength and courage. And I trust that you have raised her to hate England as much as you."

Thornhill dabbed at his mouth with his handkerchief. "What you say is true. She is fearless in battle. And she has demonstrated her loyalty to me. She hates England because I expect it of her. But this—" He shook his head vehemently. "She misses the sea and her life aboard the *Hawk*. She will fight me on this."

The visitor leaned forward. His hands clenched and unclenched at his side. "You are a shrewd man, captain. You will find a way to convince her."

"I fear—"

"Fear nothing." The visitor's attitude suddenly changed. Leaning back, he smiled. "But pretend to fear."

"I do not understand."

"Let the girl know that unless she cooperates with this request your own life will be in danger."

Thornhill stared at his guest as his meaning became clear.

"You say she is loyal to you, my friend. Use that loyalty to bend her to your will."

Thornhill nodded. "Of course. If she were to believe that without her cooperation I would be harmed, she would agree to anything." Sweat beaded his forehead, and he dabbed absently at it with his handkerchief. "Anything."

His visitor stood. "I leave it to you to arrange the time of our next meeting. But I caution you. It must be soon. I have already begun to put my plan into motion."

Courtney became aware of a subtle change in Thornhill. Each day he sent her to court while he entertained a visitor. Even old Boney, who had been with him for a lifetime, was sent away during these visits. For hours afterward, Thornhill would be quiet, thoughtful, watching her with a strange light in his eyes.

At last he summoned her to his bedchamber.

"I am an old man," Thornhill said, watching her carefully.

"You speak nonsense." Courtney settled herself in a chair beside the bed. "It is this city that is tiring you."

"Aye." He closed his eyes for a moment, then opened them once more to study her closely. "Do you find this city vexing?"

She nodded, afraid of saying something that might offend him.

"Then perhaps you should leave this place."

Courtney's mouth dropped open. How she yearned to be free of this prison. "Are we returning to the *Hawk*?"

"Nay. I must stay here and regain my strength. But you are free to go."

"I? Leave here alone? Where would I go without you?"

She thought he smiled for a moment, but before she could be certain, his lips thinned. "I have told you how I hate the English, Courtney. But I have never told you why."

Courtney waited, surprised by his unexpected candor. Never before had Thornhill taken the time to talk to her in this manner.

"When I was much younger, the English King, James I, stripped me of all my land and titles."

"But why? How could he do such a thing?"

Thornhill's eyes narrowed. "There is much more to pleasing a king than simply bowing over his hand. There are always secret plots, schemes that if carried out, can be of benefit to many."

"I do not understand."

Thornhill dabbed at his mouth with a silken handkerchief, then said softly, "When a man is king, his word is law. James had a cousin who coveted my land. Land," he added with a low growl of anger, "that had been in my family since my father's father. James declared me an enemy of the crown and stripped me of all land and titles, giving them instead to his kin."

"Why did you not fight?"

"One does not fight a king's decree. My only choice, save death, was to leave England and declare my loyalty to another crown."

"Why do you tell me this now, Father?"

His lips curled into a faint smile. He dabbed at them again with the handkerchief. "How much do you love me, Courtney?"

Love? She had never heard Thornhill speak the word. Love? He was her father, the captain of the *Hawk*, her teacher, her leader. In dozens of battles she had been willing to die rather than disobey him. But love? "I do love you," she whispered. Even to her own ears the words sounded hollow, and she felt an immediate sense of shame.

"And our king, Louis?"

Courtney was shocked. To admit to anything less than love for the monarch was treason, a crime punishable by death. "I have sworn love and loyalty to my king."

"Ah." He sank back against the pillows and closed his eyes for a moment. When he opened them, he pinned her with his gaze. "You shall have an opportunity to prove your love to me and to our king."

Courtney felt a shaft of fear pierce her. The fear grew when she heard Thornhill call, "Boney, send in our guest."

Guest? She had seen no one when she had entered their apartment. Yet she could hear the sound of the old man's voice, and the deep rumble of an answering one. A moment later a tall man in the red robes of a prince of the church was ushered into the bedchamber.

The man was tall and carried himself with a stiff, almost military bearing. He had sharp features, with a pinched mouth and a hawklike nose. His mustache was curled at the ends, and a pointed beard added a satanic look to his face. But it was his eyes that commanded attention. Fierce black eyes stared unblinking at the young woman before him.

"My daughter, Courtney." Thornhill gazed beyond her to the man who looked more like a man of the sword than a man of the cloth. "Courtney, this is Cardinal Richelieu."

When the man extended his hand, Courtney curtsied and kissed his ring. She was grateful for the chance to bow her head and hide her expression of surprise. Everyone in France had heard of Richelieu. He was the most powerful man in all of France. At court it was said that he actually made most of the decisions for which the king took credit. There was no doubt that Richelieu was the power behind the throne.

"Excellency," she murmured.

"So, this is the lovely Courtney." The cardinal waited until old Boney had pulled up a chair beside hers. Indicating the seat, he waited until she was seated before settling himself on the edge of his chair, facing her in such a way that she had no choice but to return his look.

His dark eyes pierced her. He used them to his advantage, staring deeply into hers, holding her gaze even when she tried to look away.

"Your father has long praised your loyalty to our beloved king."

Despite her dry throat, Courtney gave what she hoped was a convincing smile. "My loyalty is beyond question, Your Eminence."

"Good. Very good." He glanced over her head at the man in the bed, then said in a conspiratorial manner, "Your father and I have something of utmost importance to ask you. Upon your answer rests the safety, the very future, of France itself."

Courtney swallowed.

"Though it is not yet known, Louis has decided to permit his beloved sister, Henrietta Maria, to become the bride of the Prince of Wales, who will one day succeed his father, James I, as King of England."

Courtney gasped. Having been privy to the gossip at court, she was aware that the lovely young princess knew of her brother's plans. It was said that she was terrified of the plotting and scheming that existed at the English court. Henrietta Maria would become a helpless pawn in a power struggle between two warring countries.

Seeking to cover up her sympathy for the young princess, she said softly, "What has that to do with me, Eminence?"

"It is my wish that you accompany Henrietta Maria to England as her personal lady-in-waiting and confidante."

"A lady-in-waiting? But, Eminence, I have had no training in such things."

"I have been assured that you are a clever young woman. You shall be taught all you need to know. Your father assures me that you speak fluent English. Henrietta Maria will have need of your skills. A Frenchwoman in England will be in need of a . . . a loyal friend."

When Courtney fell silent, the cardinal added, "Your lessons will begin immediately. You will have all the necessary training before you leave France."

Leave France? Leave the *Hawk* and the only life she had ever known? Courtney turned pleading eyes to Thornhill, but he regarded her in stony silence.

"I will, of course, ask a favor in return for this splendid life I am offering you."

Courtney thought she detected a glint of amusement in his dark eyes.

"Once you arrive in England, I will expect you to meet regularly with my...representatives and keep me informed of all that transpires at court."

For a moment Courtney's breath seemed caught in her throat. At last she understood what was actually being asked of her. Her knowledge of French and English was not intended to make the young monarch comfortable. In fact, this man had no interest in the comfort of Henrietta Maria. The young princess was merely a pawn. Richelieu expected Courtney to spy for him. For France. And to do it under the very noses of the king of England and his court.

"You wish me to—" She swallowed, afraid even to speak the word. But one glance at Thornhill's narrowed gaze gave her back her confidence. "You wish me to become an informant?"

"Does that offend you?"

Courtney paused. She had heard about Richelieu's temper. A single word from him was enough to cause a man to lose his lands or his life. "I think, Eminence, that I would be a very clumsy spy."

He shifted slightly; it was the only sign of his annoyance. Still holding her gaze with his, he lifted one eyebrow. "Perhaps I neglected to tell you how important this assignment is. It is crucial to the safety of all Frenchmen to know what transpires at the court of England. It is so crucial, I am willing to sacrifice the lives of a few for the sake of many.''

Her head came up defiantly. "I do not fear dying, Eminence.''

"Good." He cut her off quickly. "That is very good. But it is not your life that will be sacrificed.''

She stared at him, puzzled.

"Unless you agree to my request, Captain Thornhill will forfeit his life.''

"My father?'' Courtney turned to study the pale face of the man in the bed. "You would demand this task of me under penalty of his life?''

"We are all soldiers, fighting the good fight. What we speak of here is a matter of survival. For France. And death to the enemy. And to those who are not willing to make the supreme sacrifice for France. I brand as enemy any citizen of France who will not fight for his country.''

Courtney went very still. She had no thought of her own life now, not when that of her father was hanging in the balance. Still, she had to ask. "What if I am caught? Is this not an offense punishable by death?''

The cardinal's mouth turned up into a smile. His eyes, she noted, were as cold as ice. "I am told you are a very brave, very clever woman. You will not be caught. But if you are,'' he added, "perhaps the princess can intervene with her new husband for you. It would be to your advantage to ingratiate yourself with Henrietta Maria. Have you any questions?''

She shook her head, too stunned by this turn of events to think clearly.

Glancing once more at Thornhill, Courtney thought she saw a gleam of triumph in his eyes. Had he feared she would refuse and seal his death? Nay. He had been counting on her to do the cardinal's bidding. What choice had she been given? None. This had all been arranged before she had ever been approached. Even if she could have refused without sealing Thornhill's fate, she would have felt the wrath of a father who had never once shown her a moment's tenderness. A father who would have turned away from her and never again have attempted to bridge the chasm. The sting of the lash would have been as nothing compared with the pain of his ultimate rejection. Through the years she had often felt the sting of his displeasure. And his lash. And although he had never managed to break her spirit, she had learned that in order to survive one often had to submit to another's bidding.

She had survived all these years without a single display of tenderness from Thornhill. Richelieu was another matter.

At court she had seen and heard what happened to those who incurred his wrath. The man's desire for power was insatiable. There was no way she could refuse—and live.

Richelieu stood, dismissing her. "I shall make all the necessary arrangements. The marriage is to take place very soon. You will arrive in England with Henrietta Maria's party within a fortnight."

As the cardinal extended his hand for her kiss, she whispered, "It shall be as you wish."

"Of course." He smiled, and she thought it the evilest smile she had ever encountered. "Instead of being forced to forfeit his life, your father shall be richly rewarded for your loyalty. And as long as you continue to please me, your father will be allowed to live in comfort."

Courtney studied Richelieu and felt a wave of revulsion. She backed from the room, eager to escape those dark eyes, that wicked, frightening demeanor. In his presence she felt as if she were with the devil himself.

She hurried to her own room and began pacing, feeling again the old sense of loneliness and desperation that she had felt as a child. Before the new moon, she would once again find herself alone in a strange new world, where she would be caught up in a web of intrigue and deceit. And if caught, her princess could not be counted on to come to her aid. If caught, Courtney knew, she would pay with her life. But if she shrank from this deadly task, Thornhill would pay with his.

There was no end to this vicious circle.

Chapter Five

Because the king of England was a Protestant, it was agreed that the marriage between the Prince of Wales and the French princess would be performed in France by proxy. Due to Cardinal Richelieu's influence, the ceremony could not take place within a Catholic church. So Courtney found herself standing beside the slender, dark-haired princess on the steps of Notre-Dame de Paris, where the marriage ceremony would be performed.

Flanked by her two brothers, King Louis XIII and Gaston, Duc d'Orléans, the pretty little princess was stunning in a gown of priceless cloth of silver and gold trimmed with diamonds.

Courtney was equally stunning. In a gown of scarlet and gold, with gold and rubies at her throat and wrists, she stood in the May sunshine and marveled at the pageantry spread out below her.

The streets teemed with citizens who strained for a glimpse of their beautiful princess. On every corner vendors hawked their wares, from food to drink to souvenirs of this fateful day.

An honor guard of a thousand soldiers stood at attention, their crimson tunics fluttering in the slight breeze. Behind them streamed nearly a hundred ladies-in-waiting and women of the royal household, their gowns a glittering sea of color.

The ceremony on the steps of the cathedral was brief. The lord chancellor, an elderly member of the English court who presided over the House of Lords and who served as private secretary to the king of England, repeated the vows in the Prince of Wales's place. Afterward, those members of the entourage who were not Protestant proceeded inside Notre-Dame for mass.

When the ceremony was finished, Courtney and Henrietta Maria entered a magnificent coach-and-four in which they began a procession through the streets of Paris. From there, the wedding party would wind its way through the French countryside, ending across the Channel, where Henrietta Maria would make her new home.

As the crowd cheered and the young bride waved, Courtney sank back against the cushions of the carriage and gave a great heaving sigh. It would take a fortnight at least to reach their final destination. A fortnight to master all the lessons swimming through her brain. Protocol at court would be difficult enough to master, but it was all so strange and new to be in the company of women. For so long now she had lived in a man's world. She was easy in their company. But women... She found herself tensing when they began whispering about the latest fashions, the latest court gossip.

She sighed again, hoping to release all the tensions. There had been no time to rest, to relax, to think. For days now she had not been allowed to give in to the luxury of dwelling on the slave, Rory MacLaren. Even at night, her exhausted sleep was rarely invaded by thoughts of him.

She felt a terrible ache around her heart. He was lost to her. He was part of that other life. Life aboard the *Hawk*. All that was now lost to her.

The ache grew as she realized that the journey had now begun. A journey to a strange new world. A journey that would present danger at every turn.

James I, king of England, succumbed to death. His son, Charles I, the Prince of Wales, was immediately proclaimed king. All of England mourned his passing, then cheered its new monarch. Shouts of "Long live the king!" echoed through the streets. And, the people added cautiously, may he find much joy with his French-born bride, Henrietta Maria, new queen of England.

In every town and village it passed through in France the wedding party was greeted by pageants, parades and fireworks. Though the young queen bore up bravely, Courtney was aware that this journey was as difficult and frightening for the young monarch as it was for her. What lay ahead for the two of them? Distrust, villainy, scheming? Love, Courtney prayed fervently. Please God, let Charles love his timid young queen.

Henrietta Maria and her weary entourage touched English soil at Dover. The following day their journey was hastily postponed when word reached them that the king was on his way to meet his wife.

"Courtney." Henrietta Maria gripped her chief lady-in-waiting's hand tightly and lifted wide eyes to her. "Why is the king coming here? It had been agreed that we would have a second wedding in London before the marriage was to be consummated."

Courtney felt the tremors that the young queen could not hide. Her heart went out to her. "This has been a difficult time for England's monarch. Perhaps," she said, as tactfully as possible, "the king wishes some time alone with his bride before presenting her to his subjects."

"Do you really think so?" Henrietta Maria's eyes were round with fear.

Courtney dropped an arm around the young woman's shoulders. In the past few weeks they had drawn together out of need, but they had become much more than monarch and lady-in-waiting. A deep friendship had been forged. In Courtney's company the young queen confided all her fears and hopes for the future. And though Courtney kept her own counsel, she now understood that the young queen suffered from the same worries as ordinary mortals.

"Come, Majesty. You must prepare yourself for your husband."

"Husband." Henrietta Maria stopped a moment and tugged on Courtney's hand. "What if I do not please him?"

"Your Majesty." Courtney smiled and turned the queen toward a looking glass mounted on a gold stand. "Could any man look upon your lovely face and not be taken with your beauty?"

The reflection in the mirror smiled back at her. "Ah, Courtney. How did I manage all these years without you?"

"How indeed?" Courtney rang for the maids, and the suite of rooms became a riot of activity as the queen's bath was prepared, her hair dressed and her best gown laid out for the most memorable night of her life.

The sun had long ago set in the western sky. Feathery clouds scudded across a full moon. Except for the cry of an occasional night bird, the evening was hushed, expectant.

"What could be keeping him?"

Courtney glanced at the young queen, who looked as if she might cry at any moment. "Perhaps the king has been slowed by crowds of English citizens waiting to cheer him as he passes."

"But he is the king. He can do anything."

Courtney smiled gently. "Anything except fly."

Henrietta Maria put a hand to her mouth and giggled. The image of Charles flying through the air filled her with mirth.

Courtney was relieved to see her friend laugh. There had been little humor in the young queen's life, and, Courtney feared, there would be even less in the future.

The blare of trumpets startled them. Henrietta Maria's eyes were suddenly round with fear. "It is the king. Oh, Courtney, what shall we do?"

Courtney stood and rang for a maid. While a servant helped the queen into an ermine-lined cape to ward off the chill of the evening, Courtney studied her carefully. "The white gown, with diamonds and pearls, is perfect for your first meeting with your new husband. And your hair—" she paused and tucked up a curl "—is lovely held away from your face with combs."

The queen moved to a mirror and nervously studied her reflection. Courtney felt a thrill of anticipation for her friend. She absently slipped her arms into the cape being held by a maid, taking no notice of her own gown or hair.

"If we hurry, Majesty, we can greet the king and his company in the courtyard."

"Courtney, you must stay by my side," the young queen said, catching her lady-in-waiting by the arm. "Do not leave me, even for one moment. Their language—" she gripped Courtney's hand tightly "—it is so strange. I fear I will not know a single word being spoken."

At the sound of dozens of footsteps in the great hall below and the deep rumble of masculine voices, Courtney squeezed her young queen's hand. "It seems your king makes haste to greet his bride." Then, seeing the look of terror in the young queen's eyes, she whispered, "Have no fear, Majesty. I will be at your side."

As the two young women descended the wide marble stairs, they found themselves staring into a sea of faces.

Where had all these men come from? Had the king brought his entire court with him?

Halfway down the stairs, the young queen hesitated. The babble of conversation had ceased. The attention of every man in the room was focused on the two beautiful women. From the diamond tiara in her dark curls, it was obvious which of them was the new queen. But the beauty of the woman beside her was enough to cause more than one man to reach for his ale and wet a throat gone suddenly dry.

When the women reached the bottom of the stairs, the sea of men parted and one lone figure moved forward to greet them.

"My lady," the king said, taking Henrietta Maria's hand in his. If he felt the slight trembling of her tiny palm, he took no notice. "Welcome to your new home. Welcome to England."

Courtney glanced from the young queen to her new husband. Tall and thin, he had an almost frail appearance. Curly brown hair softened a wide forehead and an angular face. A beard covered his chin and framed his wide, sensuous lips. His hazel eyes held a gleam of humor and appreciation as he gazed at his new bride.

"I thank you, sir."

When Henrietta Maria had spoken, Courtney repeated her words in English.

The king stared at this pretty young interpreter for a long moment before turning once more to his bride.

The young queen made a slight bow as he brushed his lips over the back of her hand.

"I trust your voyage across the Channel was a pleasant one?"

"Very pleasant, my lord. The winds were gentle, and the sea calm."

Again Courtney repeated in English what the young queen had said.

"And who might this be?" the king demanded.

"My friend, as well as my lady-in-waiting, Lady Courtney Thornhill."

"Lady Thornhill," the king said, staring at Courtney so intently that she felt her cheeks flush, "I trust you will accompany the queen to court until she has mastered our language."

It was almost too easy. Did he not suspect that she had been planted in this company by Richelieu? Was it his intention to ensnare her in a trap of his making? Or was he merely being kind to his new bride? Courtney felt her heart race, her palms sweat. "It would be my pleasure, Majesty."

"Before we dine, I will present my council." Taking Henrietta Maria's arm, the king faced the men in the room. As each man was presented to the queen, Courtney, positioned by her side, translated their remarks into French.

Courtney had just finished repeating what the elderly Lord Smathers had said when she became aware of a change in the king's inflection. There was a warmth in his tone that had been lacking in the earlier introductions.

She looked up and felt the blood rush from her face, leaving her pale and trembling. For a moment she thought her legs might not support her. It took all her willpower to keep from crying out.

The man who had just stepped into her line of vision was tall, with shoulders so broad he dwarfed the men standing near him. His skin was tanned and healthy, and his hair, thick and luxurious, curled softly around the collar of a short cape tossed carelessly over one shoulder. At his throat and wrists were snowy lace. His tall leather boots were polished to a high sheen. Even in this company of England's finest men, he stood out from all the rest. In his hand was a plumed hat, which he held before him as he bowed to his new monarch. But when he straightened, his eyes, the bluest eyes Courtney had ever seen, were fixed on her. And though he gave no indication that he recognized her,

Courtney had the distinct impression that he was laughing.

"Do not mind this rogue's rough edges, madam. He has always preferred a life of adventure to the more mundane life at court. This ruffian is the son of my father's good and loyal friend. The new chief of the MacLaren clan in Scotland, Rory MacLaren."

Gripping her hands together so tightly that the knuckles grew white, Courtney repeated in French what the king had just said. But when she was forced to repeat his name, she was unaware that her voice softened and that her eyes filled with a fine mist.

Chapter Six

Rory fought to control a tidal wave of emotions. Outrage. How dare this pirate invade the sanctity of the king's own castle! Wonderment. How had that wild creature turned herself into this beautiful, composed woman? Fear. How many others of her kind had managed to intrude themselves into the king's inner chamber? Determination. He would have his answers, if he had to strangle her lovely throat to get them.

Rory barely noticed the young queen whose hand he kissed. It was with great effort that he forced his gaze to her. She had dark hair, he realized, and a timid smile in a fresh, winsome face. Her hand was trembling slightly, and he wished there was some way he could put her at ease. But though he smiled gently and spoke a word of proper greeting, his mind was on the young woman who stood beside her. What was the beautiful pirate doing here on English soil?

"And her lady-in-waiting," Charles said to Rory.

Lady Courtney Thornhill indeed. Her father had spent a lifetime killing English sailors and looting their ships. And his daughter had spent a lifetime aboard a pirate ship. Had she not told him that although she was a French citizen she called the *Hawk* her only home? What, then, was she doing masquerading as the queen's lady-in-waiting?

The king's introduction was all the excuse the Scot needed. Taking Courtney's palm, he bowed grandly, then lifted her hand to kiss it.

"My lady."

Trapped. Courtney felt as trapped as a fish on a line. She tried to back away, but there was nowhere to go. She stiffened her hand, resisting the touch of him with all her might. As his lips brushed the back of her knuckles, she felt a rush of heat along her arm. When she tried to pull away, he held her in an iron grip. Trapped. For the moment. But the hunt was not yet over.

"My lord." She bowed slightly and lifted wide, pleading eyes to his.

Her discomfort was obvious. Satisfied, he smiled and ran his thumb across her wrist. It pleased him to note the way her pulse leaped at his touch.

"What think you of England, my lady?"

"It—" Her throat was so dry that the words would not come. Swallowing, she tried again. "It is a lovely green country. There will be much for us to admire in your land."

"I will be happy to show you as much as you wish to see. I am yours to command."

"You are too kind." She firmly extracted her hand from his and straightened her shoulders. Now that the initial shock of seeing him had passed, Courtney strove for more control. She lifted her chin in a familiar defiant gesture and met his smiling gaze.

Rory saw the little glint in her eye and swallowed back the laughter that bubbled in his throat. By the gods, she was stunning. Only moments ago she had been shocked by the sight of him. Of that he had no doubt. To her credit, though, she had retained her composure. And even as he watched he could see her fiery spirit returning.

He studied the woman who had occupied so much of his thoughts, both waking and sleeping. He had feared that with each passing day he was magnifying her beauty in his mind. But he had not. She was even more beautiful than he remembered—if that was possible.

Gone were the tight men's breeches, the flowing crimson shirt, the brilliant sash at her waist. Gone, too, was the wild mane of hair that had fallen nearly to her waist.

Now her hair was coiled neatly around her head, with one saucy curl spilling over her shoulder. Her gown was a rich shade of green, with a bodice encrusted with emeralds and pearls. At her throat was a pendant with an emerald as large as a duck's egg. A gift from the queen? Rory wondered. Or had it been part of a pirate ship's plunder?

"...chief among my councillors," the king was saying by way of introduction to the queen, "Lord Burlingame."

The man being presented was tall and exquisitely attired in a crimson jacket inset with fur. His breeches were expertly tailored to show off his trim body to its best advantage. Even the king, who was himself splendidly dressed, paled beside this man. Fine golden hair spilled over a wide forehead that was furrowed as he bent over the queen's hand.

"Welcome to English soil, mademoiselle," he said.

Though the words spoke of welcome, when he straightened, Courtney, standing beside the queen, could read no welcome in his slate eyes.

"Lady Courtney Thornhill," the king added.

"Lady Thornhill. It was worth the hard ride to Dover just to gaze upon your beauty."

Courtney felt no pleasure at his honeyed words. They lacked sincerity. His mouth, she noted, was thin-lipped and pursed slightly. A cruel mouth. As Burlingame brushed his lips over the back of her hand, it took all Courtney's willpower to keep from cringing.

"I think it shall be most interesting, entertaining our French-born queen and her company." Burlingame smiled, and Courtney felt a quiver of apprehension. Instead of adding a measure of warmth, his smile only made him look even more dangerous.

There had been few men in her young life whom Courtney had instantly disliked or feared, but she trusted her instincts. This man, though close to the king, would be a man to watch.

"Come," the king bellowed to his company. "We will sup."

As the royal pair led the way to an enormous dining hall, Courtney stared at the arm being offered by Rory. To do other than to accept would be to invite the stares of the others. And the one thing Courtney must not do was draw undue attention to herself. If she were to become an effective spy for France, she must not invite close scrutiny by the king's council. And in order to stay alive, she must not only please Richelieu, she must ingratiate herself with the king of England, as well. Courtney stared at his arm and felt a growing panic.

Seeing her distress, Rory gently took her hand and lifted it to his sleeve. "By your leave, it is proper for a lady to accept the offer of a man's assistance."

Through clenched teeth she muttered, "Damn, I know what is proper. But you have no right to touch me, Rory MacLaren. I would as soon cut off your arm."

"We are not aboard ship now, my lady. Here in England we do not abide by the rules of Captain Thornhill."

"I am well aware of that."

His voice was warm with laughter. "Then remember that a lady does not swear. And I suggest you be quick about following your king, or he may have your head for supper."

She gingerly placed her hand on his arm. Instantly she felt the corded muscles beneath the ruffled shirt and the brocade jacket. Though MacLaren dressed like the others at court, she was aware of the difference. In a fight he could best any man in the room.

Seeing the smug look on his face, she gritted her teeth and moved along by his side.

"Is taking my arm such a terrible punishment, my lady?"

"Aye." She heard the rumble of his laughter and glowered at him. "When it makes you so happy."

"I can see that it is going to be entertaining having you at court."

"I am not here for your entertainment, Rory MacLaren."

"And just why are you here?" At her tight-lipped silence, he whispered, "Why is the Mistress of the Seas passing herself off as a lady-in-waiting to the new queen of England?"

He saw the little jerk of her head, the slight narrowing of her eyes, before she brought her lips together in a tight line.

The lady was a puzzle. A beautiful, beguiling puzzle. Rory felt the stirrings of his Scottish warrior's blood as it heated at the thought of a duel with this woman. And he realized that for the first time he was actually looking forward to spending some time in the company of the king's council. For so long now he had hated this position. He missed his country, the company of his clansmen, the thrill of battle. But suddenly the thought of spending time at court seemed better than tolerable.

"MacLaren," the king commanded, "you and Lady Thornhill will join us at table."

"As you wish, Your Highness."

Rory escorted Courtney to a long wooden table set with tankards of ale and platters of roast pork, tender lamb and goose. Serving girls milled around, offering thick gruel and gravy, as well as steaming trays of bread pudding.

Courtney stared in awe at the antics of some of the men seated with Lord Burlingame, who brazenly pinched the serving girls as they bent to their tasks or peered lewdly down the necks of their gowns.

"The king's men have been many days on the road, my lady," Rory said, seeing the direction of her gaze.

"And you, my lord. Will you not join the king's men in their...pleasure?"

He heard the growl of anger in her voice and nearly laughed aloud. "It is pleasure enough to be at the side of the mysterious Lady Thornhill."

Courtney glanced at him to see if he was laughing at her once more. But when she saw, along with the laughter, a smoldering look in his blue eyes, she lowered her lashes to veil her own feelings. She must not allow herself to feel anything for MacLaren. While she ate mechanically she cautioned herself that she must not let this rogue sway her from the course already charted for her. A friendship with Rory MacLaren could only get in the way of the work she had been sent to do.

"Are you pleased with the quarters provided you?" the king asked his bride.

Although Henrietta Maria understood English well enough, she was reluctant to speak it because of her thick accent. With a blush, she simply nodded.

"I trust you are not overtired from the reception being given you during your travels?"

The new queen shook her head and averted her gaze.

"By the gods, woman, are you mute?"

Henrietta Maria's eyes widened at his tone. Never had she been spoken to in such a manner. She had, after all, been raised a royal princess. And was she not now queen?

With an accent thickened by anger, she sputtered, "I find this lodging merely adequate. But I 'ave been trained since birth to withstand the rigors of state visits in foreign lands. And as for your last impertinent question, I can speak as well as anyone. I prefer the language of my homeland until such time as I can speak yours without ridicule."

The king lifted an eyebrow and regarded his bride with new interest. So. She was not a little mouse who would bow and scrape before him. Good. He'd had enough of those in his life. What he wanted was a woman with spunk. A woman of spirit who would stand up to the fools at court.

"As you wish, madam. In public you may allow your lady-in-waiting to speak your words." He leaned closer and added, "But when we are alone, I want to hear your voice. It pleases me."

Color stained her cheeks. "If it pleases you, sir, it pleases me, as well."

For a long, silent moment the king regarded her. Abruptly he stood, negligently pushing back the heavy oak chair. "Come. I wish to be alone with my bride."

"If you please, sir," the queen said haltingly, "I desire the assistance of my lady-in-waiting to prepare me for our wedding bed."

"Prepare you?" His impatience with such rituals was obvious. Everything in his life had been attended to with pomp and circumstance. Glancing beyond her, he made no effort to veil the sarcasm in his voice. "MacLaren. You and Lady Thornhill will accompany your king and queen to their rooms."

"As you wish, Your Highness."

Rory stood. Once again Courtney was obliged to take his arm. With her head held high, she swept from the dining hall behind the royal couple. Behind them, Lord Burlingame watched through narrowed eyes.

Upstairs, a suite of rooms had been prepared for the king and queen. While Charles and Rory lounged before a blazing fire, drinking from tankards of ale, Courtney moved around the private bedchamber, helping the queen prepare. A tub of water had been installed before a second fireplace. While one maid removed the queen's clothes, another waited with scented soap and soft towels. When the bath was completed, Courtney helped Henrietta Maria into a satin-and-lace night shift with wide sleeves and a high neckline that gave only a hint of the firm young breasts beneath. Her tiny waist was accentuated by a wide satin sash. The skirt was yards of handsewn lace. When her hair had been brushed into soft waves that fell below her shoulders, Courtney took her hand. It was cold. So cold.

"You are a vision of loveliness, Majesty. The moment he sees you, your husband will fall under your spell."

"God willing, Courtney. God willing."

Taking a last look in her mirror, the queen lifted her chin, straightened her shoulders and strode regally into the sitting room.

Courtney followed.

The two men were bent close, in quiet conversation. When the queen entered, their voices faded. Both heads came up. On the king's face was a look of surprise that quickly changed to one of pleasure.

He placed his tankard on a table beside his chair and walked over to her. Taking her hand, he murmured, "You are truly beautiful. My subjects will be pleased with their lovely new queen."

"Thank you, my lord."

Turning to Courtney, the king said, "Thank you for your assistance, Lady Thornhill." His voice warmed with humor. "I believe the queen will have no further need of you tonight. What we have to say to each other will be understood without the aid of your translations."

"No, my lord. I mean, yes, my lord." Blushing furiously, Courtney bowed her way toward the door. "Good night, sir. Madam."

"By the gods, madam," the king said to his bride. "I believe your lady-in-waiting is a blushing virgin."

Courtney's cheeks grew crimson.

"MacLaren." The king's voice was choked with laughter. "Invite the council to come and give witness to the fact that the royal marriage has been consummated according to the laws of England and the holy church." Before he could turn away, he added as an afterthought, "You and Lady Thornhill are invited to witness the event, as well."

Seeing the stunned look on Courtney's face, Rory caught her roughly by the arm and drew her firmly from the room. "Aye, Majesty. I shall summon the council. But I believe that Lady Thornhill should retire for the night."

When they were out of earshot, Courtney pulled her arm from his grasp. "I am certain that the crude men downstairs will find great humor in their king's pronouncement."

"Do not be offended. It has always been the custom to guarantee that the royal marriages are consummated, in order to assure the royal lineage."

"Go then and spread the word to the men who await word of their precious king and his future issue."

Rory's tone was gentle. "Do not be angry."

"I am not angry. I am offended for the queen."

His tone lowered. "I know that you have been sheltered from such things. But Henrietta Maria has not. She will understand and accept. Come." He took her arm. "I will escort you to your room."

"I am quite capable of finding my own way."

"I am certain you are." She heard the deep rumble of his laughter as he added, "But I am curious to see the quarters given the queen's chief lady-in-waiting. Besides, I fear if I allow you to linger here you may decide to storm the king's bedchambers to protect your queen."

"She is young. And frightened."

"She is the queen of England. No harm shall come to her."

Courtney studied him for a long moment. In the light of the flickering torches set along the hall, his face was touched by shadows, adding to his dark and dangerous looks.

"I think even you, Rory MacLaren, cannot guarantee the safety of your queen."

He knew all too well the wisdom of her words. "Come, spitfire, I will do as the king ordered and see you safely to your room."

They walked down a hallway lighted by torches. When Courtney stopped before a set of double doors, Rory reached around her and threw them open. The suite was nearly as large as the one occupied by the royal couple.

Staring, Rory exclaimed, "Such luxury, my lady. After your years aboard the *Hawk*, it must be quite strange to have so much room."

Hearing the mention of the *Hawk*, Courtney felt a lump growing in her throat. Her voice was choked for a moment. "Aye. Strange."

Instantly Rory touched a hand to her shoulder. With a reticence born of years of habit, she pulled away and drew her arms around herself. She walked to the window, determined to put some distance between herself and this man who continued to threaten her composure.

He watched as her gaze was drawn to the blackened sky outside her window. Seeing the hungry look in her eyes, he repented the questions he'd come here ready to have answered. He had fully intended to challenge her position, to demand to know what a pirate's daughter was doing in the company of the queen. But now, feeling a flood of tenderness for the beautiful young woman, he decided to wait. There would be many other opportunities to question her. Of that he had no doubt. There was no way he would allow her presence in this country to threaten his king.

Tonight he would speak of things that would soothe rather than irritate. The lady showed every sign of exhaustion.

His voice, when at last he spoke, was low with emotion. "It takes time to adjust to a new place."

"I shall have plenty of that here in England." She gave a long, deep sigh that tugged at his heart. "I am a French citizen, squandering my time in England."

He moved closer until he was standing directly behind her. He was careful not to touch her. He had already seen and felt her reaction to his touch. And though the mere thought of touching her caused an ache deep inside him, he resisted.

His voice, low and deep, whispered over her senses. "And I am a Scotsman, forced to live in England."

"Why?" She turned slightly and was surprised to find him so close. She backed away until her back brushed the cold stone wall. A tiny thrill raced along her spine at the nearness of him. Fear? she wondered. Or anticipation?

"Because the king desires my counsel."

His voice was so deep, deeper even than she had remembered. "And your own people?"

"They grow restless without their leader."

He was far more handsome than she remembered. Had his shoulders always been so broad? Had his manner always been so threatening? "What happened to your brother, Malcolm?"

It pleased Rory that she remembered his brother's name. How much else did she remember? His touch, perhaps? His kiss? He must not think of such things. As a member of the king's council, it was his duty to learn why she was here.

"Dead. He died in a battle with a party of Englishmen who crossed the border and tried to loot our crops."

She saw the pain that clouded his eyes momentarily. Death. It was always painful. And the pain could be resurrected at the oddest times. "But you are friend to the king of England. How can such a thing occur between friends?"

"To prove his friendship, Charles's father, James, punished the villains. They paid with their lives. But that does not bring back my brother."

"And your land?"

"It is secure. For the moment. But if I stay away too long I fear the villagers to the north will take advantage of a leaderless clan."

"Then you will soon be returning to Scotland?"

"Aye."

At his words she felt a sudden sharp ache around her heart. Why should she care whether or not this Scotsman stayed in England? Did she not have important work to do? Work that could only be slowed or distracted by his presence?

"You are now the MacLaren?"

"Aye." His gaze was drawn to her mouth. He longed to pull her roughly against him and kiss her soundly. For months he had thought of nothing else. But he cautioned himself to go slowly. From the looks of her she had been through much these last weeks. Her hands were clenched into tiny fists at her sides. There were circles beneath her eyes that indicated a lack of sleep. And there was a puzzling tension in her that had not been there aboard her ship.

There would be other times, other places, he reminded himself. And, at least for a while, they would be together often at court.

"What you need is rest, my lady. I will leave you now."

He crossed to the door and placed his hand on the pull. Pausing, he turned. His voice barely more than a whisper, he said, "Welcome to England, Courtney. And a taste of my world."

Before she could respond, he was gone. She studied the closed doors, then turned to stare out the window.

What had she gotten herself into? How could she ever do this thing demanded of her?

She was suddenly bone-weary. Too weary to stand. Summoning a maid, she undressed and tumbled into bed.

All through the night her dreams were haunted by visions of a king and queen at opposite ends of a long table. And seated in the middle was a swordsman who held an entire company of soldiers at bay. When she grasped a sword and tried to help him, he thrust it aside and ordered her to sit quietly like a lady.

Which side was she on? And he? The rules had all been changed. A voice, warm with laughter, shouted, "Welcome to my world, my lady." And though the swordsman's face was not clear, she awoke whispering his name. Rory. Rory MacLaren.

Chapter Seven

Breakfast, Courtney learned the next morning, was enjoyed by the king and his entourage with as much gusto as supper. Aboard ship she had often worked two hours or more, shivering in the morning mist, before stopping for a bowl of gruel. Here on English soil a member of the king's household staff announced that the morning fast would be broken immediately upon arising. The king, resplendent in a hunting jacket and tight-fitting breeches, sat beside his wife at the head table. Though she said little, Henrietta Maria smiled at her husband often and blushed furiously when he bent to whisper in her ear. There was no doubt in Courtney's mind that the young monarchs were enormously pleased with each other. Except for the homage paid them by the others in the room, they looked like any newly married couple wrapped up in their love for one another.

"How slept you?" the young queen asked as her lady-in-waiting took a seat beside her.

"I slept well, Majesty."

Rory glanced at the dark circles beneath Courtney's eyes and saw through her lie. It was obvious that this journey to England was taking its toll on her. And though he burned with questions, he vowed to go slowly. Given enough time, he would uncover the truth. Time. He smiled to himself.

Had not the Fates brought him here to this place at this time?

He leaned closer. "Perhaps, my lady, you would like to see some of the lovely countryside today. The cliffs of Dover afford a magnificent view of the sea, as well as this fair island you will now call home."

Home. Courtney swallowed the protest that sprang to her lips. How could this place ever be home when she had come here with the intention of spying for its enemy, France?

"My duties lie with my queen. She relies on me for personal assistance, as well as translation of your confusing language. I have no taste for frivolous diversions from the task at hand."

Rory forced himself not to laugh at her haughty tone. The words she spoke were Thornhill's. It was obvious that she had learned her lessons well.

"As you wish, my lady. I would not want to waste your time with pleasantries."

Across the room, Lord Burlingame studied the man and woman who sat with the king and queen at the royal table. With narrowed eyes he watched as their heads bent in intimate conversation. Was not he, Burlingame, the king's chief councillor, the one to whom the king turned for advice on matters of state? And yet each time MacLaren returned to England's shores the king showered favors upon the Scot. Favors that should have been bestowed only upon Burlingame. If it were not for MacLaren, Burlingame thought with a growing sense of frustration, he would be the one seated beside the beautiful lady-in-waiting to the queen.

His gaze centered on Courtney. It was not just her beauty that fascinated him. All his life he had been surrounded by beautiful women. Not as beautiful as Lady Courtney to be sure, for she was a rare beauty. And women of every age and size intrigued him. Nay, it was more than the pretty picture she presented. It was her cool dismissal of him that both fascinated and angered him. He had never had that effect on a woman before. Here in England, the wives and daughters of the noblemen with whom he associated were aware of his position of power. Even if they were more attracted to another man, they were clever enough to give Burlingame their undivided attention until such time as he tired of their company and dismissed them. But this woman...

He studied Courtney more closely. Lady Courtney Thornhill was an altogether unusual woman. He had once come upon a band of gypsies in his travels. There had been something about them—a flash of fire in their eyes, a defiant toss of their heads, a look of fearlessness—that had intrigued him. The queen's lady-in-waiting had such a look. There was much more to the lady than met the eye.

Burlingame lifted his goblet to his lips and drank his fill. When he looked up, the lady in question glanced his way. For a moment their gazes met and held. Then, without expression, Courtney turned her attention to the king and queen. Burlingame's lips tightened. No woman, and especially no Frenchwoman, could treat him with such disdain. He would wait and watch. And when the time was right he would teach Lady Courtney Thornhill a lesson she would never forget.

Rory and Courtney trailed behind the king and queen as Charles introduced his bride to the household staff. Courtney paid close attention to the way the servants reacted to the queen. There might come a time when she would have to call upon one of them for a favor. A stranger in a strange land often had to depend upon the kindness of others.

When the introductions were complete, the king led his bride to the gardens. There, away from the prying eyes of the king's council, Charles and Henrietta Maria clasped hands and moved slowly through the rows of carefully tended hedges. To afford them their privacy, Rory and Courtney walked some distance behind.

"You are quiet, my lady. Are you tired?"

"Tired? Nay. For the first time since our journey began, I feel rested. There is something peaceful about this place."

"Aye. After the chaos of London, Dover is like a sleepy little village."

"Tell me about London," Courtney said, pausing in the shade of a gracefully curved trellis.

Rory studied the way the breeze teased her hair, longing to reach out a hand to touch her. But he had seen the way she stiffened each time they were forced together. Would she ever relax enough in his company to allow him the privilege of holding her hand? Of touching her lips with his?

"It is a busy, bustling city," Rory began.

"Like Paris?" She swallowed her disappointment. How she hated Paris.

"Nay. London has a flavor all its own. On the streets you will meet shopkeepers, fishmongers, pickpockets and thieves, as well as highborn men and women." He smiled at her look of surprise. "The people there have a keen sense of right and wrong, and an even keener interest in their monarch. If the king ever wants to know what the people are thinking, he need only walk down any street in London and the citizens of that fine city will tell him."

"Is the king free to walk the streets of London?" She tried to imagine Henrietta Maria moving freely around Paris. Whenever the French royal family left the palace they traveled in closed carriages to avoid seeing the poverty of the common people.

"Aye. Unfortunately, Charles chooses to heed the advice of his council and hold himself apart from his subjects. It would do him good to walk among them and hear what they have to say. In my country the head of a clan works alongside his people, sharing their pain, as well as their joy."

Courtney heard the note of pride in Rory's voice and wondered about a land that could foster such passion in its people.

"You must miss Scotland very much."

"Aye." Unable to resist any longer, he touched a hand to her hair and watched through narrowed eyes as the silken strands sifted through his fingers. "Though at this moment I must confess I do not regret being in England."

His words caused a tiny flutter deep inside her. She berated herself for the weakness in her that permitted such honeyed words to penetrate her heart. But before she could utter a sharp retort she heard the sound of footsteps along the garden path. Rory and Courtney looked up as the king and queen approached.

"We have decided to retire to our suite of rooms," the king said.

Courtney took a step away from Rory. "Then I shall go with you." She would be relieved to put some distance between them. Whenever they were thrown together she was reminded of the night aboard the *Hawk* when he kissed her. And she had the distinct feeling that he remembered it, too.

Courtney saw the queen cast a dubious glance at her husband.

He gave Henrietta Maria a look that spoke volumes. "We wish to be alone. We will have no further need of your company until we sup tonight."

Courtney felt her face go scarlet as the realization of their plans dawned. They hoped to slip away so that they could love without interruption.

Rory nearly laughed at her confusion. "Then this would be the perfect opportunity to introduce Lady Thornhill to the beauties of Dover."

"But I—"

"Excellent." Henrietta Maria accepted her husband's outstretched hand, then turned to Courtney with a bright smile. "You must tell me everything you see, Courtney, so that I can learn from you about my new home."

Courtney refused to meet Rory's eyes. There would be laughter there, she knew, just below the surface. Laughter at her naïveté. And at her predicament. But despite her anger at being trapped into spending more time alone with him, she felt a sense of relief. For a little while, at least, she could forget about her duties as lady-in-waiting and enjoy the simple beauty of this strange land.

"As you wish, Majesty." To Rory she said, "I will need time to change into something suitable for riding."

"I will have a carriage at your disposal when you are ready."

She kept her gaze averted as she turned away and hurried to her room.

"Come. A visit to Dover is not complete without a view from here."

Taking her hand, Rory assisted her from the small, sleek carriage and led her to the very edge of the cliffs.

Courtney stood beside Rory, staring out to sea. In the course of the afternoon they had passed through shady glens and green meadows. In the villages they had witnessed women, babies at their hips, carrying baskets of freshly baked bread to market. Women and children milled around a sparkling stream, wringing out clothes or bathing young ones, while the older children shrieked and giggled, chasing each other in games of hide-and-seek. Men labored in the fields or hunted game. Everywhere she looked, Courtney saw happiness and contentment on the faces of the English people.

"Is it not a glorious sight?" Rory pointed to the spot on the horizon where sea met sky.

She swallowed the lump that rose to her throat. "Aye. I shall miss the sea."

"It is all around you here in England. This land is an island that depends upon the sea for its very existence."

She nodded, trying desperately not to cry. "I know. And I have been given a fine life here with the queen. I have no right to grieve for a way of life that was harsh and demanding."

"We all grieve for what we leave behind, Courtney." Rory took her hand in his and was pleasantly surprised when she offered no resistance.

As she stared out to sea he studied her hand, tanned from a life in the sun, callused from years of labor. Yet, despite all that, it was a small hand, decidedly feminine, and the mere touch of it sent his pulse racing.

When she firmly withdrew her hand, he said casually, "I hope the ride through the countryside has whetted your appetite."

At her puzzled expression he walked to the carriage and lifted down a trunk. From within he produced a thick coverlet that he spread on the ground beneath a gnarled old tree. Taking Courtney's hand, he settled her comfortably on the coverlet. Then he proceeded to unwrap the linen coverings to reveal a complete meal. Cold venison and mutton, thick, crusty bread still bearing a trace of warmth from the oven and delicate fluted tarts spread with honey were arranged neatly in front of her.

"How ever did you do all this?" Courtney could not hide her surprise. "It is a feast fit for royalty."

"And prepared in a royal manner. I told the cook that it was to be a special treat for the queen's favorite lady-in-waiting."

"She has outdone herself. I must remember to thank her when we return."

Rory glanced toward her and realized that she was serious. "The cook will like that. Too often the king forgets to thank those who labor for him."

Biting into the warm bread, Courtney sighed. "I have never eaten outdoors in such a manner before."

"Then I am doubly glad that I thought of it. When the king goes on a hunt, he often has his servants fetch tables, chairs and dishes so that his every comfort is assured."

"I am not accustomed to the excesses of royalty."

At the realization of what she had just said, Courtney nearly groaned aloud. Such remarks could only lead to more questions. Questions she dared not answer.

As if he had read her mind, Rory easily changed the subject. "What do you think of your first long look at England?"

Courtney swallowed, grateful for his kindness. "I find the people of Dover surprisingly cheerful."

"Why are you surprised at their good cheer?"

"I was told—" She swallowed and tried again. "I heard that the people of England were sorely oppressed by their king. But perhaps the people in the countryside are not as oppressed as those in cities like London."

Wisely Rory kept his thoughts to himself. It was obvious that Courtney had been fed a diet of hatred for many years. The damage could not be undone overnight. "You shall soon see for yourself, my lady. When you arrive in London you will have a chance to compare the people there with the citizens of France."

For a while they ate in silence, enjoying the sunshine and the excellent food. For Courtney this was something new and strange, a chance to savor good food in the company of a man who was relaxed and charming. It was obvious that Rory was doing everything he could to put her at ease.

Suddenly Courtney was on her feet, staring out to sea. "Look! Oh, Rory, look!"

He came to his feet beside her. Without thinking, she touched a hand to his arm. Though he was startled by her action, he said nothing, absorbing the warmth of her touch, allowing himself to follow the direction of her gaze.

"It is a Spanish ship, I think." Her voice was low with wonder. "How bold, to sail so close to English soil."

"Bold and foolish. Look." Grasping her shoulders, he turned her slightly so that she became aware of a second ship farther out to sea. "An English ship, I'll wager, forcing the Spanish boat to risk the cliffs and rocks that ring this shore or meet their attack."

Courtney nodded. "It is what Thornhill would have done. A wise move on the part of the English dogs."

When she realized what she had said, she covered her mouth. Instantly Rory's hands tightened on her shoulders. She looked up to see him studying her through narrowed eyes.

"Careful, my lady. If the king hears such blasphemy he will have your head."

"Oh, Rory." She closed her eyes a moment to shut out the intense light that burned in his gaze. How could she hope to keep her secret from this man? He knew her. He knew what she had been. It was only a matter of time before he guessed the reason for her presence on English soil.

"Courtney."

At the softness of his tone, she blinked her eyes open. He was staring at her with a tenderness she had never seen before.

"I know that your years with Thornhill have ill prepared you for England. But give it time."

She took a deep breath. "Aye. Time." She swallowed, feeling her pulse begin to accelerate. Why did the hands at her shoulders not offend her? Why did the lips so close to hers not repel her? "I feel so alone here."

"You are not alone. It is obvious that you have endeared yourself to the queen."

"But I cannot speak of my fears to the queen."

"You have me."

The hands at her shoulders gentled, their thumbs making lazy circles on the tender flesh of her upper arms. He bent toward her until his lips were mere inches from hers. As he spoke, his breath mingled with hers, making her pulse quicken again.

"If you let me, Courtney, I will be your friend." His head lowered until his lips brushed hers lightly. "And more."

She stiffened and drew back for a moment, surprised by his boldness. She brought her two fists to his chest as a barrier between them. Then, remembering that she was no longer aboard the *Hawk*, she let out a long, shaky breath. They were in England, far from Thornhill's reach. They were in an isolated spot in Dover, where no one could see them.

How long had she wondered about this man and dreamed about his touch, his kiss? Now, finally, she had the chance to relive that moment aboard ship when he had held her and kissed her until the very breath had left her lungs. She had replayed that scene in her mind for so long that she was certain she had magnified it beyond reality. Right now, at this moment, Rory MacLaren was here. He was no longer just a dream, he was real and warm and inviting.

Without her realizing it, Courtney's hands unclenched. With her fingers splayed against his chest, she moved imperceptibly closer.

Feeling her reaction, Rory brought his arms around her and drew her into his embrace.

"Much, much more than a mere friend," he whispered as his mouth covered hers.

Courtney felt a rush of heat that left her flushed and breathless. The air around them smelled of the sea. It was a scent that always evoked strong feelings in her. Unconsciously she breathed it in as he drew her closer, then closer still, until her breasts were flattened against his chest. Seemingly of their own volition, her hands moved up until her arms found their way around his neck. Her body strained against his, no longer stiff and unyielding, but warm and pliant.

As he took the kiss deeper, she lost the ability to think. She lost herself in a mindless pleasure unlike anything she had ever experienced.

His teeth nipped her lower lip. His tongue probed the sweetness of her mouth, and she boldly followed suit. She heard his quiet moan as he tasted, nibbled, explored. And then, suddenly, his lips left hers to rain kisses over her cheeks, her eyelids, her temple. When at last his mouth returned to hers, she responded eagerly, her lips avid, searching. The passion that flowed between them caught them both by surprise.

He hadn't expected to feel this way. Until now it had been a challenge to touch her. But a touch led to a kiss. And this kiss was leading him to something higher. Passion? Yes, and much more. Need. A wild, driving need that threatened to shatter his cool control.

The exotic fragrance of French perfume drifted around her. It seemed to weave a spell around him, leaving him weak. And her taste. Like a primitive wildflower. He was drowning in the taste of her. In his arms she was the perfect woman, soft, pliant, feminine. But there was something different about her, something that set her apart from all others. Innocence, he reasoned, with a hint of wicked willfulness. He steeped himself in her and found that he wanted more.

His hands moved to her hips, dragging her closer, tormenting them both. Soon, he knew, kisses would not be enough. His hands moved seductively upward until they found the swell of her breasts. As his thumbs caressed her hardened nipples, he felt her stiffen. He swallowed her little gasp of surprise. Immediately he brought his hands to her back and held her close when she tried to pull away.

He had to end this—had to, before he lost control and took her too far, too fast. Still, he lingered, savoring the sweet taste of her. He was holding heaven in his arms, and the thought of relinquishing her caused an ache around his heart. Rory allowed himself one last drugging kiss, then slowly drew away.

They were both shaken, and they were both trying desperately not to show it. Courtney's pulse continued to hammer in her temples. Because she was not quite steady, she drew herself up very straight. And because her breath was still coming in short little gasps, she filled her lungs with the salty sea breeze.

Rory waited a moment, hoping his voice would be normal when he spoke. "If you will wait in the carriage, my lady, I will have this trunk packed in no time."

Courtney did not argue. She needed to sit down until her breathing returned to normal. Besides, now that she could think again, she was cursing herself for acting every kind of fool. Only a fool would allow the enemy to get this close. And whether she liked it or not, Rory MacLaren was the enemy. Richelieu had seen to that.

As she walked away, Rory bent and began packing the food and the coverlet back into the trunk. The thought of her was driving him slowly mad. He had to have her. Had to. Touching her, kissing her, would never be enough.

Chapter Eight

The king and queen tarried two days at Dover. And though Courtney invented reasons to hide in her suite of rooms, it was impossible to avoid Rory MacLaren completely. He was there at every meal, staring at her, his blue eyes searching hers, seeking answers to questions she knew he would soon ask. Each time she looked at him she thought about his touch, his kiss, and her blood warmed.

As the king's favorite, he was often invited to sit beside the king and queen. And because Henrietta Maria insisted upon having Courtney always at her side, it was inevitable that Courtney and Rory would be thrown together constantly.

Besides mealtimes, Courtney was expected to attend the queen whenever she was forced to be in the company of the king's council. Though the queen clearly understood all that was being said, she often used the ploy of asking Courtney to translate the English into French, which allowed her a few extra minutes to formulate a clever response. The queen was especially cool to Lord Burlingame. It was as if, Courtney thought as she watched them, each saw the other as the enemy. Henrietta Maria obviously resented the influence Burlingame exerted on the king. And Burlingame, as chief among the king's councillors, plainly feared that the new French bride would drive a wedge between the king and his trusted advisers.

Often, when the queen was alone, she invited her lady-in-waiting to sit with her. At these times Courtney witnessed the depth of the young queen's loneliness. Wed to a man she had never met, forced to live in a foreign land, the young woman had few friends in whom she could confide. She was well aware of the plotting and scheming that would greet her in London. She would wisely take her time sorting through the people close to the king, to decide which were the villains and which could be trusted.

"The Scot, MacLaren."

At the mere mention of his name, Courtney went very still.

The queen glanced up from the painstaking stitches she was working. The embroidered pillow was to be a present to her husband upon their arrival in London. "The king considers him a trusted friend."

Courtney waited, keeping her gaze on the needlework in her hand. She detested sewing. Detested this silly busywork that all other women seemed to enjoy. She yearned to stand on the deck of her ship and feel the fresh wind fill her lungs.

"He is handsome, is he not?"

Courtney glanced up to find the queen studying her carefully.

"He is, Majesty."

"Are you attracted to him?"

Courtney swallowed. She was not accustomed to such directness from a woman. "I have little time for the attentions of men, Majesty."

"I have noted as much, Courtney. But it would please the king if you were to be...more receptive to Rory MacLaren's attentions."

"Why?"

"He feels that his friend is lonely away from his land and the friendship of his clan. I think also that the king desires his friend to acquire some...attachments in England, so that he will not resent the time he must spend here."

"And you, Majesty? What think you?"

The queen gave her a knowing smile. "I would please my husband."

Courtney nodded and averted her gaze. "As you wish."

The queen's laugh caused her to look up suddenly. "I am not asking you to shed your blood for me, my dear friend." Her smile faded. "Though that is not beyond the realm of possibility one day." Her smile grew again, as if she were determined not to dwell on the perils in this new life. "There are many women, I think, who would be delighted to have such orders from their queen. The MacLaren is a man who makes maidens' hearts flutter."

Courtney's own smile faltered. "My heart does not flutter so easily, Majesty."

"So I have noticed." The queen brought her needle through the cloth and glanced at the bowed head of the young woman seated across from her. She had also noticed the way Courtney blushed whenever MacLaren caught her eye. "I have had enough handwork, Courtney. Walk with me in the gardens."

"With pleasure, Majesty."

The queen could not help but note the speed with which her lady-in-waiting disposed of her embroidery. Courtney had obviously had little training in the art of being a sedate, patient woman.

As they walked through the sun-drenched gardens, the queen paused to admire an early rose. When she looked up, she saw Courtney staring intently at a man who stood with his back to her just a few feet away. When he turned, she noted that Courtney quickly averted her gaze.

The queen greeted him warmly. "Rory MacLaren. Will you walk with us awhile?"

"It would be a pleasure, madam." He bowed slightly before the queen, then turned to include Courtney in the gesture. "The English weather is cooperating to make you feel at home here."

"We are most grateful." The queen walked several steps in front of MacLaren and Courtney, lifting her skirts slightly as she glided along a grassy path. "The gardens are lovely."

"All of England seeks your approval, madam."

The queen turned and gave him a knowing smile. "Surely not all of England is rejoicing over their new French-born queen. I sense that there are many, like Lord Burlingame, who would have preferred a gentle English lady at their king's side."

"All loyal English rejoice that their king has found a woman worthy of him."

Henrietta Maria's laughter trilled on the afternoon air. Turning, she placed a hand on Rory's sleeve and glanced up into his handsome face. "Now I know why Charles is so fond of you. Are you always so gifted with sweet words?"

Rory returned her smile. "'Tis said that a Scot's words are like his sword. Both are straight. And both are true."

The young queen studied Rory for a long, lingering moment. "If you speak the truth to your king, you shall always be his friend." Dropping her hand to her side, she added softly, "And mine." When she lifted her skirts, she turned away from the garden path. "I believe I will rest before supper."

"I will accompany you," Courtney said eagerly.

"No." The queen gave her an innocent smile and turned away. "There is no need. Wake me before the sun sets."

With a sinking heart, Courtney watched her walk away. Had the queen planned this? Again she felt trapped. Why were the Fates forcing her to be so near the one man who could reveal her past and destroy her future?

Rory waited until the queen had departed before speaking. "The king makes ready to leave on the morrow."

"The queen's trunks are packed and ready."

"And you, Courtney? Are you ready for London?"

She pretended to admire a neatly trimmed hedge. "You told me I will find the city interesting."

"It grows lively once more." He studied the shape of her hips and cursed himself for his weakness. "The plague and the spotted fever nearly emptied London. Those who did not die fled to country houses and outlying villages. But the illness is gone. London has again become a place of gaiety."

Gaiety. There was none in her heart when she thought of what awaited her in London. "How did you escape the illness?"

When she turned to him, he was achingly aware of her eyes, eyes that reflected the sun like molten gold. "I was in Scotland, attending to business."

"Does your business often take you away?"

"Aye." He offered her his arm and was aware of her slight hesitation before she placed her hand gently upon his sleeve. They moved along the path, stopping frequently to admire the early-blooming flowers.

"And does your clan prosper without the leadership of the MacLaren?"

He heard the challenging note in her voice but refused to take the bait. "The MacLarens are a hearty, industrious clan. Our cattle are sleek, our crops heavy in the fields."

"Ripe pickings for those more willing to steal than to work. Is that not why your brother was killed?"

"Aye."

Courtney saw his eyes narrow slightly and realized she had struck a nerve. That fact should have given her pleasure. Instead, she was eager to change the subject to one less disturbing. "I shall miss this place. The queen has been light of heart since the arrival of her husband, the king."

"The king, too, seems more relaxed since leaving the cares of London behind. Parliament and the king's council give Charles no rest."

"Could he be persuaded to stay a while longer?"

Courtney knew even before Rory spoke that her question was pointless. But how she yearned to stay here, away from London, away from her destiny. She wished with all her heart that she could be free of this terrible burden that Richelieu had placed upon her young shoulders.

Rory's words were prophetic. "The king has a duty. As do you and I."

Rory turned and led her back along the grassy garden path. At the entrance to the courtyard, he bent low over her hand.

"I have given you this time of reprieve, my lady, knowing that your journey was a trying one. But when we reach London, know that we must speak privately."

Courtney felt her heart lurch and strove to show no emotion. "As you wish, my lord."

She watched as he strode toward the stables. With one last lingering look, she gathered her skirts to turn. She knew what questions Rory would ask. And she knew that he would not rest until he was satisfied with her answers. Lying did not come easily to her. But if the truth were ever discovered, she would surely pay with her life.

She turned away, unaware of the man who stood in the shadows, watching her intently. As he moved across the garden, the sunlight glinted on his pale hair and touched his gray eyes with a cold, opaque light.

Courtney stood beside the king and queen as the royal barge sailed up the Thames. Thousands of people lined the shore, waving and cheering. Ships of the king's navy formed an escort, following in the wake of the barge. The bells of every church in London began pealing joyously.

As the barge pulled up to the seawall, the army, resplendent in crimson tunics and gold braid, fired a volley, followed by the thunder of cannons. Courtney felt the queen flinch as the sound reverberated across the sky.

"See how they come to greet you?" the king said, his voice booming above the din. He was magnificent in a regal purple tunic and a many-plumed hat.

"And you, my lord." The queen smiled shyly. "How they must love you."

"Soon they will love you, as well." He studied her for a moment, trying to see her the way these strangers would. Her long black hair was secured by a jeweled tiara. Her gown was purple satin over petticoats of silver and gold thread. An ermine-lined cape had been placed around her shoulders to ward off the slight breeze that blew off the water.

"Come." Tucking her hand through the bend of his arm, the king led her up the steps toward the crowd of ornately dressed lords and ladies who had assembled to greet the royal couple.

"MacLaren," the king called over his shoulder. "See that Lady Thornhill stays close to the queen."

"Aye, Majesty," Rory said, offering his arm to Courtney.

Straightening her spine, Courtney prepared herself for what was to come. There would be the fears of Henrietta Maria, of course. Meeting so many strangers, speaking in a strange tongue, would weigh heavily upon the young queen. Also, France was sending the queen's personal confessor to attend the queen and her company of servants, all of whom shared her faith. The presence of clergy would add greatly to the queen's burden. But Courtney had fears of her own that she had to deal with. This was the enemy, she reminded herself. And she must constantly be on her guard.

In the gardens of Stafford House, Viscountess Biddle, an aging cousin of the king's, led the parade of well-wishers. For hours a never-ending stream of men and women bowed and curtsied as they were introduced to their queen.

Courtney's head began to swim with names and titles. How could Richelieu expect her to remember which of these men were loyal to their king and which ones might be willing to share their secrets for gold?

Cardinal Richelieu had assured her that there were many in England who wanted Charles dead, as they had wanted his father, James I, dead. And these men would care little how it was accomplished as long as the deed could not be traced to them. It would be her job to ferret them out and approach them at the proper time. When Richelieu commanded it. The very thought of him caused a shiver along her spine.

"You are pale, my lady," Rory whispered, bringing her out of her reverie. "Drink this."

He handed her a glass of ale and watched as she sipped gratefully.

"It will soon be over," he said, taking the empty glass from her hand, "and you will be able to let down your guard and rest."

His words made Courtney want to weep. She was so weary. And yet she would never again be able to let down her guard.

"I have met so many lords and ladies, they have become a blur to me."

"But only for a little while. Soon," he said, glancing around the gardens, "some of them will become friends."

He felt the little tremor in her hand and wondered about it. Did she really fear that no one would befriend her? Was she not aware of her own beauty? Had she not noticed the envious looks of many of the women as they passed her? Or the way their men looked at her? Not with envy, but with admiration? Rory studied the way she looked, with the warm May sunlight bathing her in a golden glow. Despite his reservations about her, despite the many questions that danced through his mind, he could not deny that he was attracted to her. She was clearly the most striking woman in this company.

It was difficult for him to imagine a dark side to the beautiful woman beside him, but he knew of her past, and that knowledge would forever lie between them. He had to know her reason for being here. Yet he dreaded the answers to his questions.

"We will rest," the king said when the last of the well-wishers had passed the receiving line. "There is a grand ball tonight in our honor."

As she and Rory followed the king and queen to their waiting coach, Courtney felt herself reeling. Was it not enough that she must wear these ridiculous clothes and spend endless hours listening to the idle chatter of women she knew little or nothing about? Now she would be expected to dance. A feeling of near-terror gripped her.

"Are you ill?" Rory asked when he saw her pale face.

"Nay, my lord. I am perhaps overtired."

Placing a hand beneath her elbow, he assisted her into the coach and took the seat beside her. With a sinking heart, Courtney realized that Lord Burlingame was already seated across from her.

"It is good to be home, is it not, Majesty?" Burlingame asked with pretended innocence.

"It is."

"I hope the palace is to your liking," Burlingame said to the queen.

She said nothing.

"I see that you spend a great deal of your time outdoors, Lady Thornhill," Burlingame said with an icy smile.

When Courtney did not respond, he added softly, "I have never seen an English lady with such high coloring.

Almost as if—" he sneered faintly "—you had spent your days in the sun, rather than in the company of your queen."

"That is because I am not an English lady. Have you forgotten that we are French?" Courtney strove for a lightness she did not feel.

"I have forgotten nothing, my lady."

An uncomfortable silence settled over the passengers in the coach.

Though he said nothing during the long ride to the palace, Courtney could feel the solicitous glances Rory sent her from time to time.

When they reached their destination, Courtney began to make her way toward the coaches that carried the maids.

"Where are you going?" Rory caught her arm roughly, forcing her to pause.

"I must see to the queen's trunks."

"There are maids to see to that."

"But it is part of my duties."

Though the hand holding her gentled, his voice was gruff. "You are no longer aboard the *Hawk*, my lady. You are not expected to work until you drop. Thornhill is not looking over your shoulder at every turn."

If only he knew.

She glared at his offending hand. "I can still work all day and half the night if need be."

"Of that I have no doubt." His voice lowered. "But it is not necessary. Come."

She studied the hand he extended to her. With a sigh, she accepted it and allowed herself to be led inside the castle. As they climbed wide wooden stairs, she managed to glance around her at the imposing tapestries on the wall. Some showed colorful scenes of the hunt, while on others were scenes of battle. Still others bore images of beautiful maidens and handsome knights.

Courtney blinked and closed her eyes. She could still see the haunting images, and she felt as if she were caught up in the scenes they depicted. She knew them. All of them. Yet she had only glimpsed them for a moment.

Along the upper gallery were hung portraits of past monarchs, men who had occupied the throne of England before Charles. Seeing them peering down at her, Courtney had a sudden sense that they knew her, knew what she was planning to do in their country, their very home.

Rory felt her hand tighten upon his arm and glanced down at her. Her skin was the color of alabaster. Her eyes glittered a little too brightly. Concerned, he placed his hand over hers and felt the slight trembling that she could not control.

When they reached the suite of rooms that had been prepared for her, Courtney thanked Rory for his assistance.

"You must rest, my lady. I think you are feeling overwrought."

"Yes." She turned away, eager to be alone. "A little rest and I shall be fine."

Rory watched as she quickly closed the door to her room. For a long moment he stood in the hall, debating whether to leave or to knock and assure himself that she was indeed all right.

When the door was closed, Courtney glanced around the ornate suite of rooms that had been prepared for her. In the sitting room, two chairs, elegantly draped with brocade, stood on either side of a fireplace. Between them was a settle covered in furs. Despite the warmth of the day, a log crackled invitingly on the grate.

There was a cheerfulness, a cozy warmth, to this room that touched a chord deep inside her. Home. Except for her tiny room aboard the *Hawk*, she had never had a home. She felt tears mist her eyes. Instantly she brushed them away and moved toward the bedchamber.

Two maids were silently unpacking her trunks, which had been set in one corner of the room. They looked up as their mistress entered, then returned to their work.

Courtney stared at the huge bed that dominated the room. Pale ivory silk draperies had been tied back at each corner of the bed. The bedcovers were of ornately embroidered satin in a design made especially for the royal family. Grapes, leaves and fruit signified fertility. Cattle, forests and lakes were symbols of wealth. And swords, daggers and longbows symbolized strength in battle.

In the bedchamber, as in the sitting room, two ornate chairs were drawn up before a blazing fire. Between them was a settle draped with fur throws. Above the fireplace hung the portrait of a beautiful woman. Courtney's gaze was drawn to the woman's eyes. They were staring at her as if they could see through her.

Courtney's heart began to beat rapidly, and she was aware of a sudden dampness on her skin. Summoning one of the maids to undress her, she stood limply as her clothes were removed.

"Would you care for some refreshment before you retire, my lady?"

Courtney felt a strange buzzing in her head. The young maid's voice seemed to fade, then grow stronger, then fade once more.

"Begging your pardon, my lady. Are you ill?"

Courtney glanced toward the portrait. Had not the woman in the picture been smiling when first she had seen her? Why, then, was she now staring at her coldly?

"My lady?" The little maid was staring at her with that same strange, probing look.

The buzzing grew louder. The room seemed to tilt and sway. Lifting a hand to her forehead, Courtney attempted to speak. Nothing came out except a faint croak.

And then she was falling, falling into a blackness that threatened to envelop her. She cried out, fighting against the darkness. And then she began to drift, drift into blessed unconsciousness.

Chapter Nine

Courtney felt the coolness of a hand on her forehead. How was it possible that, although her eyes remained closed, she was aware of everything in the bedchamber, a room she had seen only briefly?

Against one wall would be the trunks, empty now of their contents. A settle, covered with fur throws, offered a cozy haven for sewing or relaxing.

The fragrance of woodsmoke drifted to her nostrils. In these drafty castles, fires were always kept burning to ward off the chill. She knew that two small carved lions rested on either side of the hearth, a symbol of the royalty who resided within these walls.

In a niche in the corner there was a small recessed window that looked out over the courtyard. A child, standing on a trunk, could see for miles. How could she know that?

A smile touched her lips.

"Ah, I see you are feeling better."

At the familiar sound of Rory's deep voice, her eyes fluttered open. His clear blue eyes were watching her with a look of concern.

"Sir, what are you doing here in my bedchamber?"

"When your maid cried for help, I summoned the king's physician. He says you are fatigued from your long trip and must rest."

"I am fine now." She glanced around and realized that they were alone. "Where are the others?"

"The physician ordered your chambers cleared so that you might rest."

"Yet you stayed."

Rory studied her as if memorizing every curve and line of her face. "I stayed."

She abruptly sat up, and the bedcovers fell away. Her delicate night shift revealed the soft curves of the body beneath. Rory allowed his gaze to drink in the sight of her, so pale, so vulnerable. It was a picture of Courtney he had never seen before.

"I feel rested. As if," she said, swinging her legs to the floor, "I had slept for days."

"In truth, you have slept barely an hour."

When she tried to stand, she swayed slightly. Instantly Rory's arms were around her. Courtney felt a rush of heat and blamed it on the warmth of the fire. She would not allow herself to enjoy the feelings his touch evoked. The trembling in her limbs was merely the result of her weakness. It had nothing to do with the nearness of this man.

"I am fine." She tried to push away, but he held her firmly against him.

"You are trembling, my lady."

"I do not tremble." With as much dignity as she could muster, she pushed herself from his arms and took several halting steps. When her gaze strayed to the portrait over her bed, she quickly looked away.

"What is it, Courtney?" Rory crossed to her and was about to take her arm when he saw her cringe and draw away.

She took several deep breaths. When she was sure she was strong enough, she said, "I do not want you to touch me, MacLaren."

He stiffened. She was the old Courtney once more. Gone was the pallor, the weakness. In their place he saw her strength and determination. Two bright spots of color dotted her cheeks.

"Very well, my lady." As he strode across the room, he said, "The king's physician orders you to stay in bed until he returns on the morrow."

Her words caused him to turn around.

"There is a ball tonight, and I intend to be where I belong. At the queen's side."

"Courtney, you must—"

"I know what I must do," she snapped. "You may inform the king that I shall be there."

Rory studied her for a long, silent moment. Then, bowing, he muttered, "By your leave, my lady."

As soon as he was gone, Courtney rang for her maids.

The great room was awash with color. The men, in tight-fitting breeches and rich brocaded jackets, were as splendid as the ladies in their gowns of watered silks, shimmering satins and lush velvets. The light from a thousand candles was reflected in the diamonds, rubies, sapphires and emeralds that adorned the guests.

Never had Courtney seen such a spectacle. All the English nobility had turned out to welcome their king and queen.

Driven by a sense of duty, Courtney stood beside Henrietta Maria, determined to make her young queen's introduction to English society as painless as possible.

"You look lovely, Courtney," the queen whispered. "I was told that you were ill."

"Only tired, Majesty. I am now quite rested."

"That eases my mind. I feared I would have to face the English alone."

"Fear not, Majesty. I will never desert you."

Courtney felt her voice fade as she watched Rory MacLaren enter the room and begin making his way toward them.

He was clearly the most striking man in the room. In the light of the candles, the russet strands in his dark hair seemed touched with fire. His blue eyes were made even bluer by the indigo satin jacket he wore over dark fitted breeches. Mounds of snowy lace at his throat and cuffs softened the harsh planes and angles of his face.

He paused a moment to speak to a strikingly beautiful woman. Courtney saw the look of admiration in the woman's eyes. While he spoke, Rory looked idly around the room. As his gaze swung past Courtney, he paused, glanced beyond her, then back at her. Their gazes met and held. She felt a shaft of pain pierce her heart as surely as an arrow would have, and found herself wondering at the swift pain. How was it possible that this man could touch her in such a way, touch her as no one else ever had or would?

Courtney forced her mind back to the task at hand and continued translating the words of greeting being spoken to the queen. While the last of the guests passed by, she allowed herself the luxury of studying the spectacle spread out before her.

Finally the king and queen led the way toward the banquet hall. As if on cue, Rory was at Courtney's side, offering his arm.

"You look lovely, my lady."

Lovely. He thought the word much too pale to describe her. Her gown, of lush scarlet satin, seemed to give off sparks in the candlelight with each movement she made. The bodice, encrusted with rubies and pearls, drew attention to the high, firm breasts beneath. Her waist, encircled by a matching satin sash, looked small enough for his hands to span. It took all Rory's willpower to keep from touching her.

"Thank you. You look dashing, my lord."

His gaze searched her face for any trace of the pallor that had been there earlier today. Her cheeks were flushed, her eyes glowing.

"Do you feel rested, Courtney?"

She heard the warmth in his tone and felt herself softening. It was such a beautiful night. And just for a little while she longed to forget why she was here.

"Aye. I feel wonderful."

He smiled at the excitement that trembled in her voice. This was, after all, her first ball at the English court. For this one night he could put away his questions, his concerns, and allow himself the luxury of relaxing and enjoying the pleasure of her company.

"The king has asked me to sup with him."

Courtney glanced down at his arm and placed her hand lightly upon his sleeve. He steeled himself for the warmth he felt each time she touched him. Together they followed the royal couple to a raised platform where everyone in the room could watch the king and his new bride.

The tables groaned under the weight of whole roasted pigs, deer and calves. Pheasant, partridge and doves were arranged on platters of chard and other greens. Every servant in the castle, and additional serving girls from the nearby villages, hurried around the room, seeing to the needs of the guests.

Cakes heavy with fruit and moistened with malt brew were sliced and passed out to the guests. Tankards of ale were refilled before they had a chance to be emptied.

Musicians moved around the dining hall, entertaining the assembled while they feasted. And when the feasting was over, the men and women moved on to the great hall, where they formed sets for dancing.

The king and queen were expected to lead the couples in the first dance. As Charles led his bride onto the floor, Courtney gave Henrietta Maria an encouraging smile.

"You need not act the mother hen," Rory whispered. "I suspect our new queen has much more strength than appears at first glance."

"Aye, she is strong." Courtney watched as the queen began the first steps of the dance. "But the journey, and the strain of so many new faces, have sorely sapped her strength."

Like another he knew. Pushing back his chair, Rory held out his hand. "Will you dance, my lady?"

Courtney bit her lip. Her lessons had included the dances she would need to master. But, like sewing, dancing did not come easily to her.

"I fear I will embarrass you, my lord."

Rory bit back the smile that threatened. "How so?"

"I am not a graceful dancer."

He took her hand, forcing her to stand. "I am. Just follow my lead."

Left with no choice, Courtney lifted her skirts and was led to the dance floor. Placing her hand on his arm, Rory bowed grandly. Following the lead of the other women, Courtney curtsied. With his other hand behind her, he turned her in a circle, then brought her back to face him. With his arm around her waist, he began leading her in a slow, sensuous dance.

His lips were mere inches from hers. She could feel the warmth of his breath feather the hair at her temple.

"You are very good, Courtney."

The deep timbre of his voice caused a little pulse to flutter deep inside her.

"There is no need to tease me."

"I do not jest. You are like a flower in the wind, moving as I move."

Like a flower in the wind. That was how she felt in his arms. Weak, trembling, needing to cling. Not at all like the Courtney of old.

"You also are very good at this. But then, my lord, you have probably had much experience."

"Aye, Courtney. Much experience." Especially if one counted the times he had danced away from an opponent's sword. Or the times he had danced free of the trap some clever female had set for him.

He wanted to laugh, but she was serious. "I see Lord Nevell looking our way. I expect he intends to ask you for a dance."

Her fingers gripped his hand so tightly that he looked up in surprise. "What has come over you, Courtney?"

"Please, Rory. I cannot dance with Lord Nevell."

"And why not?"

She felt panic rise in her throat until it threatened to choke her. "I have never been touched by a man before."

"And what am I?"

"You know what I mean." Her voice rose, and she felt herself close to hysterics. "Please help me."

"Courtney." Rory stopped and stared down into wide, terror-filled eyes. "Is this the same woman who climbed the rigging of the *Hawk*, defying the winds that whipped her, the storms that threatened her?"

"That took no courage." Her voice lowered. "The *Hawk* had been my whole life. But this—" She glanced around and realized that the man who had sent her into this panic was nearly beside them. "Please, Rory. Take me away. To the gardens. To the dungeons. Anyplace where I can escape this torture."

"I am truly sorry, my lady." His eyes crinkled with laughter. "But you will have to pay the wages of a lady-in-waiting to the queen. Especially a beautiful one. Every man in the room is eager to dance with you."

When the dapper Lord Nevell, who thought of himself as one of England's most eligible bachelors, captured her hand in his, Courtney looked for a moment like a frightened deer. As she was whirled away in Nevell's arms, Rory chuckled to himself and accepted a tankard from a serving tray.

When the dance ended, the earl of Essex bowed and took Courtney's hand, leading her immediately into another dance. As she whirled past him, Rory noticed that she was looking up into the handsome duke's face, laughing easily.

Four dances later, when Courtney finally pleaded that she needed to catch her breath, there were at least six gentlemen escorting her to her place beside Rory.

His smile had long since disappeared. His voice held a barely controlled thread of anger. "It seems Lady Thornhill has mastered the dance."

"It would seem so." She accepted a goblet of ale and drank it quickly. "You were so wise to goad me into trying, my lord. Once my feet began to move, they forgot to stop."

"So I noticed."

If Courtney was aware of the scowl on Rory's face, she paid it little mind. When the music started again and the handsome earl of Brighton took her hand, Courtney melted into his arms and began gracefully circling the room. Each time she passed Rory she sent him a radiant smile.

Damn the woman. He emptied another tankard and watched as she went from Brighton to Lord Newton and then to the fat, aged duke of Milford. Even Milford seemed mesmerized by her charms.

When at last she paused to rest, Rory took her hand.

"I cannot dance another step," she protested.

"You did not seem tired when Brighton asked you to dance." His voice held more than a hint of anger.

"What a handsome man," Courtney sighed as Rory turned her into his arms.

"But betrothed, and to the king's niece. Perhaps you should consider the Duke of Milford," Rory said sarcastically. "He is widowed now, and very wealthy."

"Ah. I shall take that into consideration," Courtney said, surprised by his sudden display of temper. What could be wrong? She had done nothing more than follow his advice. With a dreamy smile, she added, "I am beginning to like the English ale."

He gave her an astonished look. "Just how much have you managed to drink?"

She shrugged and moved closer to him, loving the way it felt being held in his arms. "Just three or four goblets, my lord."

"Three or four—"

Trumpets sounded as the king and queen made their way from the great hall. As soon as they were gone, several of the aged guests took their leave. Protocol decreed that none of the guests could depart until the king and queen had taken their leave. Of course, many of the revelers would stay until the early hours of the morning, drinking and dancing.

"Come," Rory said, taking Courtney's hand.

She looked up in surprise. "Where are we going?"

"I am taking you to your room, my lady. While you can still walk."

She shot him a look of cold fury. "I do not need you to take me to my room. I know the way. And I shall go when I am ready."

With that she lifted a goblet from a tray and drank half its contents before accepting the hand of a passing gentleman. As they whirled around the room, Rory could hear the lilting peal of Courtney's laughter.

Two dances later, she turned from one partner's arms into the arms of another. Looking up, she found herself staring into the cold gray eyes of Lord Burlingame.

"I am not a patient man," he said, pulling her close against him, "and I do not like to be kept at bay."

"But there are many lovely women waiting to dance." Courtney struggled to keep her tone light but felt herself recoil from his touch.

"I wanted you." The hand at her waist tightened. When she looked up, he was studying her carefully. "The mysterious Lady Thornhill."

"Mysterious? My lord, there is no mystery about me."

"Is there not?" Something flickered in his eyes. Something dangerous. Something frightening. "As chief among the king's councillors I must know everything about those who get close enough to the king to influence his thinking."

"I am here to assist Henrietta Maria. I expect I shall have little or no influence on the king."

His voice chilled her. "The woman who sleeps with the king can never hope to exert more influence than the entire council. Unless," he purred, "that woman forms an alliance with the chief councillor."

Her tone revealed her outrage. "Are you suggesting a tryst with the queen, sir?"

"Nay." He was obviously enjoying her shocked reaction. "With the queen's lady-in-waiting."

Courtney's mouth opened, but no words would come. For the first time in her life, Courtney found herself speechless.

Burlingame studied her reaction with amusement. Was it possible? Could this woman be as innocent as she appeared? Or was it all a careful act?

The women who surrounded the royals at court had been exposed to life's truths since they were very young. Most of them had enjoyed alliances with several men, vying with the others at court for power. Yet his woman, a lady-in-waiting to the queen, seemed stunned by his suggestion.

His eyes narrowed thoughtfully. An innocent. A virgin. What sport she would make.

"We must meet again later, Lady Thornhill. I will wait for you after the ball."

When the music ended, he held her a fraction longer than was necessary. Pushing free of his arms, Courtney turned and began shoving her way blindly through the crowd of dancers.

"The music has not ended. Are you just pausing a moment between dances?" Rory clenched his teeth. He had watched her swaying in the arms of Lord Burlingame. As chief councillor, Burlingame was one of the most powerful men in England. He also prided himself on being a brute with the women at court. Over the years he had made a point of boasting of his many conquests. And the look in his eyes had left no doubt about his desire for this latest beauty. "Or are you now ready to leave the ball?"

Courtney turned to glance at him. Her face was flushed, and her hair was in disarray. Rory thought she had never looked more beautiful.

"I am ready, my lord." She shook her head, almost as if she were trying to shake off any lingering fears about Lord Burlingame. The fool thought too highly of himself. Perhaps other women had fallen at his feet, but she was not like the others. Despite his power, he could not force her into an alliance she did not desire.

She firmly put Burlingame out of her mind. She was with Rory MacLaren now. She was safe.

She offered him her hand, and he grudgingly placed it upon his arm. Nodding and smiling to old friends, he led her from the great room and up the stairs. The babble of voices and the roar of laughter grew faint.

The hallway outside her door was lit by a torch. Rory studied her in the flickering light. Her hair was a cloud of rich sable that tumbled in curls to her waist. Her eyes glowed, as warm and bright as a cat's. Her lips were pursed in a little pout.

His hands curled into fists at his sides. He was furious at her for having had such a marvelous time in the arms of other men. He wanted to shout at her. He wanted to kiss her. The thought startled him with the intensity of a blow to the midsection. He went very still. It was true. He ached to touch her. To plunge his hands into her hair. To draw her head back and kiss those lips that had haunted him all through the journey from Dover. Yet he was almost afraid to touch her.

What if he felt himself losing control once again? What if she so bewitched him that he forgot about the questions that needed answering? What if by doing so he endangered his king? Would it not be better to cling to the memory of their last kiss?

She was trouble. Of that he had no doubt. And there had been trouble enough in his life. If he were wise he would turn away from her. Walk away and never look back. If he were wise.

"I think, my lady," he murmured, placing his hands on her shoulders, "that you dance the way you do everything else."

"And how is that, my lord?"

With his thumbs he stroked the soft skin of her naked shoulders and felt the tremors she could not hide. "With great enthusiasm."

She struggled to ignore the little thrill that raced along her spine. "I have you to thank."

The hands at her shoulders tightened. He drew her closer. "I was not the one who taught you to live your life on the very edge of danger."

She looked up into his eyes and saw them narrow slightly. A little trickle of ice curled along her spine. Fear? Anticipation? "You were the one who urged me to dance when I would have fled."

"Perhaps," he said, drawing her closer still, "I should have escaped with you into the gardens when you asked."

"Nay. I would not have wanted to miss the dance."

"Nor would I."

Why had she thought herself safe with this man? Rory MacLaren was the only man who could make her heart pound and her blood run hot with a mere touch.

He drew her firmly against him and covered her mouth with his. Startled, she tried to pull away, but he had anticipated her resistance. His hand cupped the back of her head, holding her still.

Instinctively she brought her hands up to his chest, as if to hold him back. But she quickly forgot about resisting. His mouth was soft and warm, his lips persuasive. Seductively he moved his mouth over hers until he felt her lips soften and part.

Her hands, which moments ago had been balled into little fists, now opened, curling into the front of his shirt, drawing him even closer. She had had every intention of resisting him. To allow Rory MacLaren to get close to her was madness. Madness. Feelings washed over her, feelings she had never even known existed. All thought of resistance fled. She sighed and gave herself up to the kiss.

He felt a rush of heat that left him stunned. She was so slender, so delicate. He felt her softness melting into him. Her breasts were flattened against his chest. Her thighs were pressed to his.

She smelled of expensive soaps and fragrant perfume. Even her hair smelled like crushed rose petals. His hands moved over the exposed flesh of her shoulders and back. Soft. She was so soft, he worried that he might bruise her tender flesh.

Sighing, she pushed away and let out an unsteady breath. For the space of a heartbeat, he lifted his head and studied her.

"I think, my lord—"

"No, Courtney," he whispered, lowering his mouth to hers. "Tonight, do not think. Feel."

His mouth found hers, and he swallowed the last of her protest.

The kiss was hard, demanding. Courtney felt the scrape of his teeth as he gave in to the passion. His hands at her hips dragged her close, reminding both of them of the passion barely held in check.

Courtney had never known such needs. Wild, raging needs that shuddered through her, leaving her weak and clinging.

She felt the thundering of her heartbeat. And his. She tasted his warm breath as his mouth roamed her face, teasing, nibbling, until she sighed and brought her lips to his for another drugging kiss.

She tasted the ale on his tongue, and darker, mysterious tastes that only made her hungry for more. She thrilled to the strength of his arms, arms that held her firmly against the length of him. She heard his little moan as he plunged his tongue deeply into her mouth and took her higher, and then higher still, with a single kiss.

Rory had never expected to feel such driving urgency. Challenge, passion, were not new to him. They excited him. But never before had he known such a dark, savage need. This was not at all as he had planned. He must walk away, now, before it was too late. And yet he could not seem to leave. He wanted one more kiss. Needed one more moment to hold her.

For a minute longer he lingered, loving the feel of her lips on his. Then he lifted his head and forced himself to step back.

Neither of them was willing to admit how shaken they were by this encounter. Courtney prayed her legs would continue to support her weight. Standing very straight, she lifted her head to meet his gaze.

Searching for something to cover the slight trembling in his hands, Rory reached around her and threw open the door to her suite of rooms.

"Good night, my lady," he said, his voice low. "It has been a memorable evening."

"My lord." She swept past him and stood just inside the open doorway. Her head was lifted in that haughty manner he had come to expect. "Good night."

"No matter what," he said, suddenly snaking out a hand and capturing her arm in a viselike grip, "on the morrow we shall talk."

When she tried to pull away, he caught her chin between his thumb and finger, forcing her to meet his stern gaze. "You have put off my questions long enough."

She met his look without flinching. "As you wish."

She turned away without another glance. He waited until the door was closed. Only then did he allow himself to lean weakly against the wall for a moment.

He had to have her. It was no longer a simple flirtation, a challenging seduction. It was need, a need as basic as hunger or thirst.

And yet... He knew that Lady Thornhill was not the person she pretended to be. When he learned the truth, would he still be free to keep her secret? Or would he be bound by honor to reveal her to the king?

Straightening, he strode along the dim hallway. His eyes narrowed fractionally. Beware, MacLaren, he cautioned himself. The lady is much more than she appears. You may just have met your match.

Farther along the hallway, a pair of eyes peered from a doorway, watching until Rory had passed by. From what he had just witnessed, perhaps the lady was not nearly as innocent as she seemed to be.

Chapter Ten

Courtney awoke dreading what was to come. Today Rory MacLaren would confront her with questions. Questions that would demand logical answers. She had spent half the night formulating responses to every conceivable query.

In the early afternoon she was summoned to the garden. As she gave the serving maid her response, Courtney felt her heart quicken. The time had come. She must convince Rory that she was here in England merely as an assistant to the queen. Her life, and that of Thornhill's, depended on her ability to lie convincingly.

In her eagerness to be done with the task at hand, she lifted her skirts and nearly flew down the wide stone steps leading from the great hall to the gardens beyond.

Rory paced the garden path, his head lowered, his hands locked behind his back. He had put off these questions for too long now. This time, by the gods, he would have his answers. At the sound of footsteps, he looked up.

Her gown was palest pink watered silk, drifting around her ankles in a gossamer cloud. She had not bothered to tie back her hair. It shimmered around her face and shoulders and streamed down her back in soft waves. Her cheeks were flushed, and her lips parted in an unspoken exclamation at the sight of him.

She was so lovely, she took his breath away. He steeled himself against feeling anything. He must not waver, must not veer from the course he had set for himself. He clenched his hands into fists at his sides. For these few minutes he would remember only that he was the king's true friend. He was feeling things for this woman he had no right to feel until he was certain that her purpose here in England was true and just. He would have his answers, or he would bring her before the council.

"My lord." She paused, clasping her hands together.

"Courtney." It pleased him to note that her hands were trembling slightly. And that he was the cause of her consternation. He indicated a bench below a gnarled oak. When she was seated, he sat beside her.

Courtney found herself fascinated by the leg that nearly brushed her skirt. How strong his limbs were. How muscled his thigh. Where had such thoughts come from? She had to be clear headed if she was to survive this inquisition.

"You know why I have summoned you?"

She forced herself to meet his steely gaze. "Aye. You desire answers."

He nodded, forcing himself not to notice the slight heaving of her breasts. "How is it that a pirate is now the queen's lady-in-waiting?"

She lowered her lashes, veiling her eyes. She could not bear the look on his face. "My father felt that it was time to introduce me to a proper way of life."

He scoffed. "As lady-in-waiting to the queen? Is that not quite a leap from lowly pirate?"

"My father has done many favors for the French court. As a way of repaying him, King Louis generously offered to allow me to accompany his sister to England."

Any trace of warmth was abruptly wiped from his voice. "To a country Thornhill hates? Did you not find this absurd?"

"Our two countries are attempting peace. Did not your sovereign marry a French princess?"

Rory nodded in agreement. "Aye. It is a beginning. A first step toward peace between England and France. But I find it hard to believe that this alone would change Thornhill's mind."

Courtney looked up, her eyes flashing fire. "My father was badly wounded in his last battle." Her voice lowered, and she glanced around the garden before adding, "The same battle in which you managed to gain your freedom."

He fell silent, remembering the bloody battle, the quick, exciting kiss and the exhausting swim to shore. It had been worth all that he had suffered to once again taste sweet, precious freedom.

When Rory merely waited for her to continue, she added, "Thornhill is changed, weakened. He needs much time to heal. The *Hawk* sails no more."

He heard the thread of pain in her voice and steeled himself against offering comfort. He must not lose sight of his reason for summoning her here.

"I am sorry, Courtney. I know how much you loved the *Hawk*."

"Aye." She swallowed the lump in her throat. "It was my only home."

Without his realizing it, Rory's voice softened. "Tell me now, in all honesty, why are you here in England with Henrietta Maria?"

"Because of my travels, I have learned many languages. It was suggested that I could be of some help to the queen in translating the difficult English into her native tongue."

Did it not make sense? Rory thought. Or was he simply hoping to find a plausible reason for her presence on English soil? Could illness have caused Thornhill to soften his hatred of the English? Or was there a dark, chilling plot being carried out beneath the very noses of the king and his council?

Rory caught her chin and lifted her face for his inspection. Her eyes softened, reflecting the golden sunlight. Her lips parted in an unspoken invitation.

Aboard the *Hawk* she had been an artless innocent. It would have been impossible for her to mask her emotions. Could she have changed so in the short months they had been apart? With his thumb he traced the outline of her lower lip.

At his tender gesture, she swallowed convulsively. "If you do not believe me, take me now before the king and his council. Lord Burlingame would be grateful for the opportunity to interrogate me further."

At the mention of Burlingame, Rory's eyes narrowed. He knew, as did all of England, that the man was a brute who relished the chance to inflict pain and humiliation. The thought of seeing Courtney in the chief councillor's clutches left him with ice in his veins.

"There is no need to go to the king with my suspicions."

Courtney felt a wave of relief. Her gamble had paid off. When she tried to pull away, Rory tightened his grip on her chin.

Her eyes widened at the unexpected hardness in his tone. "But if I find that you have lied to me, Courtney, the wrath of Burlingame will be nothing compared with my anger."

She twisted away from his grasp and stood, smoothing down her skirts. "Will there be any further questions, my lord?"

He stood and touched a hand to the sword at his side to keep from reaching out to her. "I am satisfied. For now."

"By your leave, my lord." Without another glance, she turned and flounced away.

Behind her, Rory watched the sway of her hips beneath the sheath of silken hair that fell below her waist, and cursed himself. Questions, too many of them to count, begged to be answered. And he had accepted the word of one beguiling, headstrong woman. A woman who had him so besotted that the only thing he could think about in her presence was taking her to his bed.

The queen and Courtney looked up from their handwork as a maid ushered an elderly priest into the queen's sitting room.

"Father LeFarge."

In her excitement at seeing the priest who had been her confessor since childhood, the queen stood, dumping yarn and needles to the floor. Instantly the maid bent to retrieve the fallen articles.

"How was your journey?"

"Difficult and tiring." The white-haired priest crossed the room and stood over the queen, raising his hand in a blessing.

Immediately the queen fell to her knees, and Courtney and the maid did the same. When the traditional Latin words were intoned, Father LeFarge made the sign of the cross over each woman.

As they took their seats he added, "The Channel was very rough. I was ill the entire way."

"I am sorry, Father. We will try to make you as comfortable as possible here in England. Are your rooms to your liking?"

"Adequate, my dear. Most adequate."

Courtney thought about the elegantly appointed suite of rooms the queen had had prepared for her confessor and mentally compared them with the sparse cells most priests occupied.

"I met with your brothers before I left France," the priest said, almost casually. "They send their greetings. And, of course, each sent a personal message." He handed the queen several sealed letters, and she stared at them with naked hunger.

How the queen missed her home, Courtney thought. And how she would devour those loving words from her family.

Courtney waited, hoping there would be some message from Thornhill and the crew. When the priest ignored her and continued talking to the queen, she swallowed back the disappointment she felt. Of course there would be no communication from Thornhill. He was ill and weak. And perhaps Richelieu had forbidden any communication between them until she had completed the task for which she had been sent here. Perhaps, she thought, suddenly alarmed, Thornhill was actually considered under house arrest until such time as she proved her loyalty to France.

"I would speak with you in private, madam," Father LeFarge said to the queen with quiet authority.

Noting the change in his tone, Courtney glanced from the priest to the queen. Although Henrietta Maria's expression never changed, Courtney sensed a tension in her that had not been there earlier.

Turning to Courtney, the queen said quietly, "You may leave us. I will summon you when I wish you to return."

"Yes, Majesty."

Setting aside her hated handwork, Courtney hurried to the kitchen, in the rear of the castle, where the scent of freshly baked bread permeated everything. There, as she did often, she spent a contented hour chatting with the cooks and several of the royal servants whom she had befriended.

When the door had closed behind the maid and the lady-in-waiting, Father LeFarge pulled his chair closer to the queen and lowered his voice.

"Before we discuss anything, I will hear your confession."

"My confession?" The queen touched a hand to her throat in a gesture of confusion. "But why?"

"You have been without the sacraments for too long, my dear. This journey to a godless country will have tested your faith."

"My faith is strong, Father. And I would speak of my brothers and hear the news from France before I confess."

Father LeFarge folded his hands carefully in his lap. Henrietta Maria had always been a headstrong child. A pity she had not been born a boy. But she had a role to play in France's destiny. And he would not permit the fact that she was now queen of England to diminish the authority he had always wielded over her.

"I realize what you have—" he cleared his throat "—been forced to endure at the hands of the king. The holy mother church and France are most grateful for your sacrifice. As wife you must, of course, submit. It is enough that you do your wifely duty and, God willing, bear an heir to the English throne who will carry on the faith of his mother. But I must caution you, my daughter, not to give in to carnal desires."

Henrietta Maria felt herself coloring at his words. All her life she had listened to this priest preach about the necessity of chastity if she was to attain her eternal reward. Yet this same priest had said nothing about the dozens of mistresses her brothers had taken. And now, when she was finally married to a man who not only pleased her but excited her, she was being told that it would be wrong to enjoy his attentions. Why must the church intrude itself even in her marriage bed?

Father LeFarge mistook Henrietta Maria's silence for repentance. Leaning forward, he said gently, "I will hear your confession now, my child."

"Nay, Father." The queen stood and, with quiet dignity, walked to the window. With her back to him she said, "I must prepare myself, with prayers and contemplation. I will send for you when I am ready." Turning back, she said brightly, "Now, tell me the news from France."

The priest made no effort to hide his displeasure. Richelieu had given him his orders. He must wield authority over the queen and, through her, see that the light of the faith was kept burning brightly in this Protestant country. Further, Father LeFarge had been given the task of garnering information that France could use against England should the two countries break the fragile peace between them. Of course, he would never betray the secrets of the confessional. But he hoped that if he remained close to the queen she would confide in him and thus innocently pass along useful information. This little show of resistance, so soon after his arrival, was irritating. This headstrong female was standing in the way of his success.

Changing tactics, he said, "All of France prays for you, my child."

When he saw Henrietta Maria's look of surprise, Father LeFarge went on, "Our loyal citizens fear that their Catholic princess will be persecuted in this land."

"Are you suggesting that my husband would do me harm?"

Father LeFarge saw the queen's expression alter slightly. Though she appeared outraged, he saw the flicker of fear that came and went in her eyes.

He decided to prod her further. "Your husband need not be the one to plunge the knife. It is necessary only that he look the other way while one of his henchmen does the vile deed."

"Think you that my husband would allow his own wife to suffer at the hands of religious fanatics?"

The priest spread his hands in a gesture of futility. "The holy mother church has a history of burying martyrs for the cause."

At his words, Henrietta Maria lifted her head in a way the old priest had come to recognize. She would permit no further discussion of this matter. She had effectively shut out his words. For the moment. But there would be other days, other times, to plant the seeds of distrust. Richelieu had given Father LeFarge his orders before the old priest had left Paris. Now that Henrietta Maria was queen of England, she must be persuaded to use her influence in the interests of France. And against those of England, if possible. Above all, the cardinal had stated, Henrietta Maria must not be allowed to fall under the spell of King Charles. If that happened, the cause of France, and ultimately that of the Catholic church, would be lost for generations to come. Charles was a man. A worldly man, from the stories the old priest had heard. And Henrietta Maria was hardly more than a child. From her confession before the wedding, Father LeFarge knew that she had been a virgin. A girl in her position would have no defense against a man like the king.

"Come, my child." The priest stood, placing a hand on her shoulder. "We will walk in the gardens and speak of pleasanter things. Your brothers. France." His tone lowered. "The familiar things of your childhood."

Reluctantly the young queen allowed herself to be led to the gardens. It galled her that the old priest still thought of her as a child. She was a woman now. Very much a woman, at least when she was in her husband's arms. But as the old man recited the things he thought his young queen wanted to hear, she berated herself for her impatience with him. It was sweet of Father LeFarge to remember her youth. He was a dear old man whose friendship she should not abuse. With a sigh she sat on a stone bench and gave the old priest her full attention.

Pleased with himself, Father LeFarge searched his mind for topics that would interest the young woman entrusted to his care. Richelieu had warned that unless he was able to gain her complete confidence he would send reinforcements. Younger, cleverer clerics, a bishop among them, were already being trained in the art of spying.

Spying. Father LeFarge detested the term. A man of God should not inject himself into affairs of state. Had not Christ commanded, "Render therefore unto Caesar the things which are Caesar's; and unto God the things that are God's."? But this was a necessary evil. What he was doing, the old priest consoled himself, was saving the faith, by any means available. Had not Cardinal Richelieu himself promised that the priest responsible for bringing the queen around to the proper attitude would be rewarded, not only in heaven, but here on earth?

Bishop LeFarge.

A smile lit the old man's eyes. It was a lovely title. One he intended to earn before going to his eternal reward.

As the old priest and the young queen bent close in earnest conversation, the king stood by his window and looked down at the figures in the garden with a growing sense of unease.

Henrietta Maria had been a surprise and a delight. Unwilling to prolong the suspense until she had arrived in London, Charles had journeyed to Dover, harboring the secret fear that she would resent the union that had been arranged between their two countries. He had been prepared for someone cold and unfeeling who would demand payment of a political or religious nature for every favor in her bed. Instead he had found a warm and tenderhearted woman who responded to his advances with an unexpected passion. His fiery little bride excited him in a way that no woman ever had.

Charles frowned as his bride listened attentively to the words of the old priest beside her. He tried to shake off the feeling of anxiety, berating himself for acting like a jealous lover. But the feeling persisted. He could not shake off this sense of impending doom. Through the years it had been his experience that the clergy had a habit of dredging up things that only muddied the waters.

The days and weeks became a blur of long hours spent at court interspersed with banquets and balls to honor the king and his new queen. As always, Courtney and Rory MacLaren were thrown together and forced to spend long hours in each other's company. Although the sexual tension between them grew until it was nearly intolerable, they managed to hold each other at a polite distance.

As she had on her infrequent visits to Paris, Courtney found herself both fascinated and horrified by the vast amount of state business conducted publicly at court.

The king dispensed justice, awarded lands and titles, mediated disputes and lashed out at enemies, both real and imagined. His power was absolute. His word was law.

Henrietta Maria sat beside her husband, watching, listening, as Lord Burlingame flaunted his position as chief among the king's councillors. Since the arrival of her private confessor, Burlingame had been especially cruel toward the queen, using every opportunity to cause her pain or humiliation.

"What of our laws forbidding Catholics to practice their faith, Majesty?" Burlingame hissed when a Catholic earl was stripped of his lands. "The queen herself flaunts her religion, insisting upon her priest being present at court."

A murmur arose from the crowd.

"We shall discuss this later, Lord Burlingame," the king said quietly.

Burlingame knew that the king had not made public his agreement with France that the queen and her retinue be allowed free access to their clergy. With a boldness rarely seen at court, he prodded the king further.

"Your wife makes a mockery of our laws."

Burlingame's words sent an uncontrolled ripple of excitement through the crowd present at court. Everyone knew the chief councillor was spoiling for a fight with the new queen.

Henrietta Maria sat with her head held high, her dark eyes glittering with anger. Heaven help her, she would find a way to punish this pompous fool.

Beside her, Courtney quietly absorbed the information that would be passed on to Cardinal Richelieu's messenger. Burlingame presented a clear danger to Henrietta Maria and to anyone loyal to her.

Lord Burlingame, Courtney had realized from her first days at court, was to be feared. Harsh, unyielding, he manipulated the king into granting favors to those who pleased Burlingame and punishing those who refused to do so. If anyone was foolish enough to bring down the chief councillor's wrath on him, he felt the full power of the throne.

Burlingame continued to watch Courtney, making no effort to conceal his lustful desires. Sometimes, when she sat quietly at court, she could feel his dark eyes watching her. Always she felt soiled by his look, as though he had physically touched her in some vile way.

His cruelty shocked even the most hardened men.

Lord Henry Farthingale, duke of Abinglen, whose loyalty to the king was beyond question, was brought before the throne at Burlingame's insistence. When the list of complaints had been read, the king sat with bowed head. Was he looking for a way out for his old friend? Courtney wondered. Or did he actually believe Burlingame's accusations?

"I will take this under advisement," Charles said sternly.

"As chief councillor, I suggest we strip this ungrateful lout of both lands and title," Burlingame said, striding toward the throne.

Henrietta Maria, watching him, turned to Courtney. "The man goes too far in flaunting his power."

Shocked by the queen's boldness, Courtney could only stare. "Majesty?"

"Everyone knows that Burlingame coveted the poor old duke's young wife. When she refused Burlingame's advances, he threatened to strip her husband of all his wealth.''

"Do you mean the charges against him are false?"

"There is probably some truth to them. But the only reason they have been made public is that Burlingame wants revenge against a woman who would dare to reject him. He believes that all of England—land, wealth, and people—is his for the taking."

"How do you know all this, Majesty?"

"I have my ways."

Courtney kept silent. But in her heart she knew how the queen gathered her information. It had become the major topic of conversation at court. Father LeFarge. The priest who ministered to the queen and heard her confession kept the queen informed of everything he wanted her to know. Further, it was whispered that the old priest took his orders from Cardinal Richelieu. Although Courtney found it difficult to believe that this cleric would stoop to meddling in politics, she would have found it difficult to deny that Richelieu would do anything to retain control of the French throne.

"One day soon," the queen said through clenched teeth, "the king's chief councillor will feel the wrath of a woman who does not fear him."

Courtney watched with a mixture of fear and fascination as Burlingame persuaded the king to turn his back on an old friend and strip him of both land and title. The duke of Abinglen and his proud young wife would be dependent on the charity of relatives.

Watching Burlingame use the king's power, Courtney felt a cold finger of fear along her spine. She must do nothing to anger the man. His revenge would be swift and harsh.

She was eternally grateful that Rory had not brought his suspicions to the attention of the chief councillor. The man would enjoy using his power to have his way with her. That thought caused her to shudder in revulsion.

Chapter Eleven

Father LeFarge had never before faced failure. It was a painful thing to swallow, but swallow it he must. At his failure to send Cardinal Richelieu any useful information, the French cardinal had made good his threat to send younger, more carefully trained clerics to take the old priest's place.

Henrietta Maria welcomed the bishop and his party in her sitting room. When the maids had seen to their comfort, they were dismissed, as was Courtney.

Alone, the queen listened patiently as the bishop, speaking on behalf of the church in France, made an impassioned plea for her to uphold the faith.

"You, Majesty, can be a beacon of light in this godless land. I implore you, as do your brothers and our beloved Cardinal Richelieu, to defy the king's council and demand freedom for all the king's subjects to practice the faith of their fathers."

"I understand your concern," the queen said softly. "But my husband looks the other way at those who choose to defy the law and openly practice the Catholic faith. Is not his own wife a Catholic, who has been allowed to bring her clergy into the palace? What more do you ask of the king?"

"Freedom. Justice," the bishop said with passion. "The same freedom for his subjects that is granted to his wife."

The queen fell silent. She had indeed witnessed the punishment of some who openly defied the law. And yet she had the distinct impression that the king's council twisted the truth, using a man's faith to punish him when, in truth, they coveted his lands or titles.

"If the faith is to survive in England, madam," the bishop said sternly, "it begs a strong, eloquent leader." He paused a moment for dramatic effect, then said in hushed tones, "This is why you were born, madam. This is your destiny. To lead the flock back to the true faith."

Henrietta Maria bowed her head, avoiding the eyes of the priests who surrounded her. In truth, the bishop's words moved her. Was this her destiny? To lead England back to the church? If she assumed the mantle of authority that was being thrust upon her, what would happen to the fragile relationship between her and her husband?

Charles was a proud man. How could he allow his wife to openly defy him before all of England? Such a show of defiance might cause him to permit even more punitive laws to be enacted by Parliament. Worse, her open defiance might destroy their love, their respect and their marriage.

"Madam, I beg—"

"Enough." Lifting her hand as if to ward off the bishop's words, she stood. Instantly the men seated around her rose from their chairs and glanced at their leader in confusion.

"Majesty, you must hear me out."

"We will speak another time." Pressing her hands to her temples, she said, "Leave me now. I wish to be alone."

"As you wish, madam. But this matter cannot be ignored. It must be resolved." The bishop led the way from the queen's sitting room, the priests following in his wake like a flock of black-robed ravens.

When she was alone, the queen rang for her lady-in-waiting.

Courtney noted the paleness of her queen's skin, the troubled frown that furrowed her brow.

"What is it, Majesty? Are you ill?"

"Nay, Courtney. I am weary. So weary."

Courtney helped the young queen to her bed, covering her with a fine embroidered coverlet. Pulling a chair beside the bed, she took Henrietta Maria's hand and noted that it was cold.

"They pull at me," the queen sighed.

Concerned, Courtney remained silent.

Henrietta Maria closed her eyes for a moment, then went on in a monotone. "It is almost as if they do not wish me to be happy."

"Your priests, Majesty?"

Henrietta Maria nodded. "Old Father LeFarge. Bishop Montand. The others. They heap guilt upon me for loving my husband."

"Guilt?" Courtney squeezed the queen's hand. "But does not the church preach love and fidelity in marriage?"

"The queen, it seems, is above such ordinary virtues. They ask me to choose between my love for my church and my love for my husband. But how can I make such a choice?"

"Cannot a woman love both?"

Henrietta Maria gave a long, heartrending sigh. "According to my clergy, I am not like other women. I have no right to love the man who was chosen to be my husband. I should submit but never enjoy. And what is even worse, I should use my marriage bed to obtain whatever concessions my brothers and Cardinal Richelieu desire."

Courtney saw tears spill down the queen's cheeks. She was stunned by the sight. A feeling of fierce protectiveness welled up inside her. How dare these men cause her queen such pain!

Without thinking, Courtney gathered the queen in her arms and held her while she wept. And when at last Henrietta Maria dried her tears, Courtney sat beside her and watched until she drifted into a troubled sleep.

Richelieu. He was behind all of this. The queen was being coerced into doing his bidding, just as Courtney had been.

Standing, she smoothed the coverlet across the queen's shoulders, then stared down at the sleeping woman, feeling a kinship with Henrietta Maria. They were both pawns in this dirty business. Pawns used by men with evil ambitions. What would be their fate? Courtney sighed and sank back against the cushions of the chair. She must think of ways to help the queen escape the pressures of her position and, in the process, help her to resolve her conflicts with the king. Before their marriage was forever shattered and their youthful love buried beneath the weight of warring nations.

Whenever the queen dismissed her for a few hours, Courtney escaped to the stables, where the grooms kept a spirited chestnut mare saddled for her. When she was alone in the woods that bordered the palace, with the wind whipping her hair and the sunshine warm on her face, the cares of the day slipped away. She and her mount were one, escaping the confines of those cold stone walls. On the sun-dappled trails of the woods, Courtney felt almost happy and carefree as she had aboard the *Hawk*.

As she rode, she pondered all that she had seen and heard since arriving in London.

Rory had been right about the city. With the disappearance of the illness that had plagued London, it had become once more a place of gaiety. The advent of summer had brought a profusion of green grass and colorful flowers to the gardens and parks. How was it, she wondered, that she could have grown to love a country she had been taught to hate since childhood?

The teeming streets of London offered her a fascinating look at the gentle English people. Street vendors hawked their wares while children tugged on their mothers' skirts. Pickpockets in shabby jackets rubbed elbows with elegantly attired noblemen. Fashionable women climbed into exotic carriages followed by maids bearing boxes from milliners' and dressmakers' shops. Lovers strolled arm in arm along the Thames. Occasionally Courtney found herself watching them, achingly aware of the secret that set her apart from other young women. She must never allow a man to get close. Thornhill had taught her well. Had it not been for Rory MacLaren, it would have been an easy matter. But Rory MacLaren was not an easy man to avoid.

As if on cue, the man who occupied so much of her thoughts rode toward her astride a magnificent black stallion.

"I did not know you rode, my lady," he commented. As he drew abreast of her, his mount reared, causing her horse to shy from the path.

With expert control she reined in her mare, forcing the chestnut to stand quietly beside the stallion.

"There is much about me you do not know."

He laughed. "Too much, I fear. Come, I will show you a favorite place."

Wheeling his mount, he urged the stallion into a canter. The mare, eager to keep up, stretched into an easy loping stride beside him.

Waving to the king's guard, who patrolled the palace grounds night and day, they entered a dark, overgrown stretch of woods. Bending low over their mounts, they managed to avoid being snagged by the low-hanging branches of the trees that bordered their rough path. Gradually the thick forest gave way to thin saplings and then to a rich, verdant meadow completely surrounded by woods.

Hearing the sound of water, Courtney led her horse to a stream that meandered along one side of the hilly meadow.

"What is this place?"

Rory dismounted and led his horse beside hers. "It is part of the king's park, though he never comes here. His father, James I, and my father often met here when they wanted to be free to speak without being overheard."

"A secret park? Does no one know of it?"

Rory loved the way she looked in sunlight, her eyes and cheeks touched with color. Little wisps of her hair danced in the breeze.

"I ride here often and have never met anyone on those rides. It is, I suspect, a forgotten piece of land within the walled palace grounds, a bit neglected and overgrown, but still a lovely haven."

Courtney looked around with sudden interest. "Those woods there." She pointed to the far side of the meadow, beyond the wall. "Where do they lead?"

"To the city. They are crisscrossed with paths that eventually converge into one, leading to the Thames."

This was perfect, she thought, leaving her horse at the stream's edge. Lifting her skirts, she walked up the hill and gazed around. From the highest point she could see far into the distance. To her left, beyond the woods, she could see the castle and its grounds. To her right was a wall separating the castle from the thicker stretch of woods, and beyond that the people of London strolling along the Thames.

Right here, in the king's own park, she could meet with Richelieu's messenger without fear of being caught. She had feared that she would have to leave the palace walls, but now she would be free to carry out Richelieu's orders without even leaving the grounds. The first order of business was to devise a way to distract the king's guard. Her mind was awhirl with plans.

"You are quiet, Courtney."

She turned, and for a moment Rory saw a look of concern cross her lovely features. What she was about to do would hurt him. That was her greatest regret. Greater even than her fear of being caught and punished was her reluctance to cause Rory MacLaren any more pain. She and Thornhill had already caused him enough.

"I fear I have been away from the queen's side far too long. I must return to the castle."

As she strode toward her horse, Rory caught her arm, forcing her to halt.

"How goes it, Courtney?" His tone was soft and warm, and she found herself wishing she could take this man into her confidence. "Does the time away from the *Hawk* grow easier for you?"

Easier? Courtney suddenly felt like weeping. Each day the hours grew heavier. There was no end in sight. Ahead of her there lay only deceit and the plotting and scheming of a power-hungry man who held her life, and that of Thornhill, in his hands.

"Aye," she lied, feeling the heat stain her cheeks. "In no time I shall find myself completely at ease in your world."

He bit back his laughter. Did she not know that her eyes spoke far more eloquently than her words?

"I think," he said, placing his hand beneath her elbow and assisting her into the sidesaddle, "that before that happens, roses will grow in the snow."

She shot him a questioning look.

The laughter erupted. "You need lessons in lying, my lady."

Giving in to her own laughter, she reached for the reins and watched as he mounted the stallion. "Just for that, I shall have to beat you to the stables."

With a flick of the reins the mare was off and running. Refusing to look over her shoulder, Courtney concentrated all her energy on avoiding the branches that whipped at her hair and tore at her sleeves as horse and rider raced along the wooded path. Behind her she could hear the pounding of hooves as Rory's stallion drew closer. Negotiating a bend in the trail, Courtney leaned low over the mare's back and clung to the reins. Seeing the stables looming in the distance, she shouted to her mare, urging her on.

A snap of branches alerted her that Rory had nearly caught up with her. Murmuring words of encouragement, Courtney took the last stretch of the trail at a full gallop. As the trail widened, the black stallion pulled alongside, until both horses were running neck and neck.

"Concede," Rory shouted.

"Never."

They raced past the stables, still even, and drew their mounts to a halt. Turning, they walked the horses back to the stable, where several grooms stood watching.

"Another half length and you would have been eating my dust."

Rory handed his reins to the groom, then turned to her. "You ride like a man. Who taught you?"

"Thornhill. He said there was only one way to do anything."

"And what way might that be?"

She laughed and tossed her head. "Any way that wins."

As she turned she found herself face-to-face with a strikingly handsome man of about fifty who was staring at her with a look of complete surprise.

"Lord Edgecomb," Rory exclaimed, clapping one hand to the older man's shoulder and offering the other in greeting. "When did you arrive in London?"

"Yesterday," Edgecomb replied, still staring at Courtney. "Who is this lovely lady?"

"Lord Edgecomb, may I present Lady Courtney Thornhill, lady-in-waiting to Queen Henrietta Maria."

"Lady Thornhill." Edgecomb bent low over her hand before brushing his lips across her knuckles. "It is my pleasure."

"Lord Edgecomb is the highest-ranking judge in the king's court," Rory explained.

His title sent a ripple of fear through her. A judge was the last person she should befriend.

Courtney found herself staring into the man's intense dark eyes. His hair was thick and white, as were his eyebrows, giving him the appearance of a fierce lion. His clothes were beautifully tailored, and his manner and bearing indicated that he was a man of wealth and breeding. Though he was a judge, and the highest-ranking one in all of England, Courtney sensed instinctively that he was a good and fair man, as well. Trusting her instincts, she decided instantly that she liked him.

Edgecomb was fascinated by the beautiful young woman. Unlike the pale, timid women who usually surrounded the royal family, this woman displayed an unusual spirit. He had watched the way she rode fearlessly alongside MacLaren's big mount. She had fully intended to win. There was a wildness about her that intrigued him. And there was something about her beautiful features, especially her eyes, that tugged at his heart.

He stared at Courtney, whose loose, flowing hair was intertwined with bits of leaves and twigs. "I hope you check a looking glass before presenting yourself to your queen," he remarked, picking a leaf from her hair. "She may have a difficult time believing you were out for an innocent ride." Glancing past her at Rory, he added, "There are several hay fields near the castle, MacLaren, and there are those who cannot tell a twig from a piece of hay."

Rory threw back his head and roared with laughter. "If the lady and I were going to romp in a hay field, we would not call attention to ourselves by racing back to the stables."

"Indeed." Edgecomb joined in the laughter before staring into Courtney's eyes once more. "Do you do everything the way you ride, my lady?"

"Aye." She smiled, and her eyes warmed to the color of topaz. "I know only how to win, my lord. I have never lost."

"Never?"

She thought a moment. "Nay. I was taught to be a winner. Or die trying."

"I believe I have discovered a rare jewel. If you do not mind, my dear, I should like to get to know you better."

"It would be my pleasure, Lord Edgecomb."

Bending, he brushed his lips over the back of her hand once more, then mounted the horse that a groom had been holding at the ready.

"I am glad you are back in London, MacLaren. The king has need of some wise counsel." He lifted his plumed hat. "I look forward to seeing you again, mademoiselle."

As he rode away, Courtney stood watching until he was out of sight.

"A very wise man," Rory muttered.

"Wise in what way?"

"In this way," he said, drawing her close.

Before she understood his intentions, MacLaren began picking bits of leaves and twigs from her hair. And if the groom had not been watching, he would have plunged his hands into her hair and plundered her tempting mouth, as well.

Chapter Twelve

Courtney returned from her daily ride with Rory and Lord Edgecomb. As always, they had encountered no one during their foray through the king's private park. Each day she had become more convinced it was the perfect place to meet with Richelieu's messenger and pass information without fear of being disturbed. Days ago she had sent the coded message. Tonight, while the rest of the palace staff slept, she would begin the work for which she had been sent to England.

Flushed with anticipation, she slid from the saddle. Her gown was damp and wrinkled and smelled faintly of horse and leather. Her hair, falling in casual disarray around her face and shoulders, gave her the appearance of a wild gypsy. Her skin, rosy and sun-kissed, set her apart from the pale, colorless women at court.

"I won again. What kept you?" Laughing, she watched as first Rory, then Lord Edgecomb, dismounted.

"Now I understand how you always manage to win," Rory said, tossing his reins to a waiting groom. "You cheat."

"Why, sir, how dare you suggest such a thing?" Though Courtney's eyes flashed, there was a teasing lift to her mouth that made Rory ache to kiss her.

"You started before either of us was in the saddle."

Lord Edgecomb nodded his agreement. "And even then we would have caught up, but you took a different route."

"I never said we had to ride together." Her voice trilled with laughter. "I just said I would be at the stables before either of you."

"And I suppose you will demand payment of a gold sovereign?"

"From each of you," Courtney said firmly.

Rory glanced at Edgecomb, who winked before reaching into his riding coat for the coin.

"You drive a hard bargain, my lady."

"Aye. And the wager is not over. You, sir, promised me a game of cards."

"The woman has no mercy." Laughing, Lord Edgecomb offered her his arm.

She accepted it, then looped her other arm through Rory's. The three of them walked along the path toward the palace, their voices raised in peals of laughter.

In the beginning Courtney had met Rory and Lord Edgecomb at the stables by accident. But after only a few days they had begun making plans to ride together on a daily basis.

Courtney was beginning to think she could count on these two as friends. She had missed the camaraderie of the men aboard the *Hawk*, and especially old Boney, more than she had expected. At times the loneliness was almost a physical pain.

Though she sensed that Rory still had his suspicions about her, she knew that he was a man she could trust in times of peril. As she learned more about Edgecomb, she realized that her first impressions had been correct. He was a man of high moral principles who was privately appalled at the dark deeds of Lord Burlingame and some of the others at court.

Though during their rides with Courtney both men voiced their opinions about palace intrigue, in the company of the other members of the court they kept their thoughts to themselves.

When they left the pathway and stepped into the palace, Courtney felt the relaxed atmosphere suddenly change. Always, here in the castle, there was an air of expectant tension.

"I must hurry to the king's chambers," Lord Edgecomb said, bowing over Courtney's hand. "Perhaps this evening, after we sup with the royal family, I can accept your challenge at cards."

Courtney watched as Edgecomb hurried away, then turned to Rory.

"I sense a sadness in Lord Edgecomb. A loneliness. Has he no family?"

Rory shook his head. "His wife and child died many years ago. He has had many opportunities to wed, particularly at the urging of the king, who has several kin who would make a good match. But Lord Edgecomb has chosen to live alone."

"Perhaps he cannot afford a wife."

Rory threw back his head and laughed. "Lord Edgecomb owns one of the finest houses in all of London, as well as a country house in Sussex, with cattle, rich farmland and dozens of tenant farmers."

"Then perhaps he cannot forget his first true love."

"Aye. It would be a hard thing to forget a first love." His words caused an unexpected pain around Courtney's heart.

Rory grew thoughtful as they neared Courtney's suite of rooms. "I have heard that his wife was a rare beauty. Some say he nearly died of a broken heart at the loss of his wife and child."

"The poor man." She paused outside the door to her rooms. "Then I shall simply have to beat him tonight."

"That does not make sense, my lady."

"Losing will take his mind off his loneliness. At least for the night."

Though he roared with laughter, Rory found himself grudgingly accepting her twisted logic. This could be dangerous. With each passing day this strange woman seemed to make more sense to him.

He studied her in the golden glow of the afternoon sunlight spilling through the tall windows. Each day he found her more beautiful. And more desirable.

She felt the sexual pull and drew away. "Good day, my lord."

"Until we sup, Courtney."

This night, Courtney was determined to behave as normally as possible. If she kept her mind occupied, she reasoned, she would have no time to fret over what she was about to do under cover of darkness.

The evening passed leisurely. Courtney, Rory and Lord Edgecomb joined the king and queen at supper. Afterward, Courtney and Edgecomb sat at a table near the fireplace and played cards. The queen worked at her embroidery, while Charles and Rory sat quietly over a game of chess.

Each time Courtney beat Edgecomb, everyone looked up at her laughter.

Finally Charles pushed away from the chessboard.

"I cannot concentrate with that noise," he said sulkily.

Courtney glanced up from her cards. "Does that mean you were about to lose, Majesty?"

The king's mouth dropped open, and Henrietta Maria lowered her eyes to keep from laughing.

"The king never loses at a game of strategy," Charles intoned in the voice he used for official proclamations.

"And now we know why," she intoned. "The king refuses to finish if he is in danger of losing." Courtney's eyes danced with unspoken laughter.

Lord Edgecomb looked up from his cards. "I think, Charles, the lady has caught you."

"I do not concede," the king said, returning to the chessboard.

An hour later, Rory said triumphantly, "Checkmate, Majesty."

With as much good nature as he could muster, the king drank a tankard of ale with Rory and Edgecomb before retiring to his bedchamber.

"It is not that I resent your suggestion that I was losing," he said to Courtney before retiring. His eyes began to crinkle with silent laughter, for he had grown fond of her openly teasing manner, so unlike the fawning of those who usually surrounded the royal family. "But I am weary of decisions. I must rest."

"I must retire, too," Edgecomb said. "How much did I lose tonight, Courtney?"

"Three gold sovereigns." Her eyes glinted as he handed her the money. "And a half crown."

"When you accompany the Lady Thornhill to her suite, MacLaren," Edgecomb said softly, "see that your gold is safely locked away, or I wager she'll have it all."

"You wound me, sir. I take only what I have fairly won."

"Aye. And by this time a fortnight from now I shall be lucky to still own my house and land."

"Which I have heard is considerable," the queen said.

"I suppose by some standards I am a wealthy man." Edgecomb grew thoughtful. "Perhaps someday you will be my guest, Majesty." He shifted his gaze to include Courtney. "And your delightful lady-in-waiting."

"It would give me pleasure, Lord Edgecomb."

Edgecomb bent low over the queen's hand. Turning to Courtney, he surprised her by leaning close and kissing her cheek. "Good night, my lady. It has been a most pleasant evening."

"Good night, my lord."

Bidding good-night to the queen, Rory and Courtney took their leave.

"You have brought much joy to Edgecomb's life of late," Rory said softly as they made their way through the halls.

"Aye. I sense his fondness for me. And I return his feelings. He is a fine man. His friendship eases the loneliness."

"Do you hear from Thornhill and the others?"

Courtney went very still. She did not wish to speak of Thornhill this night. Or think about the work Richelieu had sent her here to do.

"It is difficult to communicate from so great a distance."

Rory said nothing. He had noted that Courtney received no communications from her father. Odd that a man who kept such a tight rein on his daughter aboard ship should send no messages to her now that she was far away.

When they stopped outside her suite of rooms, Courtney felt the beginnings of a tremor around her heart. She and Rory had managed to maintain a cool distance for many weeks now, but she had seen the smoldering look in his eyes when Edgecomb had kissed her cheek. And she had felt the jolt at his simple touch.

She touched a hand to her mouth, pretending to stifle a yawn.

"You are tired, Courtney."

"Aye. It has been a long and pleasant day."

She sensed his reluctance as he looked down at her.

"Then I bid you good-night."

"Good night, Rory."

As she turned away, she felt his hand at her shoulder. She longed to turn back to him, to offer her lips. But already the sky was dark, and most of London lay slumbering. This night she must be about the dirty business Richelieu had begun. There was no room in her life for romantic thoughts of Rory MacLaren.

"Courtney."

She kept her face averted. "Aye?"

She felt his hand tighten for a moment, and a thread of fear curled along her spine. The hand lifted, leaving her feeling oddly bereft.

"Sleep warm, my lady."

"And you, Rory MacLaren."

On trembling legs, she stepped into her room and turned. His face was hidden in shadow, but she could feel the dark pull of his eyes. With a half smile touching her lips, she firmly closed the door, then leaned weakly against it, her heart pounding in her chest. She waited until his footsteps receded, then hurried into her bedchamber and began changing into riding clothes.

Courtney peered into the kitchen and was relieved to see the cook setting a sumptuous feast on the scarred worktable.

The rotund cook looked up when Courtney entered. "Do you really think he will come?"

"He would be a fool to miss an opportunity like this, Mary. Of course he will come."

"How can you be certain we will not get caught, my lady?"

Courtney crossed the room and placed an arm around the cook's shoulder. "The only ones moving on the castle grounds tonight will be me and—" she paused for dramatic effect "—the gentleman I am planning to meet."

Courtney hated to lie, but this was the only way she could think of to explain her absence from the palace.

"And the gentleman?" Mary turned wide eyes to her. "Will he truly keep our secret?"

Courtney nodded. "You can count on it. Now I will go and send your lover."

"Oh, Lady Courtney. My lover." The cook giggled and blushed furiously.

"If John Fenton is not yet your lover, Mary, I have no doubt this feast will change that."

With a laugh, Courtney slipped out the kitchen door and hurried through the darkness to a point midway between the forest and the meadow where soldiers patrolled the palace grounds.

"John Fenton," Courtney called to a figure on horseback.

The rider turned. Coming toward her, he leaned from the saddle. "Is that you, my lady?"

"Aye. Mary is waiting in the kitchen with a feast fit for royalty."

"Thank you, my lady. The guards will let you pass." He lifted his plumed hat and bowed grandly, then urged his mount forward.

As soon as he was out of sight, Courtney hurried toward the stables, where she saddled a mount.

The night sky was as black as a raven's wing. No moon sliced through the darkness. No stars winked in the heavens. There was only a murky darkness that closed in around horse and rider as they picked their way through the thick forest.

Courtney could taste the air, heavy with rain. She had chosen well, she thought. It was so dark here that she was unable to peer at the sky through the canopy of branches. Yet despite the fact that all had gone well, she felt her heart beating wildly in her chest. It would not return to its normal rhythm until she was safely back in her room at the palace.

Clad in tight riding breeches she had borrowed from a stableboy and a heavy black cape with a hood, she was invisible in the darkened woods.

She felt the cool, damp leaves brush her face as she bent low over her mount. Branches tore at her, snatching the hood from her head. A night bird called, shrieking like some demented creature, and she felt her heart lurch.

The forest closed around her, a cold, damp tomb. The thought left her trembling as she urged her mount forward until the branches gave way to tender saplings and springy, moss-covered earth.

At last she was free of the forest. In the inky blackness she could just make out the hilly meadow in front of her. Leaving her horse at the stream, she walked to the top of the hill. Wrapping her arms around her, she stood facing the path that led to the Thames.

Within minutes she heard the blowing and snorting of a second horse. She strained to see in the darkness, barely able to make out the figure of a horse and rider. At her short whistle, the figure halted. A moment later a man's voice whispered, "I bring greetings from your homeland."

Courtney relaxed. It was the arranged signal. "I send greetings to our good friend."

When he stepped closer, Courtney realized that he was no more than a lad. The hand he held out to her was trembling. In it was a paper.

"The cardinal bids you to read this and destroy it."

"Aye." She handed a paper to the messenger. "This is a list of the grievances being aired by the king's council. Richelieu should be advised that Charles is being encouraged by Burlingame to prosecute Catholics in England."

"What would happen to Henrietta Maria?" the lad asked.

"They could make an example of the queen."

She heard his sudden intake of breath. All of France would take up arms if their beloved Henrietta Maria suffered any shame or humiliation at the hands of the English.

The lad placed the paper in a pouch before turning away. "Our friend will send another messenger on the morrow."

"No." With a feeling of sudden panic, Courtney clutched his sleeve as he began to turn away. "I cannot risk this again so soon."

The lad pulled a hood low over his face, masking his features. "Our friend sends his concern about your father's health."

"What are you saying?" Courtney swallowed back the ripple of fear that caused her blood to run cold.

"Richelieu anticipated your reluctance. He will brook no argument. You will meet with his messenger whenever he orders you to, or your father's health may suffer."

Courtney bit back the oath that sprang to her lips. This lad would relay everything to Richelieu, including her reluctance to cooperate. "Aye," she said softly. "I will meet his messenger on the morrow."

Without another word, the lad slipped into the darkness. Courtney stood there for long minutes, her breath coming in short gasps. After all this, she had nearly caused Thornhill's death by a simple act of refusal. When would she learn that Richelieu, like Burlingame, used the power of the throne for his own selfish desires? These two men were ruthless. They cared not who lived or died. They cared only for more power. If she and Thornhill were to survive, she would have to obey Richelieu's every command until this thing was finished. No matter how much it terrified her.

When her breathing became easier, Courtney stood a moment listening to the night sounds. She was aware of the muted hoofbeats as the horse carrying the French messenger followed the trail to the Thames.

She slipped the message into the pocket of her riding breeches, then pulled the hood over her head. Hurrying down the hill, she picked her way through the darkness to the stream. Running her hand along her horse's flank, she caught the dangling reins and turned to mount.

Soon, very soon, she thought with a feeling of relief, she would be back in the warmth and safety of her rooms at the palace.

As she placed a foot in the stirrup, a hand snaked out of the darkness, catching her roughly by the shoulder.

God in heaven, she had been discovered. Someone had been here, listening to her whispered conversation with Richelieu's messenger.

As she was twisted around to face her accuser, she heard the deep, familiar tone of Lord Burlingame's voice.

"How clever of you, my lady. And how thoughtful. No one will ever find us here." She shrank from his touch and felt a growing revulsion as he gave a cruel laugh. "And all along you led me to believe that you had rejected my suggestion of a secret tryst."

Chapter Thirteen

Courtney felt the scream die in her throat. She was too terrified to make a sound. What good would it do to cry for help? She was too far from the castle to be heard. She had sought out the most isolated place in all of London to be about her dirty work. And now that very isolation would be used against her.

"I think that you should know that many at court whisper about you, my lady." Burlingame's voice, high-pitched with laughter and slightly whiny, assaulted her nerves nearly as much as his hand, which clutched the front of her cape. "You are rumored to be an untouchable virgin. Is it true?"

When she refused to answer him, he slapped her so hard that her head snapped to one side. Tears stung her eyelids as he snarled, "Do not play the high-and-mighty with me, Lady Thornhill. I know that you did not ride out here to enjoy the weather."

As if to give emphasis to his words, a jagged streak of lightning split the sky. Moments later, thunder rumbled across the heavens, echoing and reechoing in the distance.

Courtney shivered.

Burlingame drew her close until his face was mere inches from hers. "You were expecting to meet someone out here, my lady? Whom might that be?"

"No one." With both hands she pushed against his chest, but her strength was no match for his.

Catching her roughly by the shoulders, he held her a little away from him. "Why would the lovely lady-in-waiting to the queen dress in such a fashion?" He threw back his head and laughed. "Men's breeches, my lady? And the rough woolen cape of a tradesman?" The laughter faded. His face, illuminated by another flash of lightning, was twisted with rage. "Before this night is over, you will tell me who planned to meet you here. Or—" his lips curled into an imitation of a smile "—you will be brought up before the council."

He felt the tremors she could no longer hide and felt a surge of excitement. What he wanted was to see her tremble in fear of him. He wanted her to beg and grovel. As his sense of power grew, he felt himself becoming aroused. Power. It was more necessary to him than food or drink or wealth. Power. The power to decide if a man lived or died. The power to strip highborn men of titles and lands. The power to reduce their haughty women to weeping, clinging beggars.

Burlingame enunciated every word carefully, savoring their effect. "Now, Lady Thornhill, you will do as I say."

Courtney's eyes widened. As lightning flashed again, she found herself staring into the evil face of the devil himself. His lips were twisted into a leering half smile. His eyes glittered in triumph. The hands gripping her upper arms bit into her delicate flesh, causing her to cry out in pain.

"Does that hurt, my lady?" He grasped her tighter, until he could feel the bones beneath the flesh. "Good. I want you to suffer, as you have made me suffer all these days and nights, desiring you." He drew her closer. "You had no right to refuse me. I am the king's chief councillor. You can deny me nothing." He ripped the hood from her hair and ran a hand through the silken tangles. "If you dare to deny me again, you will pay as all the others have paid."

"Do not do this, Lord Burlingame." Courtney's voice was choked with loathing. "What you are doing is wrong."

"Wrong?" His eyes darkened in fury. Tearing her cloak from her, he stared at the delicate camisole she wore beneath it. "Is it not wrong for a lady to dress like a stableboy when she rides out to meet her lover? Is it not wrong to hide her beauty beneath a crude cape?"

With one hand at each shoulder, he tore away the fine lawn and delicate lace. At the sound of her garment being torn, Courtney felt tears spring to her eyes and wiped them away with the back of her hand. It was not tears she needed now, but courage.

"The chief councillor can do no wrong," Burlingame murmured. "I make the laws, woman. And you will obey me."

Staring into his glazed eyes, Courtney knew. The man was mad. And in his madness he had set himself above all others, even the king.

As he clutched at her she brought her booted foot up, catching him in the groin. He gave a howl of pain. In that moment Courtney twisted free of his grasp and began to run.

The rain, which had only been threatening until now, began in earnest. Heavy raindrops spattered the leaves and the underbrush. Desperate, Courtney plunged into the forest, with no thought of the horse she had left behind. She could hear the heavy crashing of footsteps as Burlingame thrashed around behind her.

"You shall pay dearly for this," he shouted as he caught a strand of her hair that streamed out behind her.

Ignoring the pain, she wrenched free and continued to run. Rain soaked her breeches and chilled her naked flesh. Still she ran blindly, not caring that she had left the familiar path and was now deep in the forest.

"Now, wench, you will pay, not only with your virtue but with your life," Burlingame shouted as he pounced, catching her by the ankle.

She fell forward into the wet moss, struggling to free herself from his grasp.

"I do not like my women quite so agile." Burlingame caught her hands, pinning them above her head. With the weight of his body on hers she was unable to move.

Her breath came in short, painful gasps. Twisting her head, she resisted his attempts to capture her mouth with his.

"I see that the only way to make you stop fighting me is by inflicting pain. So much pain that you will finally accept the fact that I will be not be denied."

"The only way you will take me is by killing me."

"If need be." He laughed and, clutching both her hands in one of his, removed a knife from the scabbard at his waist. Slowly, menacingly, he ran the knife along her side.

"So slender, my lady. So . . . perfectly formed."

Never, never had she been touched so crudely by a man. All the years she had been held apart from the others. All the months she had begun to dream of a lover's touch. All would be shattered by this man's cruel desires.

She felt a warm trickle of blood as he continued taunting her with the sharp blade of his knife.

He heard the little sob that broke from her lips. "Good. The lady is not as cold and unfeeling as she appears. Now, my lady. Tell me the name of the one you were meeting tonight. I shall make it my business to inform him on the morrow that I was the one who took his place with your . . . pleasures."

Courtney bit her lip to keep from crying out.

He pressed the sharp edge of the blade against her throat. "Such a pretty throat."

She tried to swallow, but could not. Even that slight movement caused her pain.

"Tell me. Who was the man?"

A voice cut through the darkness. "I was the fortunate man, Burlingame. And now you shall answer to me."

Lightning streaked across the heavens, and Courtney looked up to see Rory standing over them. In his hand glinted the ornate handle of a sword. The blade was pointed directly at Burlingame's temple.

For a long moment Burlingame looked thunderstruck. Of all the men in England, this Scot was the only one who did not fear him. Because of his foreign nationality, the king's council held no power over his Scottish lands or title. Because of his close friendship with Charles and his country's close ties to England, MacLaren could not be intimidated by Burlingame's threats.

"Stand away from the woman," Rory said with quiet fury. What he really wanted to do was run his sword through Burlingame again and again. His hand clenched around the hilt of his sword, eager to inflict pain on the animal who had dared to attack Courtney. That was what Burlingame was. An animal that attacked without warning. An animal that enjoyed the hunt and the kill. If not for the code of honor that had ruled Rory's life from his earliest days he would have run the evil creature through without a thought. It took all his willpower to keep from killing Burlingame where he lay.

Burlingame came to his knees and shot a calculating glance at the figure beneath him. If he was quick, if he was clever, he might be able to use her as a shield against the Scot's sword. MacLaren's skill with the weapon was legend. And though Burlingame himself was a powerful swordsman, he knew he had no chance of winning against the Scot.

"Stand, coward. Or do you fight only with helpless women?"

With a stream of oaths, Burlingame came to his feet and drew his sword.

Still stunned by the sight of Rory, Courtney rolled aside and sat huddled in the wet moss. He had to win. He had to. Or she would lose twice. She would lose the man who owned her heart, and she would lose her virtue and her life to Burlingame. But if she were to lose Rory, she realized with sudden insight, her virtue, even her life, would be meaningless.

As the two men raised their swords, her own hands clenched. If she had had a weapon she would gladly have taken on the villain who had tried to have his way with her. Instead, she was forced to watch helplessly as the two men dueled.

"So, MacLaren," Burlingame hissed as he crossed swords with the Scot. "You make yourself out to be a nobleman and then sneak out under cover of darkness to tryst with the queen's lady-in-waiting."

"I answer not to you." Rory stepped back, avoiding Burlingame's thrust.

"You will answer to Charles." The chief councillor ducked and felt the Scot's blade sing past his ear. Despite the cool rain, he was perspiring profusely.

"Prepare to meet your God," Rory said, skillfully moving in for the kill. With one smooth motion he lifted his blade, slitting Burlingame's sleeve from cuff to shoulder.

Shocked, the chief councillor dropped his sword. Backed against a tree, he watched as Rory's blade cut away his tunic, exposing his chest. With the point of his blade resting above Burlingame's heart, Rory went very still.

"Do not kill me, MacLaren. I beg of you." The knife still held in his other hand fell to the ground as he lifted his arms in a pleading gesture.

Courtney heard the shrill, whining tone and felt an expectant shiver as she waited for the moment when Rory would end her enemy's life.

"You were about to take something precious from the lady," Rory said in a voice low with fury.

"Mercy, MacLaren. I beg for mercy."

"This from a man who never shows mercy? How many men have pleaded with you for their lands, their titles, the honor of their women?" Rory moved a step closer, staring with contempt into his captive's face. "How dare you beg mercy, sir?"

"In the name of my king, Charles I of England, I beg your mercy."

Dazed, Courtney scrambled forward and, with a little whimper, snatched Burlingame's knife from the ground beneath his feet.

Rory stared wordlessly for several long minutes. Around them the rain fell on a forest that seemed devoid of all sound. For the first time, he became aware of the muted sound of crying.

God in heaven. Courtney was hurt. He stared at the figure huddled at his feet, desperately clutching the dagger. She needed him. Nothing else mattered.

"Go. Before I kill you where you stand." As Burlingame bent to pick up his fallen sword, Rory said in a dangerous voice, "Never threaten the lady again. Or by the gods you will answer to me."

Burlingame sheathed his sword and began running in the direction of the palace. Even before he was out of sight, Rory had dropped to his knees before Courtney.

Safe, she thought as he wrapped his arms around her. Finally, here in his arms, she was safe.

"Dear God, what has he done to you?" Tenderly Rory removed his cape and wrapped it around her nakedness. Then, enveloping her once more in his arms, he held her, as gently as if she were a child.

She was trembling. Trembling so violently she could no longer stop the shudders. His tenderness opened a floodgate. All the tears and the fears that she had been holding inside were released. With her arms about his neck, she clung to him and cried as if her heart would break.

"He is a madman," she said between shuddering sobs.

"Aye. All of England seems to know that. All except our king."

"Oh, Rory. I want to go home."

Home. He felt a wave of tenderness for the woman in his arms. Would she ever have a place, a country, to call home?

Rory climbed up on his horse and cradled her against his chest. Slowly they made their way through the forest to the king's park, where her mount stood patiently beside the stream. Catching its reins, Rory tied them behind his saddle. Then, still holding her close to his chest, he turned his mount toward the palace.

She did not speak, merely clung to him with a fierceness that worried him. Wrapping a strong arm around her, he drew her close to his heart, as if to ward off the dark world around them.

Once they were inside the palace walls he turned their mounts over to the care of a groom and carried Courtney up the wide stairs to her rooms.

Inside, the quiet warmth wrapped itself around them, shutting them away from the rest of those who dwelled within the palace walls. In her bedchamber he set her upon a pile of furs in front of the fireplace. Placing several logs among the hot coals, he stoked the fire until it blazed. With wet cloths he gently sponged the dirt and blood from her body. Though she flinched at his touch, she was too exhausted to fight him. It worried Rory that, although she permitted his touch, she watched him through narrowed eyes.

When he had finished bathing her, he wrapped her in his soft, warm cape. Setting mounds of pillows on the fur, he lay down and drew her once more into his arms.

She spoke not a word but stared at the fire with eyes that seemed too big for her face. Though Rory had a hundred questions, he kept silent. She had been shocked and brutally assaulted. What she needed now was tender care and a feeling of security. Not to be battered by questions. Putting his own needs aside for the moment, he silently ministered to her.

As he cradled her to his chest, he felt the rush of heat, the growing desire, that always surfaced when he touched her. She would be shocked, he thought, if she knew where his thoughts were leading. If he could he would lie with her and love her until all thoughts of Burlingame were erased from her mind. They would love until the morning light broke through the windows. And then they would love again, until they were both sated.

He forced himself to put aside his thoughts. Courtney, despite all her strengths, was especially vulnerable to Burlingame's attack because she had been so sheltered from normal men's desires. Though she had lived in a man's world, she had been set apart.

The touch of that brute would leave her doubly afraid of being touched by a man. For now he would have to bank his own needs. Her needs were far more important. And what she needed now was to learn to trust once more.

At last, leaning back against the pillows, he felt her taut muscles begin to relax. Safely held in his arms, she stared into the mesmerizing flames until her lids closed. He felt the warmth of her breath as she drifted into slumber. But though she slept secure in his arms, she sighed and cried out often. And in her hand she still clutched Burlingame's dagger.

Chapter Fourteen

Sunlight slanted through the tall windows, bathing the figures reclining on the furs in a golden glow.

Courtney awoke, trembling with fear. Her hand closed around the dagger. No man would ever again treat her as Burlingame had. No man would ever again touch her without her permission. She took in a long, deep breath to calm her suddenly jumping nerves, and then remembered that Rory had saved her from Burlingame's cruelty.

She was safe here in her room. Safe beside the man who had rescued her. She felt an odd heaviness against her shoulder. Rory. She knew without looking. He was holding her, as he had held her through the long night.

Courtney could hear the hiss and snap of logs as they were devoured by flames. She felt deliciously warm. Lying very still, she absorbed all the strange new feelings that drifted through her. Soft breath feathered the hair at her temple, and strong arms enclosed her in their warmth.

She felt the warmth of the dagger still clutched in her hand. Her fingers were stiff and sore from holding it so tightly. Gingerly she switched the dagger to her other hand, daring for the first time to loosen her grip. Then she flexed each finger, feeling the blood tingle at the movement.

Her eyelids fluttered, then opened. She found herself staring into a pair of warm blue eyes.

"You are as lovely when you awake as you are when you sleep," Rory murmured.

She felt heat stain her cheeks and felt an odd, curling sensation in the pit of her stomach. How long had he been lying here watching her?

"Thank you, my lord."

"For finding you beautiful?"

She saw the laughter in his eyes and loved the way he looked, so dangerous when he was angry, so gentle when he was happy. "For saving my honor. And my life."

He surprised her by pressing his lips to a tangle of hair at her temple. With an unexpected fierceness, he said gruffly, "I should have killed him. But I could think of naught but your safety."

"Shhh." She touched a finger to his lips, sending shock waves along his spine. "Do not speak of him, Rory. His very name turns my blood to ice." After a few seconds of silence, she said softly, "I am grateful that my rescuer was a skilled swordsman."

"Were you prepared to pick up my sword and finish the task if I fell?"

She stared into his eyes, amazed that he could jest about losing his life. "I had no such thought. I knew only that you could best that villain in a fight."

"Did you?" He smiled, wondering if she had any idea just how tempting she looked. The cape had slipped from her shoulders, revealing an expanse of creamy flesh. He studied the dark cleft between her breasts and longed to press his lips to the spot. Just thinking about it had him so aroused he dared not move.

"You are nearly as skilled a swordsman as I, my lord."

He smiled at her comment, spoken so simply. "How kind of you to say so. Your skill is exceeded only by your extreme humility, my lady."

"Why should I pretend humility? Thornhill said one must never be modest about one's talents."

Rory's smile faded slightly at the mention of her father's name. He would have wagered that Thornhill had something to do with Courtney's midnight ride. He wisely kept his thoughts to himself.

"We would make an unbeatable team, Courtney."

She felt a little thrill at his words but dismissed it immediately. "I fight alone."

"I spoke not of fighting." His mouth hovered just above hers. His eyes narrowed slightly as he studied the softness of her lips. He had to taste them. Had to.

His gaze lifted to meet hers. Slowly, deliberately, he lowered his mouth to hers. With soft, caressing nuzzles he seduced until her lips softened and opened to his.

"I spoke of loving."

The kiss was swift, devastating. Heat flared between them, and they clutched blindly, clinging to each other with a fierceness that took their breath away.

He felt her heart pounding unsteadily against his. Gently he moved his hand beneath the cape. As he came in contact with her warm flesh, he felt a jolt that left him tingling. He traced the softness of her stomach, let his fingertips travel upward, across her rib cage. His hand cupped her breast, and he felt her startled response. Before she could push away, he took the kiss deeper, his thumb making lazy circles around her taut nipple.

Needs, wild and pulsing, ripped through her, startling her with their intensity. Never, never had she known such desire. It had come upon her so suddenly that she was unable to fight it.

Courtney sensed everything as if for the first time. The warmth of his lips. The dark, mysterious taste of him as he explored the intimacy of her mouth. The cleverness of his fingertips as he touched her in a way no man ever had before. Moving in his arms, she gave herself up to the feelings that seemed to have robbed her of the strength to resist.

Rory had not expected this. All night he had managed to hold himself at bay while he'd offered her comfort and safety. Now, one kiss, one touch, unlocked all the passion. It was no longer merely desire that drove him. He needed her with an urgency he had never before known. This woman crowded his mind, tormented his soul, until he could no longer think. Only feel.

She felt so good in his arms. Soft and delicate, yet with nerves of steel. A woman without knowledge of a woman's wiles. In many ways an unspoiled, artless child in a perfect woman's body.

As the kiss deepened, all logical thought fled. He savored the moment.

"My lady." A maid knocked and entered. Seeing the two figures reclining among the furs, the girl stopped, stared in alarm, then began backing from the room. "Forgive me, my lady. I only wanted to assist you in your morning toilette."

Courtney slid deeper under the furs, her cheeks a bright crimson. At her look of consternation, Rory found himself chuckling, despite his own frustrations.

To the maid he said, "Return in a little while. Lady Thornhill will be ready for you then." When the maid was gone, Rory's laughter grew. "My lady, red is an especially lovely color on you."

"Red?" She arched an eyebrow, haughtily.

"You blush much too easily, I fear. By the time the maid has finished repeating this tale to the others, everyone in the palace will know that you spent the night in my arms."

She pushed herself away and stood, wrapping his cape around her with as much dignity as she could manage.

"I will explain that I was indisposed and that you came to my aid."

Rory's laugh washed over her as he gathered up his boots and began pulling them on. "The more you try to explain, the worse you will make it."

He stood and walked over to her, touching a finger to her cheek. With great tenderness he bent and brushed her lips with his. "Offer no explanation, Courtney. Except, of course, the one you shall have to give to me."

When she suddenly stiffened, he added softly, "This changes nothing. When you are feeling stronger, we will talk."

When the door closed behind him, she turned and stared out the window, deep in thought. He had saved her life. He deserved to know what had taken her from the safety of the palace last night. And yet if he knew he would be forced to go to the king with the knowledge. Knowledge that would cost her her life.

Rushing to the discarded breeches, she found the message, still folded, in the pocket. Unfolding it, she read quickly.

My dear,
The plot to overthrow the king must be put into action as soon as willing parties are found. Relay names of those who can be trusted to cooperate. R.

Tossing the note into the fire, Courtney watched as flames devoured the paper. She was caught up in something evil. Something that might demand of her the ultimate price. And yet she saw no way out that would not cost Thornhill his life. The choice between her life or her father's was really no choice at all.

Courtney spent much of the day in her suite of rooms, feigning illness. When Henrietta Maria visited her late in the afternoon, followed by a retinue of maids bearing steaming broth and herbal teas, she told Courtney that Lord Burlingame had also been absent from court.

"It is said that he suffers from fevers and chills. The king's own physician has pronounced him well enough to attend court on the morrow. What of you?" the queen asked. "Will you be strong enough to sit beside me at court?"

The thought of facing Burlingame caused her stomach to churn, but face him she must.

"Aye, Majesty. I was merely indisposed. By the morrow I will be fine."

"You must rest, then." The queen regarded Courtney, who was reclining on a settle positioned in front of the fireplace. Sitting, she ran a hand along the fur robe covering Courtney's lap. "Perhaps the Scot can be persuaded to return to help you . . . rest."

"Majesty!" Courtney gasped.

"Oh, Courtney." The queen caught her hand and squeezed it lightly. "Do not be so offended. Everyone in the palace is whispering about it."

"But I did not . . . he did not . . ." Realizing that she was sputtering, Courtney gave up.

"My dear. Everyone does it." Henrietta Maria looked down for a moment, veiling her eyes from her friend's view. "Even the king, I am told."

Courtney swallowed the lump in her throat and wished she could think of some pretty words, some soothing phrases, that would ease the pain she heard in her young queen's voice. There were rumors that the king, urged on by Lord Burlingame, was already planning to discard his bride in favor of a more suitable Englishwoman.

"But at least," Henrietta Maria said more cheerfully, "you must learn to be more discreet. The palace is awash with gossip and rumors. If you are going to choose a lover, find a place away from prying eyes."

"But I—" Courtney bit her tongue. What had Rory said? The more you try to explain, the worse you will make it. "Thank you, Majesty. I shall remember."

The queen gave her a gentle smile. "Rest now, my dear. I missed your companionship at court today."

When she was alone once more, Courtney leaned her head back and wearily began to make her plans. Tonight, as soon as the palace grew quiet, she must face the dangers of the forest once again. Richelieu had ordered her to meet with his messenger. And, though she feared the dangers lurking in the darkness, she feared the French cardinal's wrath more.

Rory stifled a yawn and set down his tankard of ale. King Charles, lacking the companionship of Lord Burlingame, whose cynical comments always made him laugh, had demanded that Rory stay with him to pass the evening.

Rory found it sad that the king had begun to seek pleasures that would keep him absent from the queen for long periods of time. It was sad because these two lonely monarchs could have found solace in one another. Could have, but probably would not. Each was being advised by trusted aides that the other was a villain.

Henrietta Maria, closely attended to by the clergy, felt that her duty was to preserve the faith, especially in England, where Catholics were being persecuted.

Charles, prodded constantly by Burlingame, felt that his first duty was to see to it that the French intruders were kept firmly in their place. If that meant humiliating the queen, so be it.

"You grow weary, MacLaren?"

"Aye, Majesty."

"Perhaps," the king said with a twinkle in his eye, "Lady Thornhill asks too much of a man, keeping him from his bed the entire night."

Rory merely smiled. He had heard the whispers, had felt the stares of the curious and had endured the nudges and knowing smiles. Through it all, he had kept his silence.

"Good night, MacLaren." The king rose unsteadily, having emptied a good many tankards.

Together they climbed the wide stairs. The king veered to the right, toward the royal suite. Rory turned left, toward the rooms prepared for guests of the royal family.

When he reached Courtney's door, he paused. He had missed seeing her lovely face at court. So many times he had found his thoughts drifting back to her. Had the fear left her? Had she finally given up the dagger, or was she clutching it still? Was she pacing? Or resting?

He thought of her asleep in his arms, her breathing soft, her body warm and inviting. God in heaven. Every man on the king's council believed that Rory had taken Lady Thornhill as his lover. Why did he hesitate? Why not make it a fact?

He raised his hand to knock. Everyone in the palace was asleep. He imagined her, gowned in pristine white, her hair soft and streaming down her back.

Before he could bring his fist to the door, an image crept into his mind. An image of Courtney, naked and bleeding, crying as if her heart would break. She had been shattered by Burlingame's brutality. She needed time. Time to heal. Time to trust. Time to love.

He turned from her door and walked on. He could wait. Although he was not a patient man, he could put her needs ahead of his own for as long as necessary.

Courtney leaned low over the neck of her mount, urging the mare forward through the dark forest. The air was dry this night, dry and cool. As before, she wore breeches and a dark hooded cape that covered her head and masked her features.

The cook, Mary, and her lover, John Fenton, were together in the kitchen, where, after sharing a lovingly prepared meal, they would share Mary's bed. Courtney prayed that would keep the king's guard busy until her deed was done.

Her heart was beating like the wings of a caged bird. She held the reins in trembling hands. A night owl screeched, and she jerked around in the saddle, dagger aloft, ready for battle. When she saw the owl's shadow against the night sky, she emitted a weak sigh of relief.

Coming to the end of the trail, she dismounted and led her horse to the stream, then made her way up the hill. Stooping, she watched and waited. Within minutes a figure on horseback could be seen entering the meadow from the opposite trail.

"I bring you greetings from home," whispered a voice.

"How is our mutual friend?"

"He is well." The figure stepped from the shadows. Like the first messenger, he was no more than a lad, dressed in a shabby cape and worn breeches. "You are instructed to read this and then destroy it."

"Aye." Courtney accepted the paper and folded it before tucking it into the pocket of her breeches.

"Our friend said to expect no more messages for a fortnight."

Courtney could not hide the little sigh that escaped her lips. For a fortnight she would be free of this terrible business.

"Our friend orders you to observe those around you carefully. One close to the king can be counted on to betray him."

"How will I know the one?"

"By observing. Soon enough he will reveal his true feelings. When he approaches our mutual friend, you will be notified."

Courtney nodded. The messenger turned away. At the bottom of the hill he mounted and disappeared into the woods. Eager to be away from the place that had caused her so much pain, she ran down the hill and mounted her horse. Horse and rider disappeared into the overgrown path that led into the forest.

Behind her, slipping from his place of concealment, a tall figure crept to where his horse was tethered. Moonlight glinted on pale hair and illuminated a face that was twisted into an evil leer. Pulling himself into the saddle, he followed at a leisurely pace.

When Courtney arrived at the palace, she lifted the heavy saddle from the horse and returned it to the stables. Then she hurried into the palace and nearly ran up the stairs in her haste to hide herself in the safety of her room.

As she took the stairs at a run, a shadowy figure followed, observing her with calculated interest.

Chapter Fifteen

I tell you, the woman is dangerous.''

Burlingame faced the king, who was seated in a private chamber, along with the lord chancellor, who was scribbling furiously, and Lord Edgecomb, who, as chief among England's judges, had been invited to this meeting at Charles's insistence.

"You are accusing the queen's lady-in-waiting of being a spy, sir. These are very serious charges." Edgecomb made no effort to hide the displeasure in his tone.

"It is common knowledge that you have befriended the girl," Burlingame said in a voice high-pitched with agitation. "But surely you will not put friendship above duty. We are talking about the safety of our king."

"Let no man question my loyalty to the English throne. Especially not you, Burlingame. My father and Charles's father lived together, wenched together and, when they had to, fought together, side by side. The Edgecombs have been loyal English subjects for generations."

"Edgecomb," Charles said soothingly, "I am certain that Lord Burlingame does not question your loyalty to me." He turned to the chief councillor. "Why would the queen surround herself with spies?"

"For France, sir," Burlingame said quickly. "The queen's first loyalty is to the country of her birth. Those papists have convinced her that you are in league with the devil. And while they send their princess to masquerade as queen of England, they send emissaries to Spain for an alliance that will one day be used against us."

"The alliance has failed," Edgecomb added softly. "Once Henrietta Maria came to England as your bride, sir, Spain was forced to accept the fact that England and France had formed an unbeatable partnership."

"Partnership." Burlingame spit the word out contemptuously. "This marriage is not a partnership. It is an opportunity to bring spies into the king's own bedchamber."

"Careful, Burlingame," Charles said with quiet authority. "Next you will be calling the queen a spy."

An uncomfortable silence fell over the men in the room. Finally Edgecomb spoke.

"Tell us exactly what you saw and heard last night."

Burlingame stood and began to pace. He had painstakingly rehearsed his tale, being careful to mention nothing about the prior night, when he had attacked Courtney and been driven off by MacLaren.

"I heard the sound of footsteps outside my room. Knowing that all the servants had retired, I decided to investigate. Imagine my surprise when I saw Lady Thornhill, dressed like a stablehand, creeping down the stairs."

"Of course you were dressed and ready to follow," Edgecomb said sarcastically.

"I was dressed, having not yet retired," Burlingame said quickly. "I followed the lady and saw her saddle a horse in the stable. As soon as she was out of sight, I saddled my mount and followed in the direction she had gone."

"Why did the king's guard not stop her?"

"The king's guard, John Fenton, was absent from his post. I learned later from one of the footmen that Fenton and one of the king's cooks, Mary, were enjoying a tryst." At the king's dark scowl, Burlingame added, "A tryst suggested and arranged by Lady Thornhill."

Charles's lips thinned. A soldier found neglecting his duty could be punished by whipping, imprisonment and even death if the king so commanded. He would find a punishment that would forever remind Fenton of the foolishness of putting a woman's favors above the safety of his king.

"How is it that you did not lose the lady in the darkness of the forest?" Edgecomb studied Burlingame carefully, eager to catch him in a lie.

"There was a full moon." Burlingame smiled, beginning to enjoy the role of storyteller. It was apparent that he had captured the king's undivided attention. "It was easy to spot a horse and rider ahead of me on the trail. When we emerged from the forest, we were in a grassy meadow. I believe, sir," he added, turning to the king, "that it is known as the king's park."

Charles nodded. "I know of this place, though I seldom go there."

"Apparently Lady Thornhill knows of it, as well. And I must assume that she is aware that it is rarely visited. That is why she so brazenly met with the French emissary in the king's own park."

Edgecomb grew uneasy. He and Rory had often ridden there with Courtney. All three were familiar with the place. "How do you know it was a Frenchman?"

"I was close enough to hear them speak. The messenger called out in French, and Lady Thornhill replied in the same tongue."

"And could you understand what was being said?"

Burlingame smiled. "I have some knowledge of the language. What I understood left me stunned."

"What was it?"

"The messenger told her that one close to the king could be counted on to betray him."

A sudden chilling silence descended upon the group.

"That is why I insisted upon this private meeting," Burlingame said with an air of importance. "Any one of the men surrounding the throne could be plotting to betray the king."

Lord Edgecomb watched Burlingame with great interest. Though he despised the man, he could detect no false note in this report. If what he said was true, their beloved king was the object of a sinister plot against his life. They must find the traitors, and quickly.

Yet, try as he might, Edgecomb could not bring himself to believe that Courtney would plot against the king. There was a fresh, artless quality about that young woman that had endeared her to him. "What was Lady Thornhill's reaction?"

"She is a very accomplished spy, Majesty. She accepted the message and agreed to bide her time until the rest of the plot is revealed to her."

"How shall we deal with this villainy?" Charles asked, glancing at his chief councillor.

"The advantage is on our side. The lady does not know that she was followed and observed going about her vicious business," Burlingame said. Then, lowering his voice, he added conspiratorially, "Lady Thornhill is to meet with a French emissary in a fortnight. When she does, I propose that we set a trap for her."

"Tell me your plan." The king moved to the edge of his chair, caught up in the thrill of danger.

"We must devise a way in which not only Lady Thornhill and the messenger are caught, but any others in France and England who are cooperating in this vile scheme." Burlingame glanced at the king. Seeing Charles's nod of approval, he went on, "It is not completely clear in my mind yet, Majesty. But when I have it ready, I will present it for your approval."

"Good. Good work, Burlingame. Now," the king said with a trace of anger, "we must discover the man who would betray me."

"I think I know," Burlingame said, savoring the look of shock on the faces of the three men around him.

Charles fixed him with a look of quiet resignation. "Who is it?"

"You will not like what I am about to say, Majesty."

"Who is it, man?"

Even the lord chancellor stopped writing and studied Burlingame with intense interest.

Burlingame thought about the humiliation he had suffered at the hands of the man Charles called friend. No friend, no wife, no man or woman in all of England, must be closer to the king than his chief councillor. He would see to it.

"MacLaren," Burlingame said, a note of triumph in his voice.

The name was greeted with ominous silence.

Edgecomb was the first to recover. "It is not possible. I have known MacLaren all his life, and his father before him. He is like a son to me. No one is more loyal to the king."

Ignoring Edgecomb's protest, Burlingame said, "Rory MacLaren is besotted with Lady Thornhill. Even the scullery maids whisper about their tryst."

The king looked thunderstruck. "Not MacLaren." He stood and pounded a fist on the tabletop, causing the lord chancellor to snatch up the parchment that flew into the air.

"And why not, Majesty?" Burlingame was careful to keep his feelings carefully hidden behind a bland mask.

"Like Edgecomb, his father and my father were closer than brothers."

"You are not your father, Majesty. Nor is MacLaren his."

"In time of danger, there is no one I would rather have at my side than Rory MacLaren. I would trust my life to the man."

"That is precisely what he is counting on," Burlingame said.

The king stood and walked to the window, where he stared for long, silent minutes. Was it possible for a man in his position to trust anyone? Had not his own father been betrayed by one close to him? Had not Henrietta Maria turned away from her new husband to listen to the ravings of her priests and her bishop? Why should he suffer such agony over a planned treachery by a man who had once been friend? It was the fate of royalty that many of those who pretended love and loyalty were merely courting favors. But Rory MacLaren?

When the king turned his face to them, Edgecomb noted that he was pale. "Until this thing is settled I will trust only the men in this room."

"And MacLaren?" Burlingame prodded.

After a moment's hesitation, the king said gruffly, "Watch him. And report everything he does, every person with whom he meets and every journey he takes."

"Aye, Majesty." Burlingame was smiling broadly now. "And when the trap is set, we will catch everyone connected with the spies, including Lady Thornhill and Rory MacLaren."

"I pray you are wrong," Charles said gravely.

Wrong? Burlingame cared not for right or wrong. The hunt. The kill. That was what mattered. Was this not the very best of sports?

Unable to hide his growing excitement, he left the room, eager to put his plans into motion. MacLaren and Lady Thornhill would rue the day they dared to cross him. Before he was through with them, they would crawl and beg. He would see them both publicly destroyed.

"I must get away from London before I go mad." Henrietta Maria paced the floor of her sitting chamber, while Courtney watched.

Her heart went out to the distressed woman. This very day, all at court had witnessed her latest humiliation at the hands of Lord Burlingame. While the others had watched in stunned silence, the chief councillor had blatantly accused the queen's clergy of fomenting dissent among the Catholics of England, who were bitterly opposed to the latest laws banning the practice of their faith. When the queen had turned to her husband, expecting a harsh denunciation of such high-handedness, the king had simply muttered that no one was above the law.

Many of the fine English ladies at court had whispered behind their hands that Charles had already turned away from the charms of the Frenchwoman and was enjoying the favors of a highborn Englishwoman. How quickly, they scoffed, had the king tired of his French bride. How soon, they wondered, before she and her retinue would be banished to some dreary castle on the moors to languish until old age or boredom claimed her life?

"Perhaps we could return to Paris." Courtney's heart soared at the very thought of seeing old Boney and her shipmates. Even the dour Thornhill would be preferable to the gossiping women at court.

"Nay. The king would never permit it. He is convinced that all of France plots against him."

Courtney glanced away, unable to meet the queen's eyes. If only Henrietta Maria knew that one of her trusted aides had been coerced into spying. And by Cardinal Richelieu, the man closest to the king of France.

"We were happy at Dover." Henrietta Maria's voice held a wistful note. "I yearn to smell the sea air."

"Aye." Courtney stared down at the needle in her hand and fought the desire to weep.

"I must leave these rooms. They stifle me." The queen strode restlessly to the window. "Perhaps a walk in the gardens will help. Courtney, will you accompany me?"

"I will, Majesty." As they descended the stairs and walked to the garden, Courtney searched her mind for some subject that would put the queen's mind at ease.

"Majesty, perhaps you would enjoy a ride on the morrow. The palace stables are filled with exquisite mounts."

The queen paused a moment, a smile lighting her eyes. "I am an expert equestrienne. Did you know that, Courtney?"

"Nay, Majesty." Courtney felt herself coloring. "There is much about you I do not know."

"Yes." The queen regarded her in silence before moving on. "And there is much about you I do not know. But my bishop spoke highly of you. And he insisted that you would be the perfect companion in this strange land. I think," Henrietta Maria added in a low voice, "there is much more to you than I have been told."

"Majesty, I—" Courtney swallowed. Did she dare trust the queen with the truth of her position here in England? Or had the queen already been informed by her clergy? She owed Henrietta Maria the truth. "I want you to know—"

"It is not my concern," the queen said quickly. "There are many things a woman in my position should not know." She glanced at the young woman beside her. Then, just as quickly, she looked away. Bishop Montand had warned her not to grow too fond of her companion. But he had not told her why. Further, he had not told her how to avoid such feelings. Courtney had become much more than a lady-in-waiting. She had become a friend and confidante. It was whispered at court that a delicate web of intrigue was being spun. A web that could ensnare anyone loyal to France. Including this lovely young woman. The less she knew, the less apt she was to become entangled herself.

Courtney was not certain whether or not to be relieved at the queen's abrupt dismissal of her words.

"I believe I have had enough fresh air."

Courtney glanced at the queen's usually pallid features, Two bright spots of color touched her cheeks, giving her a feverish appearance. "I trust you are not ailing, Majesty."

"I am fine. But I shall rest until I sup with the king." Courtney watched as the queen lifted her skirts and turned away. Turning back, Henrietta Maria said in an almost apologetic tone, "I will not need you at my side this night."

She did not add that the king had insisted that neither Lady Thornhill nor Rory MacLaren be invited to dine with the royal family. He had given no reason for excluding them, but from the look on his face the queen had thought his reasons must be grave. To Henrietta Maria's extreme discomfort, the king had invited Lord Burlingame and several other members of the council instead.

"Aye, Majesty. I will see you on the morrow."

"Good night, Courtney."

The queen hurried toward the palace, leaving Courtney standing alone in the gardens.

"Thank you. Leave the tray here." Courtney directed the maid to set her meal on a small table in front of a roaring fire.

It was to be her first evening completely alone. As the maid left the room and closed the door, Courtney savored the thought. She could eat and drink when she pleased without having to endure the stares of the crowds that constantly surrounded the royal family. For the first time since she had assumed the duties of lady-in-waiting, she did not have to interpret the queen's every word. There would be no sly smiles from the men who watched her and whispered about her as though she were some silly bit of pastry to be enjoyed at their leisure.

She lifted the goblet and tasted the ale. It still bore the coolness of the palace cellars where it had been stored. Drinking her fill, she touched a linen napkin to her lips and thought about the men aboard the *Hawk*, who quaffed their ale and wiped their foamy mouths with the sleeves of their shirts. Instantly a wave of homesickness washed over her, so acute that her throat ached with longing.

She had heard not a word from Boney and the others. They had apparently been forbidden to contact her, just as she had been forbidden to contact anyone from her past.

She picked at the food and pushed it away. All her life she had been alone. Set apart.

She heard a sound at her window and walked over to investigate. Pale moonlight filtered through the open window, bathing the room in a golden glow. Millions of stars shimmered in the night sky. Lifting her face to the heavens, she sighed. The sigh became a gasp when a dark figure climbed over her balcony and loomed before her.

"How dare—"

The words died in her throat as a hand covered her mouth. Before she could pull away, she was dragged against the solid wall of a man's chest. Her eyes rounded, then narrowed as the familiar figure released her mouth.

"Rory."

"Aye, my lady."

"What are you doing?"

His voice was warm with laughter. "I wish to keep you company. No one should be alone on a beautiful night such as this."

Her pulse, which had begun racing at the first sight of the intruder, stirred even faster at his nearness.

"How did you know I was alone?"

"Henrietta Maria told me. The queen, it seems, has a soft place in her heart for lovers."

"We are not lovers, Rory MacLaren." As if to emphasize her words, Courtney pushed herself free of his arms and strode across the room. With some distance between them, she could think more clearly.

"We could be."

She trembled at the softness of his words.

"We could never be." Her voice was strong and firm.

"Why, Courtney?"

"Because we come from different worlds. We owe our loyalty to different thrones."

"The ones who own our loyalty are now wed. Our countries have formed an alliance. Can we not do the same?"

"Nay." She turned away, unable to meet his dark gaze.

With quick steps, he was across the room. Though he stood directly behind her, he did not touch her. Instead, he watched as she gripped her hands tightly together, as if she were fighting desperately to hold her feelings in check.

"Tell me why you were out riding in the forest the night Burlingame attacked you."

"I cannot."

"You must." He watched the way her fists clenched and unclenched.

"Do not ask me." She turned, and his gaze was drawn to her eyes, eyes that were wide with emotion. Fear? Passion?

"It is difficult not to ask." His voice softened once more to a low, seductive note.

"Leave me be, MacLaren. Why must you push and prod?"

"I care, Courtney. I care about you."

She felt the sting of tears and blinked them away. Tears? Because someone cared about her? Had anyone ever cared before? Surely not Thornhill. He had given orders and had expected them to be carried out without question. He had taught her to fight like a man and had been proud when she'd succeeded. But he had never really cared about her. Boney? Yes, the old man had cared. As a mother hen cares for her chick. But this, this simple statement from Rory, had her weeping.

She felt his hands at her shoulders, turning her into his arms. With unbelievable tenderness he drew her against his chest and pressed his lips to the tangle of hair at her temple.

At any other time she could have resisted him. It had been her intention to keep a careful distance from this man until her deed was done and she could return safely to France, where she would be forced to live with her memories. But this night, with such loneliness washing over her, she had no strength left to resist. The need to be held and comforted overcame all others.

"Let me touch you, Courtney." He ran his hands along her arms, sending tremors along her spine. "Let me kiss you." He covered her mouth with his, and she felt a rush of heat. "Let me love you," he murmured against her lips.

Her only reply was a moan that was quickly smothered as he took the kiss deeper.

He had anticipated the fire that raged out of control each time he touched her. He had expected to be flooded by feelings that only she could arouse. What he hadn't counted on was the rush of desire that left him reeling. Pulsing need drove him to clutch her firmly to him while his tongue plundered the intimate recesses of her mouth.

Rory caught his breath and took the kiss deeper still. The woman in his arms had completely bewitched him.

She tasted of honey, sweet and tempting. He drew out all the flavors of her lips before taking a swift journey across her face, pausing to nibble her earlobe and press damp, moist kisses to her eyelid, her cheek, the corner of her mouth.

Moving his mouth lower, he trailed kisses along her neck and shoulder and thrilled to her little sigh of pleasure when he buried his lips in the hollow between her neck and shoulder.

He wanted her so desperately, he could take her here, now, on the cold, hard floor. He banked his needs. There would be time. Time to taste, to savor.

With deft movements he slid her gown from her shoulders and bent his lips to the swell of her breast. His mouth lingered, sending ripples of pleasure through her. His tongue flicked lazily across her nipple while his fingertips caressed her other breast.

Never, never had she known such intense feelings. She moaned and clutched at him, her body a mass of nerve endings, aching to be satisfied.

He unfastened her gown. With a whisper of silk, it drifted to the floor and lay in a forgotten heap at their feet.

Courtney had a desperate need to feel him, flesh to flesh. With a swiftness she would not have believed possible, she removed his shirt and brought her lips to his hair-roughened chest.

When her fingers fumbled with the buttons at his waistband, he helped her, and then his clothes had joined hers.

His gaze burned over her. In the spill of moonlight, she was a glorious golden creature. "By the gods, you are the most beautiful woman I have ever seen."

Slowly, languorously, she wound her arms around his neck and lifted her mouth to his. Again the need to take her was so swift, so desperate, that he had to force himself to go slowly.

Their kisses were no longer gentle. A desperate driving need drove them both higher and higher still, until kisses were no longer enough.

Scooping her up in his arms, Rory carried her through the archway to her bedchamber, where he settled her on the bed. The coolness of the embroidered linens was a blessed relief to her heated flesh.

When Rory stretched out beside her, Courtney reached out a hand to him, eager to explore the body she had so long admired.

She eased her fingertips across shoulders corded with muscles and thrilled to his strength. When he rolled toward her, she ran a hand along his back and felt him tremble at her touch. Growing bolder, she brought her hands to his chest and traced his muscled rib cage. Her hand stilled its movement when she encountered a raised scar.

"Is this from a beating aboard the *Hawk*?" Her voice was low and breathy and sent tremors along his spine.

"There were so many beatings. In prison. Aboard ship. It matters not. They have healed."

"But there are scars." Without thinking, she touched her mouth to the flesh her fingers probed.

He sucked in his breath and caught her to him in a viselike grip. Her hair fanned out around him as he drew her face to him for a kiss. Rolling over, he raised himself up on one elbow and studied the way she looked. Her mouth was still hungry for his. Her eyelids were heavy with passion.

With lips and fingertips he explored her body, loving the satiny smoothness of her flesh. When his fingertips encountered the imprint of a scar across her back and shoulder, his hands stilled their movements.

"What is this?" His voice was low, hushed.

"It is nothing."

"Nothing?" His fingertips traced the raised flesh. "Did the evil Thornhill have even his own daughter flogged?"

At the fury in his tone, Courtney attempted to soothe him. "Like you, Rory MacLaren, I endured many beatings in my lifetime aboard the *Hawk*. It matters not."

"It matters to me." He caught her face between his hands and stared down into her tawny eyes. "Everything about you matters to me. I would die rather than see your flesh scarred again."

"Oh, Rory." She felt a welling of emotion that left her speechless.

With a kind of reverence he brought his lips to the scar, tracing its path to her breast, where he nibbled, suckled, until she writhed beneath him. Still he worshiped her body, bringing his lips lower until her stomach quivered beneath them. When his mouth moved lower still, she clutched his head in a vain attempt to stop him. His tongue shot pleasure through her entire body until, arching, sobbing his name, she climbed to the first shuddering crest.

He gave her no time to recover, but took her over crest after crest until her whispered words were no longer coherent.

The need for her had become a madness that drove him to near desperation. His body ached and throbbed.

"Tell me that you want me, Courtney."

"I do." She clutched at him, her own desperate desire matching his. "Oh, Rory. Please."

At last he gave in to his need and slipped inside her, taking her slowly, slowly, then faster and faster until they felt themselves merge with the golden moon and explode, splintering into a million tiny star fragments.

Chapter Sixteen

Rory lay back on the mounded pillows and studied the woman beside him. All night they had loved, then slept fitfully, only to awaken and love once more.

Rory was astounded by the depth of Courtney's passion. She had loved with a desperation born of loneliness and isolation.

It was true that he had come here last night determined to seduce her. But it was no longer clear who had led and who had followed. They had both been caught up in feelings too intense to deny.

He felt her stir and caught his breath for the space of a heartbeat. In the clear light of day, a night of passion was often regretted. Especially by a woman so sheltered that she had never even been allowed normal friendships.

Courtney's lids flickered, then opened. She stared into the blue eyes she had come to love. Her own eyes warmed and softened at the sight of him.

"I slept like a babe, knowing you were here."

"Aye. I've enjoyed watching you." He traced a finger along her lower lip and felt the first stirrings of desire. How was it possible that he could want her again so soon?

They heard the familiar morning sounds, maids scurrying along the cool, dim hallways, fetching food, water, clothing. Rory lifted his head at the sounds.

Courtney felt her heart lurch. He would leave her now.

"If you slip over the balcony, no one will know you were here."

Rory glanced down at her and felt his heart contract. "Are you ordering me to leave, my lady?"

"Ordering? Are you not eager to be off?"

"I would rather stay here with you."

"The maids will carry tales."

"Do you fear what the maids say?"

She smiled then, and he felt his heartbeat grow steady once more.

"I love you, Courtney. I would stay with you forever if you but asked it."

Love. Courtney felt the word explode inside her and trickle like warm honey over her heart. He loved her. And she loved him. With all her heart. Never again would she be alone and lonely. Never again would she be isolated, untouched.

"Oh, Rory. I love you more than life itself."

He caught her to him and hugged her fiercely.

Her smile faded as her heart tumbled. If she truly loved him, she must not drag him into her sinister plot. She must set herself apart from him.

Courtney went very still. It was more than a feeling. It was a responsibility. She must not do anything to bring harm to the man she loved.

His lips, his fingertips, were already weaving their magic. Try as she might, she could not concentrate on anything except a growing need to be kissed, caressed, held.

And then all serious thought fled as he began tickling her. Laughing, she struggled to be free.

"You, sir, shall pay for that." With a strength he had not expected, she rolled on top of him. Straddling him, she brought her lips to his throat. Her hair fanned out around them, skimming his naked flesh.

He marveled that this woman could bring him to such madness with a single touch. And then he was beyond thought as she took him on a wild ride to the heavens.

"Would you like me to send for the musicians, my lord?" The queen looked up from her handwork to study the king, who was pacing restlessly.

"Nay. I am in no mood for music."

From across the room, their friend watched in uncomfortable silence. Lord Edgecomb had spent a lifetime in the company of royalty. He had known Charles since the king's birth and had treasured the friendship of his father, James. He recognized the many moods of the monarch, and recognized also the weight of the duties that rested upon the king's shoulders.

Charles was tense and edgy. All this talk of betrayal was causing him to turn away from those who could best comfort him: his wife and his best friends. It was easy enough to see why. Whom could a man in the king's position trust? As if that were not enough, Edgecomb noted, the king's council, and Burlingame in particular, had become more vocal in their protests against everything that did not meet with their approval, especially the presence of the queen's clergy at court.

The clergy were not altogether blameless, Edgecomb thought as he watched the king empty a tankard and call for another. When the marriage between the two monarchs had been arranged, King James had been forced to agree that the Prince of Wales would permit his French bride to practice her faith and be attended by her clergy. This had been insisted upon by Cardinal Richelieu, affording church officials the perfect opportunity to keep their hands in affairs of state. In retaliation, the laws of England were continually moving toward a more repressive attitude. Though the practice of the Catholic faith was tolerated, some were persecuted for being too openly Catholic.

Edgecomb glanced at the queen, whose hands were continually busy with needles and yarn. Though she seemed to be concentrating on her handwork, he noted that her gaze often swept up to watch her husband. It was obvious that she was attracted to the king. And though he tried to deny it, the king was equally attracted to his lovely young bride. But there were forces working against them.

Henrietta Maria was naive and easily manipulated. It would be a simple matter for France's ruler, Louis, to instruct her bishop to use his influence to sway her against her newly adopted Protestant country. Such manipulations would, of course, drive a wedge between the young queen and her new husband.

Who would gain by such actions?

In France, Louis and his confidant, Cardinal Richelieu, would be privy to information that the queen gleaned from her husband. Information that would be critical if France decided to align herself with Spain in the future.

In England, Burlingame and the king's council, by decrying the influence of the clergy on the queen, would also drive a wedge of distrust between the king and his bride. The more they openly humiliated Henrietta Maria, the more she would lean toward her clergy and away from her husband. The more she withdrew from Charles, the more he would begin to believe the whispers and rumors about her lack of loyalty.

Absence, Edgecomb reasoned, might be the perfect solution for their suspicious minds. Not to mention their breaking hearts.

He cleared his throat. "Madam, I was wondering if you would like to visit my home just outside London. It is at its loveliest this time of year."

Henrietta Maria looked up in surprise. Since her arrival in this country she had been treated like a social outcast, receiving invitations only when they included her husband.

"Why, what a lovely idea, sir." Henrietta Maria dropped the needle in her lap and rested her hands atop the yarn. "When would we go?"

"Tomorrow, if you wish. My home is large and comfortable, and the gardens are considered some of the finest in England." Turning to the king, he added, "If you do not object, Majesty, I thought the queen might wish to extend the visit for a day or two."

Charles gave a careless shrug of his shoulders. "It matters not to me. Whatever my wife wishes."

If Henrietta Maria felt a tug of unhappiness at his words, she carefully masked her feelings. "I would bring my maids of course. And my lady-in-waiting."

"Certainly, madam."

This was perfect. It would give Edgecomb the chance he needed to get to know Courtney better and, he hoped, to dispel the ugly rumors about her spying. "And I will invite Rory MacLaren, as well. He is good company and an excellent horseman, if you wish to ride to the hounds."

The queen's spirits began to soar. A few days away from the palace and the suspicions of the king's council. A chance to be rid of the dour comments of the clergy, who gave her no rest. A chance to spend time with this English nobleman whose gentle patience and good humor warmed her. And, best of all, she would be with Courtney and Rory, whose affection for each other was a joy to behold. Their mutual attraction was obvious to everyone in the palace. If only, she thought with a sigh, it were contagious.

"Since my husband has expressed no objection, I would like that very much, Lord Edgecomb."

Edgecomb bowed. "I will leave now and make ready for your arrival on the morrow, madam. I look forward to your visit."

"As do I, Lord Edgecomb."

When Courtney first heard the news, she was reluctant to be separated from Rory. Like the queen, she yearned to escape for a little while the tensions of the palace. But her heart lay with the MacLaren. When she heard that Rory was also going to be at Lord Edgecomb's country house, she was overjoyed. She was reminded of Henrietta Maria's earlier suggestion that lovers ought to be discreet. What better way to avoid the gossip than to spend their time in the company of the queen and the highest-ranking judge in England and away from the prying eyes of the palace staff?

With a light heart, Courtney packed carefully. Two days, her mind whispered. Two days of complete relaxation away from the intrigue of the royal court. Two days with Lord Edgecomb and Henrietta Maria. And, best of all, two days with Rory.

Six carriages rolled along behind the queen's carriage, bearing her maids and an assortment of trunks. Since the queen wished to be prepared for any occasion, she had brought an assortment of gowns for morning, afternoon and evening. There were fur-lined capes to ward off the evening chill and jewels that were the envy of every high-born woman in England.

Courtney peered from the windows of the queen's carriage and watched as the lush English countryside passed by. Along the trail, wildflowers grew in profusion. Farmers and their families walked beside carts and wagons loaded with goods for the market. Occasionally Courtney glimpsed graceful country houses set far back from the road.

Rory had chosen to ride with the king's guards, who flanked the procession of carriages. Each time Rory pulled alongside the carriage, Courtney found herself thinking how fine he looked in his tight-fitting breeches and scarlet riding coat. The plumes in his hat danced in the breeze, giving him a jaunty air.

"Rory MacLaren is indeed a handsome man." The queen stifled a laugh at the blush that colored Courtney's cheeks.

"I . . . was admiring the country house in the distance."

"That, too, is handsome."

The queen was laughing openly now, and Courtney joined her. "I see I cannot keep secrets from you, Majesty."

"Your feelings for the MacLaren are written in your eyes, Courtney."

"As are yours for your husband, madam."

For a brief moment a look of sadness crossed the queen's face.

Cursing her clumsiness, Courtney searched for a topic that would cheer her. "I look forward to this time away from the palace. It will allow us a closer look at England."

"What little I have seen is lovely."

Courtney nodded. "It is not unlike the French countryside."

"I quite agree. Could it be that the people of England are no different from the citizens of France?"

Courtney thought of her travels around the world. Travels that she could not discuss for fear of revealing too much about her past. "I believe that all people desire peace, Majesty. And the freedom to pursue a life of happiness."

The queen glanced at her lady-in-waiting. "And what of you, Courtney? What do you desire?"

Freedom from Richelieu's domination, she thought with a shudder. Freedom to love Rory without fear of drawing him into something evil. Courtney shook off her dark thoughts. This was to be, after all, a respite from the troubles that plagued her. She gave an impish smile. "Gentle weather, a sturdy mount and two days of nothing more complicated than a game of cards."

The queen sat back against the cushions of the carriage and fanned herself. "What you ask sounds like heaven."

The sun drifted high in the sky before the line of carriages turned off the rutted road and paused at a gatekeeper's cottage. Instantly a weathered old man with a thin thatch of hair the color of faded wheat appeared. He snatched his hat from his head and made a graceful bow before the lead carriage.

"Welcome," he said in a voice that still carried traces of his Yorkshire boyhood. "The master is expecting Her Majesty."

Henrietta Maria lifted a hand in greeting as the carriage rolled past him. When the last of the carriages had passed by, he pulled himself up alongside the trunks and rode along.

Their procession now entered a graceful, curving path. A low wall of gray stone dipped and curved over the gently rolling land. Far ahead, Lord Edgecomb's country house loomed. It was made of the same stone as the wall and rose to four stories topped by turrets.

As they drew near, Courtney could see that the household staff were lined up to greet them. In front of them stood Lord Edgecomb, his white hair glinting in the bright summer sunlight.

"Majesty, welcome to Greystone." Edgecomb took the queen's hand to help her from the carriage.

"Thank you, Lord Edgecomb."

"Courtney, allow me to assist you." Courtney's hand was engulfed in his as she stepped down.

"I trust your journey was an easy one."

"It was most pleasant, sir," the queen said, smoothing her skirts.

Rory dismounted and handed his reins to a young stableboy before shaking his host's hand. Lifting his head, he drew in a deep breath. "How much cleaner the air seems outside London."

"I quite agree," Edgecomb said with a smile. "Though I am forced to spend far too much time at my London house, I much prefer life in the country. Come, Majesty." Edgecomb made a sweeping gesture to indicate the men and women assembled before the house. "The servants are eager to welcome their queen."

Courtney noted the way Henrietta Maria made an effort to put each servant at ease as they were presented to her. From the butler and housekeeper to the lowliest scullery maid, she had a smile and a kind word for each. Awkward stumblings and curious stares were replaced by smiles of real pleasure at having been treated to the queen's warmth.

Upon entering the house, they were led into a parlor that was large and comfortably furnished, reflecting the casual, dignified taste of their host.

"You will want to refresh yourselves," he said, leading them to chairs and a settle drawn up before a fire.

A servant came forward with a silver tray laden with an assortment of ales and teas. The queen preferred a goblet of ale. The others followed suit.

"Since the weather is so fine, Majesty, I thought we might hunt this afternoon."

"I would like that." The queen's eyes fairly shone as she added, "When I was very young, my brothers treated me like one of them. We rode to the hounds and hunted game until we dropped." For a moment her tone became wistful. "I miss that. The minute I became betrothed, I was excluded from their company." Then she smiled and lifted wide, innocent eyes to her host. "I look forward to these precious days, Lord Edgecomb."

"Then we must not tarry." He set down his tankard and rang for a servant. "Show the queen and her lady-in-waiting to their rooms. By the way, Courtney," Edgecomb asked conversationally, "did you also hunt with your father and brothers?"

Courtney swallowed back her discomfort. "Nay. I had no brothers."

When it appeared that their host would pursue the subject further, she turned and followed the queen from the room.

"When you are rested and changed, Majesty, we will begin the hunt," Edgecomb called.

The suite of rooms prepared for the queen's visit consisted of a large sitting chamber, a bedchamber and, to one side, a separate room to accommodate her maids. In each room was a fireplace in front of which were fur-covered chaises. Bowls of fresh flowers on the tables and the wide stone windowsills filled the rooms with their fragrance.

On the opposite side of a wide hallway was Courtney's suite. Like the queen's, it had a sitting room and a bright, cheery bedchamber, made even brighter by the presence of masses of flowers. To her delight, Courtney discovered a balcony that afforded a view of the magnificent gardens below.

While the maids finished unpacking, Courtney and Henrietta Maria hurriedly changed into suitable hunting clothes. The queen chose a gown of russet velvet, the full sleeves inset with ermine. The neck and hemline were also trimmed with matching ermine. On her feet were high kid boots, and leather gauntlets protected her hands and wrists. Her long hair was pulled away from her face by a veil and covered by a hat with russet plumes.

Courtney wore a simple gown of green velvet. She had left her head uncovered, allowing her hair to stream down her back in a riot of curls. As Rory helped her mount, he noted that she wore no riding gloves, choosing instead to thread the reins lightly through her fingers. If Thornhill had hoped to teach his daughter the ways of royalty, he had not succeeded. Even without the garb of a pirate, Courtney was still as wild and free as ever. The thought brought a smile to Rory's lips.

"We will cross the meadow to yonder woods," Lord Edgecomb called, taking the lead.

Beside each member of their hunting party rode a groom who carried an assortment of weapons.

"The hunt is new to me," Courtney said, eager to learn. "How will we spot the game?"

Edgecomb turned in his saddle. "The woods teem with game. Deer, rabbit, quail. I have sent the hunt master ahead, along with his assistants. When he finds something challenging enough, he will scare it up and his assistants will see that it is directed toward us."

As their party neared the woods, a shout went up. A moment later, with a whirring of wings, four pheasants flew directly above their heads. While Courtney watched in fascination, the queen accepted a longbow from her groom and aimed. Her arrow found the bird's breast, and bird and arrow fell in lazy spirals to the ground.

While Courtney watched, Edgecomb and Rory took careful aim and brought two more birds to the ground. Courtney found herself straining against the sunlight to track the path of the fourth pheasant. She was relieved when it disappeared safely behind a stand of trees.

"Excellent aim, Majesty."

The queen gave her host a brilliant smile. "I was afraid I had lost the skill after all this time."

"Such skills are never completely lost. Come." Turning his mount, Edgecomb led them into the forest while one of the grooms retrieved the pheasants.

They rode the sun-dappled trails of the woods for nearly an hour. Lord Edgecomb and Henrietta Maria took the lead, followed by their grooms. Several hundred yards behind, Rory and Courtney followed.

In boots and tight-fitting breeches topped by a burgundy hunting jacket, Rory looked at ease in the forest. A longbow was slung carelessly over his shoulder.

"I can see that you are happy to be here in the country."

He turned slightly. "This part of England reminds me of home."

"You have been away a long time."

"Aye. Too long." He caught her reins, forcing her mount to slow to a walk beside his. "But there is a woman who has bewitched me, making me forget the land of my birth."

In keeping with the hushed quality of the forest, their voices were muted.

"I think, sir, nothing in the world could do that. Scotland is in your blood."

"Aye. As is the woman I spoke of."

Courtney's eyes warmed as she lifted her gaze to his. "A certain Scots chieftain has made my stay in England easier, as well."

He made an elaborate bow. "I am at your service, my lady."

Before she could reply, a deer stepped into a clearing just in front of them, its head lifted to the wind.

Rory touched a hand to Courtney's arm to silence her. Then, removing his longbow, he offered it to her. Courtney's eyes widened when she realized what he had in mind. He wanted her to loose the arrow that would bring down the buck. She returned her gaze to the deer, then shook her head in refusal. In one swift motion, Rory placed an arrow against the string, aimed and released it. The deer's head turned toward the motion. Before the buck could dart away to safety, the arrow found its mark. The animal reared up and took several unsteady steps. Moments later it fell. By the time the grooms reached it, the buck was dead.

Courtney sat very still, spine rigid, head high, watching the animal's death throes. When at last it was over, she experienced a feeling of loss.

"Why did you refuse the shot?" Rory asked. "Surely you have handled a longbow?"

"Aye." Courtney swallowed. "But I could not kill such a magnificent creature."

Rory turned, and for the first time he was aware of her pallor. Drawing his mount even closer to hers, he placed a hand over hers on the saddle. Her hands, he noted, were cold.

"But you have killed men."

"In battle," she said quickly. "They were armed and able to defend themselves. I learned early that it was their life or mine."

"This deer will provide food, not only for Lord Edgecomb but for the villagers who depend on the lord of the manor for much of their sustenance."

"Aye. I know," Courtney said softly. "At least I know here." She touched a hand to her forehead. "But here..." Touching a hand to her heart, she continued softly, "...it is harder to accept. I cannot permit myself to take the life of a helpless creature simply for the pleasure of the hunt."

Leaning across the saddle, Rory drew her into his arms. She continually surprised him. This infamous pirate, who fought as fiercely as any man in battle, kept hidden a tender, compassionate heart. It was one more contradiction to this strange, compelling woman.

With his lips pressed to a tangle of her hair, he whispered, "Your secret is safe with me, my lady. I will tell no one that Lady Courtney Thornhill shrinks from the sight of blood."

"And I will tell no one that the fierce warrior Rory MacLaren goes weak when a maiden places her lips just so against his throat."

His low rumble of laughter suddenly died. The arms holding her tightened until she was held in a viselike grip.

"You go too far, my lady. If you are not careful I will be forced to take you here, in the lush cool grass."

She sighed, enjoying the sensations that had begun curling around her midsection. "And what of our grooms?"

"I could send them to join the queen's party. And pray that they will lose themselves in the forest until dark."

She allowed herself to relax against him for a moment, loving the way she felt in his arms. Then, playfully, she pushed him away. "You are a cruel man, MacLaren. Thinking of your own selfish pleasures while others would be forced to suffer."

"Aye. I suppose we will be forced to continue in the hunt, even though we can both think of pleasanter ways to spend an afternoon."

Courtney's laughter rang on the breeze as she carefully turned her mount away from the sight of the fallen deer.

For the rest of the afternoon she was merely a spectator while the others took part in the hunt. When Lord Edgecomb became aware of her distaste for killing, he was strangely relieved. A true French spy would have no qualms about killing.

Lord Edgecomb had wisely decided that their first evening's supper would be a relaxed, carefree meal. Instead of using the great hall of the manor, the four friends dined in the hunt room. Weapons and trophies of the hunt were hung on the walls. The chairs strewn about for easy conversation were comfortable and well-worn from years of use. As course after course was served, they found themselves engaged in the easy conversation of old friends.

Henrietta Maria, grateful for her host's consideration, regaled them with stories of her youth.

"I was spoiled," she confessed with a shrug. "By my father and my brothers. It was my mother who decided that I needed a strong hand. She placed me under Father Le-Farge's holy care, with orders that I be taught patience and humility."

"But why?" Courtney asked. "I should think your mother would be pleased to see that you were a woman of strength. My fath—" Stunned by what she had been about to reveal, she stopped, feeling her cheeks grow hot.

Seeing her distress, Rory broke the awkward silence. "In my country, both men and women are expected to be strong."

Courtney shot him a grateful look and fell silent as he continued.

"If a man dies without sons, his daughters inherit all, including his title."

The queen was intrigued. "Are you saying that a woman may become a clan leader?"

"Aye. There have been some fine ones who have led their clans to battle and bested their enemies."

Henrietta Maria met Courtney's look. "I fear we were born in the wrong place."

The young women shared a smile.

"Where were you born, Courtney?" Edgecomb asked. "Was your childhood similar to the queen's?"

Courtney fell silent, her mind awhirl. "It was such an ordinary childhood." Out of the corner of her eye she saw the surprise on Rory's face. A pirate's childhood, ordinary? "You would much prefer to hear Her Majesty's tales of her youth."

"You said you had no brothers. Were there sisters?"

Courtney shook her head. "I was alone much of my life."

"And your parents?" Edgecomb persisted.

"Such good, kind people. I miss them." When would the lies end? Courtney pretended to yawn.

"Forgive me." Lord Edgecomb stood. "It has been a long day. But it is such a delight having guests at Greystone. It has been far too long since I have entertained good friends."

The fire had long since burned low and their goblets were empty. The four bid each other good-night.

When his guests had left, Lord Edgecomb stood by the mantel, staring thoughtfully into the ashes. Had it been his imagination, or had Courtney carefully avoided any mention of herself? He drained the last of his ale and turned away. There was one more day. He would make a determined effort to find out more about her.

Upstairs, a maid helped Courtney from her clothes and prepared her for bed. When she departed, Courtney looked up to see Rory on her balcony.

With a little laugh of surprise, she rushed across the room and caught his hand. "How long have you been there?"

"Just long enough to ascertain that you were alone."

"Where is your room?"

He gave a low chuckle. "Right beside yours. How convenient that Lord Edgecomb has this balcony. Otherwise I would have had to storm your door."

He caught her by the shoulders and stared down into her eyes. He loved the way they looked, warm and inviting, with only a hint of the passion that he knew lurked just below the surface.

"I could not bear to sleep a room away—" he touched his lips to hers, and instantly the flame ignited "—knowing what heaven awaited me here."

His arms came around her, drawing her firmly against him. He took her fully into the kiss and felt her eager response.

"Nor could I have slept alone this night," she whispered against his mouth, "knowing you were somewhere nearby."

"All day I have waited for this," he murmured, slipping the silken night shift from her shoulders and bringing his lips to her warm flesh.

She moved in his arms, feeling herself opening like a flower to his touch. His lips, his fingertips, caressed her until a sob broke from her lips.

"Rory. Oh, Rory."

They dropped to their knees on the fur throw and felt the warmth of the fire. Or was it the fire of their passion that heated their flesh, making it impossible to think? It mattered not. They were beyond thought. Mouth to mouth, flesh to flesh, they slipped over the edge of madness. And, with murmured words of endearment, they came together with an almost savage intensity.

Chapter Seventeen

The early-morning light streamed through a gap in the curtains, warming the two figures who lay in each other's arms, wrapped in a tangle of sheets. As Rory's fingertips found the tiny scar at Courtney's shoulder, his eyes slowly opened.

He had endured the brutality in the French prison, as well as aboard the *Hawk*, by telling himself that one day he would escape. How had this amazing woman endured, knowing that her harsh life aboard ship would never end? What sort of inner strength did she possess that had enabled her to survive?

His eyes narrowed, and without thinking he pressed his lips to the scar. If it were in his power he would erase all pain, all cruel memories, from her life.

At the touch of his lips on her flesh, her eyes blinked open. For a moment her thoughts scattered, as dream and reality mingled. Then, with a little sigh of contentment, she drew him close and brought her lips to his ear.

"Good morning, my lord. Were you examining me for imperfections?"

"That would be futile, my lady." He ran openmouthed kisses along the column of her throat. "In you I have found perfection."

Her warm breath shuddered from between parted lips, feathering his hair. "No flaws? Not even one?"

"Perhaps one." He lifted his head a moment to study the way she looked in his arms. Thick, dark hair spilled across the linen sheets, and he plunged a hand into the tangles, drawing her inexorably closer.

"What would that be?"

He studied the laughing amber eyes, the smiling lips, and felt the passion rise within him. "I will never have enough of you, Courtney."

His lips covered hers, and the laughter died in her throat as they lost themselves in the wonder of their newly discovered feelings.

"Good morning, Lord Edgecomb."

Her host looked up from the table, then came to his feet. "Ah, Courtney. You are the first one to awaken and join me."

She swallowed back the laughter that bubbled at the thought of Rory, clad only in a sheet, narrowly escaping to the balcony before the maid had arrived to help Courtney dress.

Edgecomb held her chair as she settled herself at the table.

"I am certain the others will be here soon. I heard the sound of morning activity in the queen's rooms."

Several maids entered the dining hall carrying trays and platters of covered dishes. Courtney spent a few minutes lifting the silver lids and exclaiming over the tempting food. There were hot and cold meats, and steaming gruels and puddings, as well as biscuits and breads still warm from the oven. On still another tray were jams and jellies and an assortment of pastries to tempt the sweet tooth.

Edgecomb watched as she savored the excellent meal. "Do you find our food different from that of France?"

"Not so different. In my travels I have become accustomed to exotic foods."

Realizing what she had just revealed, Courtney touched a napkin to her lips to cover her dismay.

"How is it that you have traveled, my dear?"

"My father was—a sea captain."

"And you and your mother sailed with him?"

Courtney nearly groaned aloud at her dilemma. "My mother was in . . . delicate health. But I often traveled with my father."

"How extraordinary that a sea captain's daughter should be trained as a lady-in-waiting to a royal princess."

"It . . . was my knowledge of languages that brought me to the attention of King Louis. And he, in turn, suggested to his sister that I would make an excellent companion in your country."

"So," Edgecomb said guardedly, "you have only been lady-in-waiting to Henrietta Maria for a short time."

"Aye." Courtney avoided his eyes. She must reveal no more about herself. How she hated deceiving this good man. Searching her mind for a way to change the topic, she asked, "Has this house been in your family for generations?"

He shook his head. "I inherited several fine pieces of land from my father and a farm in Sussex. And there is the house in London, of course, as well as many other holdings. But I bought this manor as a means of consolation after the death of my wife and child."

"I was quite certain this was a man's retreat," she remarked, smiling at his arched look. "It bears no trace of a woman's hand. And it lacks the loving touches usually found in a home, portraits, handworked items, bits and pieces of family. Have you no portrait of your wife and child?"

He seemed saddened by her question. "There are many in my London house, as well as the family estates. When we were first wed, I was so proud of my wife that I had many portraits painted. She was a favorite cousin of the queen's. There are several fine portraits of her in the castle in London.''

"Was she very beautiful?"

He stared into the distance for a moment, and Courtney knew that he could see his wife in his mind's eye. "She was exceptionally beautiful. Her hair was dark, unless she was in the sunlight. Then it seemed to turn to fire. Her eyes were sometimes green, sometimes the color of amber. At first glance your eyes reminded me of hers. And her voice was soft, gentle." He smiled. "A cultured voice. She could command without ever changing the tone of her voice."

Courtney felt a shiver at the way he spoke of his dead wife. His feeling for her, even after all these years, was evident. "You loved her very much."

"I did."

"Tell me about your child."

"I cannot," he said unexpectedly.

At Courtney's puzzled look, he said softly, "Even now it pains me to speak of her. The way she looked the last time I gazed on her, so sweet and angelic, yet with a strength that continually amazed me. I think she resembled her mother, though I was often told she had inherited something of me, as well. After the death of her mother she was never out of my sight. We were inseparable. She filled my life. We traveled together everywhere with nurses and tutors."

"Did she become ill?"

He shook his head. "I was sent to Ireland as a representative of the king. It was hoped that I could use my powers of persuasion to calm a minor rebellion. But when I sensed still more unrest, I sent my child back to England, where she would be safe." He paused for a long moment before adding, "That was the last time I saw her. But I thank God that I had her for at least those few years."

"You still carry your wife and child in your heart."

A look of sadness crossed his face. Without thinking, Courtney covered his hand with hers. How right it seemed to offer comfort to this good man. How easy it was to forget Thornhill's lessons. He glanced at her with a look of pleasant surprise.

"Forgive me, Lord Edgecomb. I did not wish to bring up unpleasant memories."

He gave her a tender smile and patted her hand. "Such memories are never unpleasant. Quite the contrary." His voice took on a wistful tone. "It was a very long time ago. I should be used to it. But even after all these years I am often surprised by the flash of sudden pain at the memory."

"You must have loved them very much."

"More than life itself. I would have given anything, anything," he said vehemently, "to have them back."

"Has there been no one who could fill the void in your life?"

A maid entered and he straightened and lifted a napkin to his lips. "No one. But not for lack of trying."

He chuckled, and Courtney was relieved that he could find humor in his sorrow.

"My friends have paraded every eligible woman from ten and six to half a century before me, hoping I would marry again."

He and Courtney shared a laugh before he sobered once again. "They do not understand that one woman, and only one, owned my heart. When I lost my wife and child, I lost my own heart, as well."

Courtney thought of Rory and felt a shaft of pain that left her stunned. She knew beyond doubt that if anything happened to him she would be inconsolable.

They looked up as Rory and the queen entered the dining hall. Forcing a smile to his lips, Lord Edgecomb greeted his guests warmly.

"How did you sleep, Majesty?"

"Without interruption, Lord Edgecomb. Your accommodations are most comfortable."

"And you, Rory?"

Courtney saw the hint of laughter behind Rory's solemn eyes. "I agree with her majesty. Your accommodations are...most comfortable."

"Good. Good." Leading Henrietta Maria to the table, Edgecomb rang for the servants, who were eager to serve their queen.

"If you agree, madam, I thought we might ride to hounds this morning." Lord Edgecomb watched as the queen filled her plate.

"I would like that," the queen said between mouthfuls. "I have been looking forward to a fox hunt."

"As have my gamekeepers." Edgecomb accepted another cup of tea before adding, "I also thought you would enjoy a visit to our nearby village market this afternoon. The citizens have heard that their queen is in residence at Greystone, and they would be most eager to boast to their grandchildren that you spent a pleasant hour in their midst."

The queen found herself smiling at the picture his words brought to mind. "If you think my visit will bring the villagers pleasure, Lord Edgecomb, I will be more than happy to go."

"Good. As for tonight, the servants will prepare the game you so skillfully hunted, Majesty. I have ordered a feast prepared for this evening."

At the queen's look of pleasure, Edgecomb's voice lowered. "I know how much you enjoyed your privacy last evening. But since this is your last night in my home, Majesty, I would like to invite several of the nearby landowners to sup with us. It would be a privilege they would not soon forget."

Courtney saw the look that came and went on the queen's face and realized that dining with strangers was a strain for this shy monarch. But it was difficult even for royalty to deny this cultured gentleman a request.

"I would be pleased to dine with your friends, Lord Edgecomb."

Their host smiled broadly. Though he, too, recognized the queen's discomfort, he was certain that she would enjoy the evening once she relaxed and allowed herself to get to know the good citizens of the county.

By the time the queen had finished a leisurely breakfast and changed into riding clothes, the horses had been saddled and brought from the stables for the chase.

Courtney had not expected to enjoy the fox hunt. Yesterday's hunt had left her saddened by the killing of so much game. But she could not deny the excitement as the hounds howled and bayed, eager to be turned loose. The horses, sensing the tension, stamped and snorted in the morning air. When at last the dogs were released, they darted across the meadow with amazing speed in pursuit of a fox. Even the horses, though carefully trained for the hunt, could hardly be contained. Given their heads, they raced skillfully over the ground.

Henrietta Maria and Lord Edgecomb led the hunt, along with the gameskeeper, while Rory and Courtney followed. Just ahead of them the hounds paused, sniffed the grass, then leaped ahead as if driven mad. Each time the hounds paused, the horsemen paused, as well. Each time the hounds broke into a run, the horses were right behind them.

Courtney leaned low over her mount, feeling the wind tugging at her hair. The scent of horseflesh and leather excited her almost as much as a fresh sea breeze. Her heartbeat kept time to the pounding of the horse's hooves. When at last, after nearly two hours, the fox was cornered, she was thrilled to discover that he would mercifully be allowed to go free. The hounds were caged and the horses, sweating from their exertion, were returned to the stable.

As she glanced at the queen's happy face, Courtney felt a strange exhilaration.

"I think," Rory said, taking her arm as they made their way back to the house, "you are a woman who could find challenge even in a quiet country setting."

"We may be far from the crowds of London, but this is hardly quiet, my lord. I can see why the queen so loves riding to hounds. The sound of their baying and the thunder of the horses' hooves set my heart racing."

"I saw your face as you rode, Courtney." He paused and placed his hands on either side of her face, staring deeply into her eyes. "The sight of you is all I need to set my heart racing."

He brushed his lips lightly over hers and felt a sudden rush of heat. When their host called out to them, he pulled back.

"Remind me to finish this when we are alone."

Placing Courtney's hand on his arm, he gave her a wicked smile before leading her toward the others.

Six matched white horses pulled the queen's carriage along the road toward the village market. Alongside rode Lord Edgecomb and Rory, resplendent in velvet riding coats and plumed hats.

Word had spread among the villagers that the queen would be visiting this afternoon. All morning the road had been crowded with carts and wagons, as entire families had made the important trip in the hope of glimpsing their queen.

"So many people," Henrietta Maria sighed as the carriage rolled to a stop. "I had thought this a sleepy little village."

"They feel privileged to see their queen," Courtney said, peering from the window. "For many of them it will be the most exciting event of their lives. Their children and grandchildren will be regaled with the story, Majesty."

"Then we must make it memorable." As the door to the carriage was opened, the queen lifted her chin and offered her hand to the footman.

Pausing on the carriage step, the queen heard the cheers from the watching crowd. Her eyes widened for a moment, but then she lifted her hand in a greeting. The cheering grew louder.

From her vantage point in the carriage, Courtney could see Henrietta Maria in profile. As the cheers continued, the queen's eyes brimmed, and a tear trickled from the corner of her eye. The queen touched a finger to stem the flow, then raised her hand to the crowd. When at last she stepped down from the carriage, the crowd fell silent, watching as the queen of England began to walk among them. One step behind her, Lord Edgecomb, hat in hand, began introducing the villagers, who bowed and curtsied.

Rory helped Courtney from the carriage. With her hand on his arm, she trailed behind the queen and their host.

When the villagers had been presented, the queen moved among the stalls in the village market, exclaiming over handmade lace and beribboned bonnets, complimenting farmers on their plump chickens and ducks. Everywhere she stopped she took the time to speak with the people, listening to their descriptions of their farms, occasionally stooping to listen to the halting words of a timid child. A visit that had been expected to last no more than an hour stretched into four. When at last the queen's carriage began to journey back to Greystone, the sun had made its arc to the western sky.

In the marketplace, men slapped each other on the back while women hugged their children and whispered to each other about the queen's excellent command of the language. They openly marveled at her exquisite gown and her delicate kid boots, and talked about her warmth and kindness. Everyone agreed that their king had made an excellent choice, and that Henrietta Maria, the little French princess, had become a remarkable queen.

"Majesty, you are beautiful."

Lord Edgecomb and Rory looked up from their talk of the hunt as the queen paused in the doorway. Because she was meeting people who were not normally privileged to attend royal functions, Henrietta Maria had taken great pains with her toilette. The women expected elegance. She would give it to them. Her dark hair had been carefully twisted into a wreath of curls, forming a stunning backdrop for a tiara of winking diamonds. Around her throat and wrists and at her earlobes were more diamonds, giving off a glow that seemed to surround her in an aura of light. Her white gown was shot through with silver and gold thread that gave it a luminescent quality. On her feet were white kid slippers.

The men, she knew, expected a certain haughtiness from their queen. Again she would give them what they expected. With her spine rigid, her head tilted at a proud angle, she left no doubt of her position.

Setting aside his ale, Edgecomb hurried forward.

"There are still a few minutes before our guests arrive, Majesty. Would you join us in a drink?"

"I would, Lord Edgecomb."

Instantly a maid appeared at her side bearing a tray. The queen selected a crystal goblet.

"Your kindness to the people of the village this day will long be remembered, Majesty."

"I found your people warm and friendly, Lord Edgecomb."

"They are your people, too, Majesty. All the people of England are now your subjects."

Henrietta Maria grew silent. Could it be that for just a moment she had forgotten that she was no longer a French princess? She was queen of England. Wife of Charles I of

England. And the people of this tiny village had given her a sense of pride, a feeling of belonging.

Edgecomb and Rory exchanged a glance.

When Courtney paused in the doorway, Rory looked up and felt his heart begin to race.

She was wearing a gown of crimson satin, gathered just below the bosom to display her high, firm breasts. The gown fell in delicate folds to the tip of her kid slippers. At her throat was a necklace of rubies and diamonds that caught and reflected the light of dozens of candles. At her earlobes were matching earrings.

Crossing the room, he took her hand in his. If only they were alone. He longed to crush her in his arms and kiss her until they were both breathless. He longed to feel the heat build until the flames devoured them both. Instead he merely brushed his lips over her hand and murmured, "My lady, you will be the envy of every woman in the room tonight."

She saw the smoldering look in his eyes and felt a sudden rush of heat. "You are too kind, my lord."

The butler approached to announce the arrival of their guests. The queen handed her goblet to a maid and took Lord Edgecomb's arm. Behind them, Rory and Courtney followed at a discreet distance as they made their way to the great dining hall. Inside, everyone craned their necks for a glimpse of the queen as she passed. When they were positioned at the front of the hall, the couples bowed.

"Majesty," Lord Edgecomb said in a tone usually reserved for court, "may I present your loyal subjects."

As the couples lined up to be formally introduced to their monarch, Courtney positioned herself beside the queen in case Henrietta Maria had need of an interpreter.

Rory touched Courtney's hand and felt the slight tremble. If this evening would be difficult for the queen, it would be twice as difficult for her lady-in-waiting. A genteel manor house was not a pirate ship. And the wealthy landowners were far removed from the thieves and murderers Courtney had lived with for a lifetime. But Rory had no doubt Courtney would be able to handle any situation that arose, as she had ever since her arrival on English soil.

The women at table were prepared to dislike the queen. After having been raised in the opulence of French royalty, she now appeared indulged by England, as well. Her gown had probably taken an army of servants many weeks to sew. And her jewelry was worth a king's ransom.

The men at table were properly envious of the king. Henrietta Maria's youth, her dark beauty and the way she used her charms made them realize that Charles had made a fine bargain.

But as each course was served and Lord Edgecomb regaled his guests with stories of the previous day's hunt, both men and women gained new respect for the monarch in their midst.

"Her Majesty handles a longbow with the skill of the king's archers," Edgecomb boasted.

Courtney saw many of the guests turn to study the queen with new interest.

"And as a horsewoman Her Majesty is unequaled."

"Your lovely countryside makes it a pleasure to ride," the queen said softly. "I believe I have fallen in love with England since my stay at Greystone."

"And what of your lady-in-waiting?" The plump, red-cheeked earl of Hollingswell turned to Courtney, who was seated beside him. She felt the stares of the others as they turned their attention to her.

"Do you miss your home and family in France?"

Rory turned in time to see the smile freeze on Courtney's lips. Her voice trembled slightly, and he hoped he was the only one who noticed it.

"It is natural to miss one's home and family. But, like Her Majesty, I grow to love England more each day. The people are warm and friendly—'' she saw Rory's eyebrow arch slightly and felt herself begin to flush ''—and you have made me feel welcome.''

At the other end of the table, Lord Edgecomb felt an uncomfortable stirring of curiosity. He could no longer deny that Courtney was being deliberately evasive. Except when prodded, she never mentioned her home or family. Though she had been attentive when he had spoken of his wife and child, she had deliberately steered the conversation away from herself. Could Burlingame's accusations be correct? As the question nagged at him, he felt a trickle of fear. Yet, as he watched her, the fear faded. She was so sweet, so sincere, it was impossible that she could be guilty of the things Burlingame suggested.

It was a relief when the supper ended and they retired to a warm, cheery parlor where musicians had been assembled to entertain the guests.

It was well past midnight before the guests said their goodbyes and climbed into carriages for the long ride back to their homes. Even before the sound of carriage wheels had faded in the distance, the queen stifled a yawn behind her hand.

"It has been a long day, Majesty. I regret that you had no time to rest."

"I enjoyed every minute of it, Lord Edgecomb. There will be time enough to rest when I return to the palace."

Aye, Courtney thought as she followed the queen upstairs. This night especially, she did not wish to rest. As she undressed and prepared for bed, she watched the balcony for her night visitor. When at last he stepped into her room, she rushed into his arms.

"I have missed you here in my arms," he whispered against her temple.

"And I you." She drew him close and lifted her mouth to his. "Oh, Rory. Hold me. I wish this night would never end."

As the kiss deepened and the first stirrings of passion began to rise, he found himself wishing he could steal her away. These two days away from the palace and the problems of England and France and of their respective monarchs had been a special gift. One they might never enjoy again.

She melted against him, and he felt a welling of tenderness. If only they could go on like this forever.

All thought scattered as he brought his lips to the little hollow between her neck and shoulder. Hearing the soft moan that escaped her lips, he crushed her mouth with his and lifted her in his arms. This was their last night of freedom from the prying eyes of the palace staff. They were free to love all through the night.

Courtney was determined to put aside all her fears for this one last night. Tomorrow she would face the fact that she was deeply involved in an intrigue that might cost her her life. Tonight she was a woman in love. If love was enough, she could hold back the dawn forever.

Chapter Eighteen

Lord Edgecomb, these have been very precious days. I am forever in your debt."

Courtney was shocked to see the usually reserved Henrietta Maria embrace their host.

"They have been most special to me, as well, Majesty. We are all so involved in affairs of state, we spend too little time with friends. My home is yours whenever you have a need to escape the rigors of royal duties."

Edgecomb helped the queen into her carriage, then turned toward Courtney. "You are a rare woman, Courtney. I am pleased that we had these days together."

"I am grateful to you, my lord. You will never know what this time has meant to me."

Edgecomb embraced her warmly, and Courtney felt an ache around her heart. If only her father could have held her in like manner. How had she endured all those years without warmth and affection?

After Edgecomb helped her into the carriage, he nodded to the driver. As the carriage moved ahead, Courtney stared out the window and watched as Rory and Lord Edgecomb exchanged words and laughter before warmly saying farewell.

On the long ride back to London, the queen chatted openly about the people she had met, the things she had experienced in the country. But as the carriage drew near the city once more, the two fell silent, each lost in private thoughts.

As Rory drew his mount alongside the carriage, he saw the little frown that furrowed the queen's brow and knew that she was steeling herself for the next battle between the king's council and her clergy.

The king was in an expansive mood. Word of Henrietta Maria's reception in the country had preceded her. Several of the noblemen who had been present at dinner at Lord Edgecomb's had already visited the palace. They had lavished praise upon the king's French bride, regaling all who would listen with tales of her hunting prowess. When they spoke of the warmth she had displayed to all the citizens at the village market, the king listened attentively.

Though Burlingame had tempted him with several attractive wenches in the queen's absence, Charles had refused, saying he had too much on his mind. The truth was that he missed his bride. He missed her flash of anger when Burlingame went too far in his accusations. He missed her laughter when she regaled him with tales of her childhood. He missed her tenderness when they were alone.

Walking to the window, Charles strained for a glimpse of the carriage that would bring his bride home. Home. Would she ever accept his land as home?

He brought a fist down on the tabletop. He should have ignored Burlingame's endless list of duties and gone instead to Edgecomb's country house with her. They could have had a fine time hunting and visiting the village market. His heart quickened. They could have had a fine time loving, as they had in Dover.

He heard the trumpets announcing the arrival of the queen's carriage and hurried into the hallway.

Burlingame was waiting. "I have convened your council, Majesty."

"In a while," the king said impatiently. "My wife is returning from the country."

"I have sent an emissary to greet the queen, Majesty. She will be informed that the king will see her when affairs of state have been dealt with."

"These things can wait—"

"Majesty, there are matters of life and death to be discussed. A monarch must make many sacrifices for his country."

Charles met his chief councillor's eye and recognized the look of disdain. Burlingame was right, of course. There were far more important issues at stake here than his love for his wife. He was acting like a lovesick boy.

With a sigh, the king turned away and stalked toward the council chamber. He would greet Henrietta Maria later.

The queen stepped from her carriage and glanced around expectantly.

The stooped, aging lord chancellor stepped forward. Though he was a kindly old man, Henrietta Maria had a lingering dislike for him because he had been the one sent to stand in for the Prince of Wales at their marriage on the steps of Notre-Dame. To her he was one more vestige of the old guard who formed a wall around her husband. A wall she would never penetrate.

"Welcome home, Majesty. The king sends his greetings, and his apology that he must deal with some important matters of state."

Henrietta Maria lifted her head in a familiar gesture of defiance. She would not let her feelings show. "Thank you, my lord chancellor."

Spotting Bishop Montand, surrounded by a cluster of priests, the queen strode toward him. After greeting her warmly, he escorted her into the palace and was treated to a long visit in her private chamber.

As they walked away, Courtney overheard the lord chancellor mutter to Rory, "Look at them. Black-robed devils leading the king's own bride down a path of destruction.

Courtney thought the queen had never looked more regal. Or more unhappy.

"I still think we should hide here in my room and let the revelry and music go on without us." Courtney slipped on a gown of wine-colored satin and beckoned Rory to do up the buttons at her back.

"The king has ordered everyone in the palace to sup with him before the ball." Rory planted a kiss in the middle of her back before fastening her gown.

"Could we not beg illness?"

Studying their reflection in the looking glass, Rory placed a hand on each of her shoulders and drew her back against him. "After the tales the maids have carried about the palace these past days regarding a certain lady-in-waiting and a Scots ruffian, no one would believe such a blatant lie."

"Hmmm." She sighed and snuggled closer against him. "I tire of the king's revelry. It is merely an excuse to avoid being alone with his bride."

"Aye." Rory nuzzled her neck. "Royalty are not as fortunate as the rest of the populace. We, thankfully, are free to marry whom we choose."

Free to marry. Courtney felt a quick, sharp pain. She avoided meeting his gaze in the mirror. If he noticed, he said nothing.

"Will I be forced to stand around and watch you dance by in the arms of every man in the room again tonight?"

Courtney gave a husky laugh that shivered over his senses. "Perhaps, my lord, it is the only way to get you to take notice of me."

"I will take notice," he said, playfully tugging on a strand of her hair. "And I will put such a brazen wench over my knee when we return to this room."

"Then you are returning here with me?" She studied him through lowered lashes.

"Lady Thornhill," he said, turning her in his arms so that she was now facing him, "I intend to return to this room with you. This night and every night."

It would be wonderful having him here. She drew her arms about him, then froze.

God in heaven, it would be terrible.

Courtney thought about the next meeting with Richelieu's messenger, which was scheduled to take place in the small hours of the morning. She would have to find a way to sneak out without Rory's knowledge. As he bent his lips to hers, she relaxed, letting the feelings of love and anticipation thread along her veins as her blood grew hot. She had hours before she had to face that dreaded meeting. Hours of pleasure in Rory's arms.

"On second thought, Lady Thornhill," he muttered against her lips, "I think we can be a little late for the king's supper."

Courtney gave a delighted laugh as he scooped her up in his arms and carried her to the bed. "I wish to indulge in a little private revelry here before we join the others."

She gave herself up to the lips, the hands, that she had come to know as intimately as her own. And with a little sigh they slipped into the world that only lovers know.

"I have come up with the perfect plan," Burlingame whispered to the king in his private chamber.

"Shall I summon Edgecomb and the lord chancellor?"

"Nay, Majesty. It would be better if no one knew of this plan but the two of us. That way, there is no chance that anyone could warn off the guilty ones. I do not trust Edgecomb. The man has become too friendly with the queen and her lady-in-waiting, to say nothing of his friendship with the MacLaren."

The king could not agree. Although Edgecomb had grown very close to the queen and Lady Thornhill, he was still the highest-ranking judge in the land. He was a fine and noble man, and the king's true friend. Still... Reluctantly the king nodded. Burlingame's caution made perfect sense. "What is your plan?"

"We will send a woman, dressed like a stablehand, into the forest to meet the French messenger before he arrives at the king's meadow. The woman will carry a false message. Then we will send our own messenger to meet Lady Thornhill at the appointed time and place. He will carry the message we want her to have."

"It sounds simple enough." Charles pondered a moment. "What will the messages say?"

Burlingame's sinister smile grew. "We will order all the lady's evil associates in France to meet her aboard ship in the English Channel, where a plan to eliminate the king of England will be divulged. In reality our own navy will be waiting to send them to a watery grave."

The king digested what Burlingame had said. It would be clean. It would rid the country of spies. And, best of all, it would eliminate these villains without drawing the wrath of all of England down on Henrietta Maria. Word about French and English spies plotting against the king would certainly turn the people against their new French-born queen. Charles glanced at his chief councillor with a look of surprise. He had expected the man to try to tie the spies to Henrietta Maria's influence or that of her clergy.

"And the man who would betray me to France? Will he go to a watery grave with the others?"

"Nay, Majesty. The traitor must be brought back for public trial and execution."

"How shall we capture him?"

"I have no doubt that the lady will have him sniffing along at her heels. As you saw the other evening, Majesty, MacLaren is so besotted with her he is incapable of seeing beyond her."

"Are you so certain that the traitor is Rory MacLaren?"

"He is too close to Lady Thornhill to be unaware of her illicit activities."

The king stroked his beard and nodded. Everyone in the palace was aware of the infatuation. The two could hardly take their eyes off each other long enough to carry on a simple conversation with others.

Charles thought about his old friend, and pain twisted his heart. He had always hoped that Rory would find a woman worthy of him, an Englishwoman who would keep his mind off the country whose hills and forests and rugged people beckoned to him beyond England's borders. But now all hope had been dashed. MacLaren had lost his heart to the French-born Lady Thornhill, a woman who would entice him into rebellion and betrayal of his king. A woman who would lead him straight to the executioner's block.

"What woman will pretend to be Lady Thornhill?"

Burlingame sat back, enjoying the heady sense of power. "I have found a tavern wench with long, flowing hair and a slender frame. She has a knowledge of the French language. In the darkness, with a hooded cape, she will be believable."

"And the one who will masquerade as the messenger to the real Lady Thornhill?"

"One of your own soldiers, sir."

"She will not suspect?"

"Nay. His knowledge of the French language is excellent. Even now he memorizes the words he must speak."

Charles stood and clapped a hand on his chief councillor's shoulder. "You have served the throne of England well, Lord Burlingame. Your king will never forget this favor.''

Burlingame strode toward the great hall. He would lift a tankard or two with the members of the king's council before retiring.

On the morrow he would need no ale to lift his spirits. He would be drunk with power. When the spies were killed and MacLaren brought to trial, Lord Burlingame's name would ring throughout the country. And when, he thought with a smile, he next contacted Cardinal Richelieu in France, he would demand that the new spy network consist of professionals. He had no stomach for these puny lords and ladies who were being coerced into spying with threats on the lives of their loved ones.

He threw back his head and laughed aloud. He would rid the kingdom of everyone who dared question his authority. And then he would do what he had originally planned with the French cardinal so many long months ago. He would betray Charles and bring down the throne. With no progeny, the Stuart reign, begun by James I and continued by his son, Charles I, would be ended. A distant cousin, no more than a child, was the next in line. Yes, he thought with a smile, the next king would be young enough to mold. And stupid enough to manipulate completely.

Burlingame suddenly frowned, his eyebrows knit into straight slashes above his stormy eyes. If he could not be born king, he would settle for slightly less. He would be the complete power behind the English throne.

The revelry lasted until late in the night. The king, in an expansive mood, even led his smiling bride in several dances. With flushed cheeks and laughing eyes, Henrietta Maria finally persuaded Charles to retire to their rooms. When the king and queen had left, the party began breaking up.

Seemingly back in the king's favor, Courtney and Rory were relieved when the royal couple had departed and they could make their way toward her suite of rooms. Behind them trailed a serving maid bearing a tray containing ale and goblets. All who watched whispered that the queen's lady-in-waiting and the Scotsman planned their own revelry behind closed doors. All but Lord Burlingame. As they ascended the stairs, he watched from the shadows. An expression of triumph twisted his lips into a sneer. This night they would pay for what they had put him through.

As Rory tossed his cloak on the settle, Courtney instructed the maid to leave the ale on a table drawn up before a roaring fire.

"I shall serve," she said, showing the young woman to the door. When it was closed, she removed the small square of fabric from her waist and walked to the tray. With her back to Rory, she shook a fine powder into one of the goblets and filled it with ale. Filling a second goblet for herself, she turned and knelt among the furs scattered about the floor.

"I need no ale." His gaze scanned her face, then lingered on her lips.

"We will drink to our love," Courtney said softly. Lifting the goblet, she took a sip and watched as Rory did the same. "I do love you, Rory." She spoke the words so vehemently that he shot her a puzzled look.

"And I you, my love."

"No matter..." She watched as he drained the goblet and set it aside. For a moment she thought she could not go on. Her heart was pounding so hard, she was certain he could hear it.

He was watching her with a questioning look, one eyebrow arched, his lips parted and smiling.

She paused to lick her lips, then tried again. "No matter what happens, know always that I love you."

"The only thing that is going to happen is this." He took the goblet from her hands and pulled her close. With one hand on either side of her face, he stared deeply into her eyes. "We are going to ask the king's permission to wed. And then I will write to Thornhill stating my intention."

Courtney felt her eyes brim. "You would marry me?"

His voice was low and gruff with emotion. "Let no man say that I stole your virtue. I love you, Courtney. I want to spend a lifetime with you."

"Oh, Rory. Hold me." She felt a sob rising in her throat and swallowed. "Hold me."

He plunged his hands into her hair and drew her close. Against her temple, he whispered, "I want to know everything about you. The child you were. The woman you have become. The things you like. The thoughts that stir in your mind. I would know you as intimately as I know myself, my love."

She clung to him, absorbing shock after shock. Rory was saying all the things she had ever dreamed of hearing from him. On the very night she was about to betray his king.

Tears flowed from her eyes, soaking the front of his shirt. She loved him so desperately that she thought she would rather die than risk losing him.

"Lie with me, Courtney. Let me hold you, touch you."

As he lay back on the furs, she clung to him, burying her face against his throat. It was useless to try to fight it. She loved Rory MacLaren with all her being. She could not do anything to bring him harm.

She felt Rory's hand stroking her hair, her back. She would tell Richelieu's messenger that it was over. She would carry no more messages. For France. For Richelieu. She would spy no longer, not even to save the life of Thornhill.

Rory's hand went slack. She felt his breathing grow soft and even. Moving a little away from him, she stared down at his handsome, peaceful face. The drug she had given him had worked as promised. He would sleep through the night.

And by the time he awoke she would be lying here by his side, free at last from this evil business.

Slipping off her crimson gown, she drew on her breeches and her rough cape and crept to the balcony. Lowering herself to the ground, she began to make her way to the stables. Soon, soon, she prayed, chanting the word like a litany, she would be back in the arms of the man she loved, locked safely away from the villainy of this world.

Chapter Nineteen

Dark clouds crossed the moon, cutting off what little light there had been. Courtney crouched atop the hill, straining to see something, anything, in the shadows. A night bird called, and she stiffened and clutched the dagger firmly by her side. Each sigh of wind, each flutter of wing and scamper of wild creature, left her throat dry, her heart pounding.

John Fenton had not been on duty tonight. Mary had neither seen nor heard from him for weeks, since he had been sent on a mission by the king. But, surprisingly, it had taken little skill or cunning to slip through the network of guards who patrolled the castle grounds. They had been extremely careless.

Oh, to be rid of this dirty business. To be free to return to the arms of her lover, unsullied by the dark deeds of Richelieu and his underlings. She stood facing the path leading from the Thames, eager to catch a glimpse of the messenger.

A shadow moved, and she caught her breath. Animal? Man? She waited, watching, afraid to breathe, as it moved closer.

"I bring you greetings from home," a voice called in perfect French.

"How is our mutual friend?"

The hooded figure moved closer. This man, Courtney noted, was much older than the first two messengers. And far better dressed. How much, she found herself wondering, did Richelieu have to pay this man to do his evil deed? Or was the wicked cardinal also holding this man's loved ones hostage until the man complied with his wishes?

"I bring you an important message. Listen carefully."

It occurred to Courtney that her earlier messages had always been written, with the order to read and destroy them immediately. Abruptly an alarm went off in her mind, but was just as quickly dismissed. Apparently Richelieu was not willing to trust this to paper.

"A boat lies waiting for you in the harbor."

Courtney froze at his words. "A boat?" Rory, oh Rory. What is happening to me? To us? Why now, when we have just found love? She brushed away her fears and laments to concentrate on the messenger. "Where am I to go?"

"Another boat leaves France at this very moment, bound for a meeting with you in the Channel. Once aboard the second vessel, you shall receive your orders."

"I will be missed at the palace. Henrietta Maria…"

"…will be told where you have gone and why."

"But you do not understand," Courtney said patiently as if she were explaining to a child. "My work here is over. I will carry no more messages for Richelieu, even if he decides to carry out the threat upon the life of my father."

For a moment the messenger seemed taken aback by her words. He stared at her for a long, silent moment before saying firmly, "Your father is coming to you. He will be aboard the vessel you are meeting in the Channel."

"Thornhill is no longer a pawn?" Courtney clapped her hands and gave a little laugh. "Oh, how kind the Fates are. Now he can be here to grant his consent. Where is this boat?"

Her words made no sense to the messenger. He knew only that his task was to lay a trap for a French spy who had threatened the life of his beloved king. The man's teeth gleamed as he gave her a sinister smile. "Follow me, my lady. I will see you do not get lost along the way."

Catching her horse's reins, Courtney pulled herself into the saddle and followed behind the hooded figure. Soon she would see for herself that Thornhill was safely away from the evil clutches of Cardinal Richelieu. And to thank her for saving his life, Thornhill would surely give his blessing of the marriage between Courtney and Rory MacLaren.

The English ship was large. Twice as large as the *Hawk*. When Courtney was led aboard, she noted much frantic activity among the crew members. Weapons were being loaded, as well as casks of wine and ale, blankets, clean clothing and dressings. It puzzled her. This was much the same sort of activity that took place aboard the *Hawk* before a planned attack at sea. She had participated in such activities hundreds of times.

"Take Lady Thornhill to the captain's cabin," the messenger said in English.

Courtney glanced at him, but he was already hurrying away. She had rarely heard such excellent English from her fellow Frenchmen. No wonder Richelieu had commissioned him to spy on the English. Before she could speak with him further, a crew member led her below deck and paused before an open cabin door.

"The captain will be along shortly," the crewman said before closing the door.

Courtney glanced around the tidy cabin, then sat in the only chair. Within minutes she could hear the anchors being hauled aboard. The steady rocking movement alerted her to the fact that they were under way. Striding toward the porthole, she watched the shore recede until it was only a dark spot on the horizon.

The door opened. The captain was tall and thick shouldered, with the uniform of the king's navy buttoned over a bulging stomach.

"Lady Thornhill." He strode forward and bowed grandly. "It will be two or three hours before we reach our destination. If you would care to rest, please use my bunk."

"You are too kind, captain. I am much too excited to rest."

"Yes, I am certain this is quite an adventure for you," he said dryly. "Excuse me, my lady. I have much to see to."

When he was gone, Courtney glanced longingly at the bunk, then gave in to the need to rest. It was true that she was excited by the prospect of seeing Thornhill and the crew of the *Hawk* once more. Boney. Simpson. How she had missed them. But the journey was a long one. It would be dawn before they were all together, and midday before she was reunited with Rory. She would be wise to rest.

As she gratefully sank down on the bunk, she thought about the years she had been lulled to sleep by the gentle motions of the *Hawk*. It was so good to be back at sea. She had missed it.

Her eyes closed. Her breathing became steady. Letting go of all her tensions, all her fears, she slept.

Henrietta Maria sat in the middle of the bed and stared at her husband with wide, horror-filled eyes. This could not be happening. What he had just said could not be true.

The king had had far too much to drink. And in his drunken stupor he had just boasted that her lady-in-waiting, Courtney, and his best friend, Rory MacLaren, were at this very minute on their way to watery graves in the English Channel.

"It is a clever trap, madam. Meant to ensnare the spies working on both sides of the Channel."

She watched as the king's eyes closed. His breathing was shallow, raspy. As she began to slide off the bed, his hand snaked out, catching her wrist in an iron grip. "You would warn her, woman?" His eyes glittered dangerously.

"If what you say is true, she will no longer be in the palace, will she, sir?"

He thought for a moment, then relaxed his grip. "Go then. See for yourself. Your husband speaks the truth. As he has from the beginning. It is your evil papist clergy who spread lies."

She rubbed her tender wrist and watched as he rolled over, dismissing her. By the time she had pulled on a heavy cut-velvet cape, he was snoring blissfully.

Henrietta Maria ran along the cold, dim hallways, not even taking the time to summon one of her maids to accompany her. At the door to Courtney's suite she paused just long enough to grasp the door pull. Inside, she raced through the sitting chamber to the bedchamber. Her heart sank. The bed was empty.

As she started to turn away, she caught sight of a figure lying among the furs. Though the fire had burned down to hot coals, there was enough light to see. Rory.

"Rory. Rory MacLaren." The queen shook him roughly and watched as he slowly opened his eyes.

The light seemed to hurt his eyes, and for long minutes he blinked and glanced around the room, as if trying to remember where he was.

"Where is Courtney?" the queen demanded, kneeling beside him.

"Courtney?" He rubbed his eyes and glanced toward the bed.

"She is not in the bed. She is not in her rooms. How long have you been asleep?"

Rory sat up and groaned. "Forgive me, Majesty. There is a heaviness about my limbs. As if I had been...."

Drugged. He glanced at the flagon of ale on the tray, and then at his empty goblet. A second goblet, Courtney's goblet, was nearly full.

Lifting the empty goblet, he sniffed at it. Then, with a muttered oath, he sent it crashing against the hearth.

"She drugged you?"

Rory looked away, unable to meet the queen's eyes.

Henrietta Maria took a long, deep breath, then stood. Looking down at Rory, she said softly, "The king has just revealed to me that my lady-in-waiting, Lady Thornhill, is a spy."

"Spy?" Rory started to get up, then sank back down among the furs. The room was spinning badly, and his mind was still befuddled. "This cannot be."

"She has been sent into a trap that my husband and his chief councillor have set. She and all the other spies are sailing to a watery grave."

"Where, Majesty?" With great effort, Rory stood and gripped her arm.

For a moment the queen merely studied the offending hand. Rory, ashamed of his momentary lapse of protocol, withdrew his hand and murmured an apology.

"I know only that she sails into a trap set for her in the Channel."

The queen walked to the door. Then, with her hand on the door pull, she turned. "My husband was wrong about one thing."

Rory met her gaze. "What was that, Majesty?"

"He believed Burlingame when he said you were the one who would betray him. The chief councillor has convinced the king that you were a willing accomplice of Courtney's."

"Accomplice?" He swore low and deep in his throat. "I was her fool." Rory lifted his sword from the hearth and pulled his cape over his shoulders. "I knew nothing of her plans, madam. And I will do everything in my power to stop her. But," he added in a low growl, "by all the saints in heaven, I must save her from Burlingame's clutches, or die trying."

"Take this." The queen wrote upon a scroll and signed her name with a flourish. "Perhaps this will grant you safe passage. Or—" she looked up and met his steady gaze "—it may make you even more suspect in the eyes of the king's men."

"It is not the king's men I fear, Majesty."

In his face she saw fear mingled with pain. His eyes had grown dark and angry. But the hand gripping the sword was steady.

"It is but one man I fear. A man who will stop at nothing in his quest for power."

Burlingame. Neither of them had need to speak his name. Henrietta Maria watched as he rushed from the room and raced toward the stables.

It took hours for Rory to commission a boat and crew. Hours of calling on every favor ever owed him. Hours of invoking the king's name, of using the queen's handwritten message. In the end, the pale, hazy light of dawn streaked the eastern sky as Rory MacLaren and his hastily assembled crew set sail across the English Channel.

Rory stood by the bow, facing into the stiff breeze. He was not a man who prayed. Whether on land or sea, whether in fierce battle or quietly ruling his clan, he was a man calmly in control of his own destiny. From the time he was very young he had been taught to be prepared for all that life handed him and to accept the inevitability of death.

With Courtney, everything had changed. He loved her, needed her, with a desperation that made everything else in his life seem insignificant. With Courtney he could do anything. Without her his life would be but an empty shell.

She was sailing to her death.

Pounding a fist against the bow of the ship, he lifted his head to the heavens and prayed as he had never prayed before.

"God in heaven, keep her safe. Until I can stand beside her, keep her safe."

Keep her safe. Keep her safe. As the waves pounded and slapped against the hull, the words became a litany. Above all else in this world, Courtney must survive. Or, Rory knew, death would be his only release from the pain.

Chapter Twenty

It was that hushed, eerie time between darkness and dawn. Courtney, dressed in the stablehand's breeches and a shirt borrowed from one of the crew, paced at the bow of the ship. She studied the pearly glow that seemed to rise from the water to touch the sky. Tufts of fog danced on the waves and drifted about the boat like a shroud.

"Ship. Dead ahead." A voice from the rigging filtered down, and everyone strained to see.

"Aye. There." The captain pointed, and Courtney followed his direction.

The faint light of a torch could be seen through the hazy mist.

Her heart began beating faster. The *Hawk*. Old Boney. She had missed the old man more than she had realized. It would be so good to see him again. To tell him all that she had seen and experienced while they had been apart.

Rory. What would the old man say when he discovered that the man she now loved was the slave who had made good his escape? Worse, what would Thornhill's reaction be?

As the boat drew closer, she began to pace frantically. How could she have forgotten Thornhill's temper? She had been severely beaten in front of the entire crew because she had allowed the prisoners to escape rather than risk their death by fire. Thornhill was not a man to forget. Or forgive.

She was going to free him from the clutches of the evil Cardinal Richelieu, she reminded herself. Free him and herself. Would Thornhill not take that into account when she asked for his blessing on her marriage?

"Lady Thornhill." The captain laid a hand on her arm, causing her to stop her pacing.

"Captain?"

"My orders are to have one of the longboats take you to the French boat for boarding. When you are ready to return to my ship, signal and I will send a crew to retrieve you."

"Thank you, captain." If she were not so distracted, she might have noticed the slight curl of his lips, as though her very presence on his boat amused him. Amused or offended him. But she was too eager to board the *Hawk*, to see her old shipmates. She was blind to everything else.

As she stepped into the longboat, she wrapped the heavy, dark cape around herself, shivering in the damp air. The men leaned to the oars, and she stared straight ahead, feeling her heart beating a wild rhythm. The *Hawk*. After these many long months, she was being granted the privilege of returning to see her one last time.

The captain of the English ship, spyglass in hand, watched as the longboat rode the waves toward the *Hawk*. Turning to his crew, he shouted, "Prepare to attack."

Cannons were rolled from their hiding places beneath lengths of canvas. The sailors, all elite members of the king's navy, strapped swords to their waists and secured pistols under their jackets and shirts.

Calculating the direction of the wind and the distance between the two ships, the captain ordered the sails raised. Within minutes, under cover of the fog, the English ship began shortening the distance between it and the *Hawk*.

They would pick up the longboat and its crew along the way, after the lady had been deposited aboard the pirate ship.

In the shifting mist, Courtney could make out the figures of several men moving around on the deck of the *Hawk*. In her mind she could see them hurrying through their morning chores. She smiled to herself. How she had missed it. And how she would miss it in the future. But her home from this day on would be with Rory MacLaren. Whatever orders Thornhill and the others had been given by Richelieu, she would have no part in it. After this meeting she would leave the past behind and concentrate on the future. A bright, loving future with Rory.

Great rolling waves thrust the longboat against the side of the *Hawk*, then pushed it away again. With straining muscles, the men hooked on to the side of her and, heaving and pulling, drew closer until the two boats bobbed together on the water. A rope was tossed over the side of the pirate ship, and one of the crew in the longboat caught it and handed it to Courtney. They watched, openmouthed, as the slender young woman tossed aside her cape and grasped the rope firmly in her hands and began pulling herself up the side of the *Hawk*. When she reached the rail, she hauled herself over and disappeared from view.

The deck of the *Hawk* was crowded with staring faces, most of which were familiar to her, though there were several new ones, as well. When the men stepped back, unwilling to touch her, she was shaken by the feelings such treatment evoked. How quickly she had forgotten the loneliness, the isolation. Here, aboard the *Hawk*, she was once more the untouchable female who had been set apart by stern order of Thornhill. She was so happy to see these men that she wanted to shake their hands, to hug them. She longed to have them reach out to her and touch her, to make her feel as if she had indeed come home. But even as she walked toward them, they backed away and glanced uneasily over their shoulders, as if they were expecting the wrath of God.

"Courtney. Lass. Look at you." A gnarled old figure came careening around the corner and stood looking at her. His wrinkled old face was wreathed in a smile.

"Boney. Oh, Boney, how I've missed you."

The old man opened his arms wide, and Courtney threw herself into them. Of all the men from her childhood, he alone had ever held her.

"I wish I could have sent you a message. But it was forbidden."

"Aye, lass. It was the same for me. The cap'n forbid me to contact you." He drew her away a little and studied her carefully. Seeing the glimmer of tears on her lashes, he touched a finger to them, then looked deeply into her eyes. "Tears, lass? Just when I think ye haven't changed, I see ye have."

"Happy tears. I am so happy to be back aboard the *Hawk*."

"'Tisn't a happy place to be this day. I suggest," he said dryly, "that ye go and talk with Thornhill, lass. There's much ye need to know."

"In a moment, Boney. First I just want to look at you, to talk to you."

"That can come later, lass. Thornhill's waiting."

With a welling of emotion, Courtney made her way unerringly toward Thornhill's cabin.

Thornhill sat ramrod-straight, a tumbler of whiskey in his hand. His brow was deeply furrowed, his mouth a thin, tight line of concentration.

When he heard the slight tapping on his door, he looked up in annoyance.

When Courtney walked in, his scowl grew.

"So. You could not do this thing alone. You had to send for me and the men of the *Hawk* to finish the job."

Courtney's eyebrows arched in surprise. No smile from her father. Not even a word of greeting. "What are you saying?"

He drained the tumbler and brought it crashing down upon the desktop. "Enough. What is it you want us to do?"

"I?" Courtney blinked trying to follow his words. "I want nothing, Father. Richelieu's messenger told me I was to meet you here in the Channel. That is all I know."

Thornhill fixed her with a chilling look. Through gritted teeth he hissed, "Your messenger told Richelieu to send everyone who was involved in this operation to meet you here."

"My messenger?" For a moment, Courtney could only stare. Then, as his meaning became clear, she exploded. "And you have involved Boney and the rest of the crew in this evil scheme?"

"My men go where I lead them. Now, what is your plan?"

She shook her head sadly. "You still do not understand, do you?"

At his blank look she said softly, "I have no plan. We have been tricked, Father. Tricked by Richelieu."

"Never." Thornhill uncoiled himself from the chair and crossed the room in quick strides, gripping her arm in a painful grasp. "I have planned and plotted for years. Cardinal Richelieu and I both want the same thing. Revenge on a king who had no right to grow fat in England while I was forced to roam the seas."

"If Richelieu has not tricked us," she said softly, "then the son of that fat king whom you despised has managed to trick us."

Thornhill slapped her so hard that the imprint of his fingers was left on her cheek. Stunned, she took a step backward and stared at him contemptuously. "What a fool I have been." Gingerly she touched a hand to her cheek. "I thought I was doing this evil business to keep you safe from Richelieu's wrath. And all the while you and he had conspired together. I have been a pawn in your dirty little game."

When Thornhill said nothing, she added softly, "I have never been anything more to you than a pawn, have I?"

His lips curled in a sneer. "You were, from the beginning, a means of revenge. Such sweet revenge. Against my enemies. That is the only reason I allowed you to live instead of sending you to join your nurse at the bottom of the sea."

"Father..."

"I am not your father." His voice was cold and brittle. "And now that you have failed me, you are nothing to me."

Courtney was shocked to the depths of her soul.

A volley of cannon fire thundered above them. Thornhill's head come up sharply. At the same moment there was the sound of voices shouting on the deck above.

"We are under attack."

Thornhill strapped on his sword and raced from his cabin. Behind him, Courtney stood very still for a moment, unable to accept all that had just transpired between them. Then, hearing the sounds of battle swell above her, she grabbed a sword from Thornhill's store of weapons and made her way after him. A moment later she faced her first attacker.

She recognized her opponent in his fine red uniform, as one of the sailors from the ship that had brought her here. A trick. This had all been a clever plot, and she had allowed herself to be caught up in it.

As the sailor lifted his sword, Courtney ran him through and left him moaning. Then she ran up the steps to the deck. Several men were fighting in her way, and it was impossible to get past.

A terrible explosion sent shock waves shuddering through the ship. Racing across to the rail, Courtney was stunned to see that the bow of the ship had been blown completely away. Fire raced along the sails. Balls of orange flame leaped along the rigging, fanned by the breeze.

The deck swarmed with red-coated sailors, all brandishing arms. Everywhere Courtney looked, battles raged and men fell to the deck, bleeding and dying.

"Lass. This way."

Old Boney balanced precariously on the rickety ladder leading to the hold. Dodging small fires and sailors, Courtney ran toward the old man and followed him into the dim interior of the *Hawk*.

"Stay here, lass. I'll find us a stray longboat and come back for you."

"You cannot go up there, Boney."

"I must, lass. It's our only hope."

"There are too many of them. Our only chance is to hide until they leave."

The old man touched a finger to her cheek. "The English ship will not leave until the *Hawk* sinks below the sea. And the way that fire's raging, I'd say there's little time left."

"Then we stay and fight."

"No, lass. We don't stand a chance against that many swords. Our only hope is a longboat."

He turned and started up the ladder. As Courtney watched in horror, the old man was pushed backward. He fell, landing hard on the floor. Four sailors followed, leaping into the hold.

Rory heard the explosion even before his shipmates spotted the two ships. In the thin light of morning he saw the flames leaping and dancing high in the sky. The breeze was heavy with the acrid stench of smoke.

And then he saw them. The *Hawk* was listing badly, and its deck swarmed with activity. The English ship beside it appeared to be almost deserted. He saw the English lookout high in the rigging and knew that his ship had been spotted.

"Faster," he urged the captain of his boat. The sailors crowded the deck, straining for a glimpse of the battle.

When they drew abreast of the two ships, Rory alone swung over the rail and boarded the *Hawk*. The crew members who had brought him this far stood silently, watching as their fellow English sailors fought valiantly against the French pirates.

"That man must be one of them," a red-coated sailor shouted, and three sailors took up swords against Rory.

God in heaven, where had they all come from? To Rory it looked as if half the king's navy was fighting aboard this small pirate ship.

He ran his sword through the first swordsman and sent the second to the deck, howling in pain. The third attacked with a vengeance, and Rory stepped aside, avoiding the blade by inches. When at last he disabled the third attacker, he searched frantically for any sign of Courtney. Each time he came upon a tangle of bodies his heart stopped. Each time he satisfied himself that none of them was Courtney he felt a jolt of relief until he approached the next scene of carnage.

When he was certain that Courtney was not on deck, he cautiously made his way to the cabins. All were empty, except for the bodies that littered every ladder, cabin and passageway.

Hearing a terrible battle raging below deck, he raced toward the hold. Ignoring the steps, he leaped into the fray. What he saw left his heart hammering in his chest.

"Courtney. Behind you."

At the sound of his voice, she turned, barely escaping the blade of a sword that sang past her head. With one swift thrust she brought her sword up and through the chest of the English sailor. As he fell, she turned to face two more attackers.

Rory felt a sharp sting as a blade pierced his shoulder. For a moment he felt nothing. Then a warmth began spreading along his arm, followed by hot, searing pain. He glanced down to see blood spilling down his sleeve and soaking the front of his tunic.

With one arm dangling uselessly at his side, he fought on. Seeing that he was wounded, five swordsmen surrounded him, making it impossible for him to reach Courtney's side. Though he fought bravely, he could not stave off the thrusts and blows of his attackers. Within minutes, Rory was bleeding from four separate wounds. The figures before him swam in his vision. Words became muted, fragmented, until he could no longer trust what he heard. He felt the sharp thrust of a blade and dropped to his knees. Pain enveloped him. Courtney. Why had he come? To save her? Or to punish her? The answer came, swiftly, shockingly. Though she was a spy who had threatened the safety of his friend and king, he loved her. God help him, he loved her with a desperation that bordered on insanity. She was the enemy. And the enemy owned his heart and soul.

A strong arm lifted him, pinning him against the wall.

"You are not one of them. I have seen you with the king. Why do you fight your own men?"

Rory's voice was choked with pain. "I fight to save the lady. The Mistress of the Seas."

The swordsman barked a command. Several strong arms held Rory in a death grip, pinning him against the cold, wet wall of the hold. Though his life was spared, he prayed for a swift death. When it did not come, he was forced to watch helplessly as the woman he loved continued to fight against overwhelming odds.

"Lass."

Courtney heard the old man's strained voice and turned to see old Boney holding a sword nearly as big as he. He had already managed to drive off two attackers who would have run her through. Now, with three more sailors advancing upon them, he was brandishing the weapon like a madman.

"Leave the lass alone," he shouted, leaping in front of her. "She is innocent."

The tallest of the sailors lifted his sword. "Be gone, old man."

Courtney heard a grunt of pain and turned. The sword had gone clear through the skinny old man. He was staring at it, clutching it with both hands as if to stave off the pain.

When he fell to the floor, Courtney screamed and dropped to her knees beside him.

"No, Boney. No." She cradled his head in her arms and began to cry.

"I loved you, lass," the old man said. His words were barely more than a whisper. "Truly loved you."

"I know, Boney, I know." Tears streamed down her face, mingling with the dirt and blood to form little rivers that stained her cheeks and soaked her shirt. She brushed back the hair from his forehead and crooned softly to him as his breath rattled in his throat.

"You never hurt anyone. You were always so fair, so gentle." She began rocking him as the tears continued to flow.

The swordsmen, startled by this turn of events, stood by helplessly and watched as the beautiful, wild creature cradled the lifeless form of the old man in her arms and sobbed as though her heart would break. How had she turned from a wildcat to a weak, whimpering kitten in the blink of an eye?

"This is the leader of the spies," a man's voice said. An English sailor knelt and pressed a pistol to her head. "Our orders are to send all of you to a watery grave. And you, woman, most of all."

With all the strength left in him, Rory let out a shout of pain and frenzy, struggling valiantly with the men holding him. One of them pressed his sword to Rory's chest. "Struggle once more and you will forfeit your life."

Across the room, Courtney went very still, waiting for the explosion that would end her life. As the sailor's finger tightened on the trigger, a gleam of metal flashed by her line of vision. The sailor fell backward as the gun was torn from his hands by a metal hook.

Stunned, Courtney could only stare at the man who had saved her life and now was kneeling to face her.

"Ian." Still holding Boney's lifeless body in her arms, she touched a hand to his cheek. "Ian Horn. I thought you had died when Thornhill cut off your hand. But look at you."

The big blond youth removed the heavy burden from her arms and helped her to her feet. "I was too filled with hate and loathing for Thornhill to die. I decided that the best way to seek revenge was to swear fealty to the very king he detested. I am a loyal English subject now." His tone hardened. "And our orders were to send all the spies to their death in the Channel."

"The lady is no spy," Rory shouted.

At the sound of his beloved voice, Courtney turned. When she saw the blood that stained his tunic and breeches, she tried to go to him. But Ian held her fast.

"Does that man speak the truth?" Ian asked softly. "Or are you part of Cardinal Richelieu's plot to overthrow England with spies?"

"Aye." Courtney looked away, unable to meet Rory's eyes. "I was a spy. Though I had come here to renounce my evil work. But that man, Rory MacLaren, had no part in this."

Ian Horn studied the way the man looked at Courtney and the way she avoided meeting his eye. So, he thought, the lonely little girl had grown up. And had at last been touched by a man.

"We cannot take the word of an admitted spy," Ian said briskly. "You will both be taken to Fleet Prison, where you will be held until you are proven innocent." He looked away, unwilling to meet Courtney's eyes. "Or found guilty."

As the prisoners were led on deck, Courtney saw the figure of Thornhill lying near the wheel. With a little cry, she ran to him. Immediately dozens of swordsmen surrounded her. With a word from Ian Horn they drew back and allowed her a moment of private grief.

"Father." She knelt and touched a hand tentatively to his cheek. Odd. She had never before touched his face. They had never embraced. He had never held her, kissed her, never even squeezed her hand. And now, in death, there was nothing familiar about him. She did not know him. And never had. What had he said just before the attack? He was not her father. And she was nothing to him. Nothing.

As she started to rise, she noted the gleam of gold at his throat. Opening his shirt, she stared at the gold medallion and felt the faintest stirring of memory.

Lifting the gold chain from his neck, she placed it around her own and felt the medallion slip between her breasts.

"Come, Courtney," Ian urged gently. "This ship will soon lie at the bottom of the Channel. We must hurry to safety."

Safety. The safety of prison. The safety of the executioner's block.

She watched as Rory was led away to the ship on which he had come. For a long moment their gazes met and held.

She tried to smile, but her lips quivered, and she felt the beginning of tears once more.

How you must hate me, she thought as the crew began leading Rory away. *I love you, Rory MacLaren, more than life itself.* Though she spoke not a word, her mind shouted the words, willing him to hear. *And if I could I would undo all the harm I have brought to you. If only I could.*

He turned, fighting the chains that bit into his flesh. His eyes narrowed as he studied her, willing her to memory. *I will never see you again, Courtney. But I shall never forget you.*

The wind tousled his hair, and Courtney thought about the first time she had seen him aboard the *Hawk*. Even in a prisoner's chains he had had a strength, a dignity, that no one could take from him.

She saw the slight narrowing of his eyes as he stared at her. She lowered her gaze, unable to bear the knowledge that he hated her because she had betrayed him and everything he stood for.

The sailors pulled her roughly away and dragged her aboard the English vessel that had brought them to this battle ground. Behind her there was nothing left of the *Hawk* as she had known it. Black smoke billowed from its skeleton, sending dark clouds hovering above the water. The charred remains of the deck were littered with bodies. The carnage left her stunned and reeling. Every man with whom she had ever lived and worked was gone. The ship was listing badly and had only minutes left before it would slip beneath the waves.

As she was led to the hold and chained to a wall, she heard the anchor being raised. She felt the waves swell as the *Hawk* shuddered and sank beneath the ocean.

The cover of the hold was drawn shut. Alone, in total darkness, Courtney huddled, fighting a terror that left her paralyzed. From the farthest reaches of her mind, a memory struggled to awaken. She had the feeling that she had been through all this before.

She struggled to hold on, but she could feel herself slipping deeper and deeper into the dark recesses of her mind. Dark places she had kept carefully locked these many years.

Chapter Twenty-one

Courtney lay on the filthy pallet in the small cell and listened to the screams and moans of the other prisoners. Because of the serious nature of her crime, she had been segregated from the others and placed in isolation. But through the small window cut into the stone door she could see what went on beyond her cell.

If there was a hell, Fleet Prison was truly it. The cold stone walls bore the names of hundreds of prisoners who had written them in their own blood before breathing their last. Water trickled constantly down the walls, leaving the prisoners damp, as well as cold. With chattering teeth she watched rats scurrying over bodies too wasted to even recoil at their touch.

She had been here three days. In that time she had seen no one except the jailer. She could bear the cold, the rats and the loneliness. But not knowing what had happened to Rory caused her endless pain.

Had he been returned to England, or had he been quietly disposed of during the voyage? Courtney shivered. And if he had made it safely back to port, was he too, rotting away in a prison cell? Was it her fate to bring pain to the ones she loved?

She heard the heavy iron doors being forced open. A tiny sliver of light spilled through the small window of her cell.

Footsteps echoed on the stone steps, coming nearer and nearer still, before stopping outside her door.

Her heart began a wild fluttering in her chest, and she swallowed back the terror that threatened to choke her. If they were coming to take her to her death, it would be welcome after these last days of horror.

The stone door swung open. A bright light momentarily blinded her. Courtney blinked, then forced herself to look up. Framed in the doorway stood the jailer. For a long moment he studied her by the light of his lantern. Then, turning to the figure behind him, he spit, "Here she is. Or what's left of her. Though I can't imagine what you'd want with her."

From behind the jailer came the low, taunting voice of Burlingame, and she fought to control the shudders that convulsed her.

"My business is with the lady. Begone, man." He took the lantern from the jailer and pulled the cell door shut. Through the small window he ordered, "Do not return until I summon you."

He waited until the jailer had climbed the stairs and disappeared before turning to face Courtney.

"So." He lifted the lantern to study her. She was still wearing the stablehand's breeches and the borrowed shirt.

He noted the way the fabric of the shirt pulled tautly across her breasts and the breeches outlined her slender waist and rounded hips. Her hair was a tangle of dark curls, giving her the look of a wild creature.

He set the lantern on the floor and moved closer. Warily Courtney watched him, feeling like a trapped animal. The flickering flame of the lantern cast light across his cruel mouth but left his upper face in shadow. As he moved menacingly closer, she shrank back against the cold stone wall.

"Why have you come here? To gloat over your victory?"

He smiled, and she felt a trickle of fear.

"I am here to help you, Lady Thornhill."

"Help me?" She tossed her head, sending the wild mane of hair drifting tantalizingly around her face.

In the shadows, she missed the feral look that darted into his eyes.

"You are completely alone." He inched closer and lifted a hand to her cheek.

He felt the way she flinched at his touch, but to her credit she did not slap his hand away. Instead, she steeled herself against all feeling and faced him squarely.

"I am not alone," she said.

"Ah, but you are. The queen, Henrietta Maria, has disavowed any knowledge of your evil deeds. She will make no effort to come to your aid. And of course you have heard about poor Rory MacLaren."

He felt her stiffen at the mention of Rory's name.

"Did no one tell you?"

For a moment Courtney thought she would be unable to speak. Swallowing the lump in her throat, she whispered, "Rory? What has happened to Rory?"

"He is dying, my lady."

"No." Placing her hands over her ears to blot out his words, she turned away. Her heart contracted. Rory dying. How much more pain would she have to bear before death claimed her, as well?

"From wounds inflicted by your evil pirates, I hear."

She spun around to face him. "That is a lie."

"Do you call King Charles a liar?"

Courtney could only stare at him.

"From all accounts, MacLaren remained a loyal subject. The king is convinced that Rory MacLaren had no knowledge of your evil scheme."

At those words, Courtney felt tears sting her eyes. Rory had been exonerated. At least his reputation would remain untarnished. The MacLaren clan would not have to bear the stigma of having had a traitor as a leader.

"The king believes him?"

Burlingame's eyes narrowed. "It seems the queen found MacLaren drugged on the floor of your bedchamber. The king is convinced that you acted without your lover's knowledge."

Drugging Rory was the hardest thing she had ever done. Now she rejoiced that she had found the strength to do it.

Seeing the joy that momentarily lit her eyes, Burlingame added dryly, "But even the king cannot save his life. If he has not done so by now, MacLaren will die, as surely as you will die at the hands of the executioner. Unless—" he moved closer and placed his hands on her shoulders "—you convince me to spare your life."

"You?" Her voice was filled with contempt. "Why would I beg mercy from you?"

"Because I am the one closest to the king." His eyes glittered with a strange, almost feverish light. "In fact, I have more power than the king."

"That is blasphemy."

"Is it?" He gripped her shoulders painfully and, ignoring her little gasp of pain, drew her to him. "When I have rid us of this weak-willed king, I will be the most powerful man in all of England. Men will live or die at my whim. Ancestral lands will be given to those who are loyal to me. Gold and precious jewels will be mine. And women."

He laughed deep in his throat and stared down into her startled eyes. "The woman who is fortunate enough to please me will be given everything her heart desires."

"You," she said, her eyes wide with sudden knowledge. "You are the one who would betray the king. Why—" She licked her lips and forced herself not to give in to the loathing she felt at his touch. "Why are you telling me this?"

"Because it can all be yours, my dear." He ran a hand over her hair, then grabbed a handful of it, pulling her head back sharply. "If you beg."

She blinked back the tears that stung her lids. "And if I choose not to beg?"

"Then you will die. And, I assure you, it will be a slow and painful death."

As she tried to pull free of his grasp, he pinned her against the wall with his body and caught her face in both his hands. When she struggled to avoid his descending mouth, he gave a cruel laugh.

"No woman has ever denied me and got away with it. After that incident in the forest I vowed that I would have my revenge. And now I shall have it. First I shall take you." He laughed. "The way I planned to take you when first I set eyes on you. And because you dare to refuse me, when I am finished with you, I will show no mercy. I will kill you."

He laughed harder when she struggled to pull away. "Yes. Kill you. And tell the king's council that I was forced to defend myself when I came here to prepare you for trial."

"You are evil. More evil than Richelieu."

"Richelieu is merely a player in my game." He brought his mouth down on hers with such force that she could taste her own blood.

Strong hands tore at her shirt, and she heard the ripping sound as the fabric gave way. Then his hands found the soft, naked flesh of her shoulders, and she cried out as he gripped her painfully.

She struggled desperately, twisting, clawing, fighting, but he was too strong for her. Within minutes she was pinned beneath him on the cold stone floor. And as she struggled to be free of him, her hand encountered the dagger she still carried in the pocket of her breeches.

"Unless you stop now, I will kill you." Her words were issued between shaking, tumbling breaths.

"Kill me?" He threw back his head and laughed. "You are not even strong enough to put up a good fight. You will submit."

She plunged the knife into his chest and felt it tear through cloth and flesh. For a moment Burlingame stared at her as if unable to believe what she had done. Then, as blood spilled from the gaping wound in his chest, he struggled to his feet and stumbled across the cell toward the locked stone door.

Pounding frantically on the door, he shouted, "Jailer. Come. At once."

Courtney struggled to her knees and watched in dazed silence as the door was thrown open by a burly jailer. Throwing his arm around the jailer's neck, Burlingame leaned heavily on him and fixed Courtney with a steely look.

"You have sealed your own fate, woman. First you will endure a public trial. Then all of England will want to watch the hanging of the evil, infamous Mistress of the Seas."

As the door slammed shut, Courtney heard his words ringing in her ears. Mistress of the Seas. There was only one man who had known about that. The man who had once declared his undying love for her. How he must hate her now.

As she lapsed into unconsciousness, his name echoed in her mind. Rory MacLaren.

"No matter what happens, no matter what you hear, you must not allow them to find you. Is that understood?"

Through the mists that clouded her mind, Courtney fought to listen intently to the words of her nurse. As the heavy cape was placed over her, she squeezed her eyes shut. She heard a door close and waited for what seemed an interminable time before opening her eyes. She could see nothing. Only blackness. She blinked and tried again, but there was still only blackness. She was in a small, tiny space. With the heavy cape completely covering her, she felt as if she were smothering. There was no air, no light. The tiny space closed in around her until at last she was squeezed into nothingness.

There were voices beyond the darkness. Harsh, strident voices. Dangerous voices. Her nurse's voice, low, controlled, but trembling with fear. Men's voices, taunting, laughing. Then there was sudden silence.

Courtney knew she had a willful streak. Papa said she had inherited it from her grandfather. Papa. She could almost see him. Almost hear his voice. And then the image faded. She tried to hold on to his dear face. Tried so hard. But he slipped away. His handsome face. His warm, loving voice.

Just beyond her hiding place there was silence. And although she knew from Lady Montieth's tone of voice that she had been given a very important order, Courtney was compelled to disobey. Lifting the cape, she peered through a crack in the wardrobe.

Lady Montieth was lying on the floor. Her lovely pink gown was stained with red. Men she had never seen before were standing around her, staring at her with surprised looks. And though Courtney had little knowledge of death or what it really meant, she knew with a childish certainty that her nurse was dead. Trembling, she pulled the cape over her head and shrank back against the wall of the wardrobe. She did not move. She barely even breathed. If she had to, she would die in this black space before revealing herself to these barbarians who had caused her nurse to die.

Beyond her hiding place she heard a voice of authority barking commands, clearing the room of all sound.

How long could she endure this blackness? How long before there was no more air and she suffocated? Her lungs were screaming for fresh air, and still she refused to move. She was resigned to die. To die like Lady Montieth.

"How is she?" Henrietta Maria stood beside the bed and peered down at the pale, drawn figure.

On the opposite side of the bed, Rory MacLaren sat holding Courtney's limp hand in his. A scraggly stubble of beard darkened his chin. His eyes were red-rimmed from lack of sleep.

"She suffers even in her sleep. She talks often, but the words make no sense."

"You must rouse her soon, Rory. Lord Edgecomb needs time to prepare her defense."

"She is not strong enough to stand trial."

"Then she will be hanged without one. All of England is calling for her execution. And the king is losing patience."

The queen looked down at the beautiful young woman lying so still against the linens. "I think I have known from the beginning that she was a spy. Richelieu recommended to my bishop that Courtney be trained as a lady-in-waiting, claiming her excellent knowledge of languages." Henrietta Maria brushed a lock of damp hair from Courtney's cheek and met Rory's questioning look. "She once tried to tell me more about herself, but I stopped her. God help me, I had already learned to love her. I did not wish to hear the truth."

Rory nodded. Had he not been torturing himself for the same reason? "Aye, madam. I, too, knew that Courtney was not what she claimed to be. But I am even more guilty. I knew that she was the famed Mistress of the Seas. I was once a prisoner aboard her father's pirate ship."

At the queen's startled look, he nodded. "I chose to keep her secret because my love for her blinded me to all else."

The queen felt a wave of kinship with this man. Holding back her tears, she turned away. "I will send my maid with some broth. Beyond that, I can do no more for her."

"You have done more than enough."

When the queen stepped through the doorway, she moved stiffly past the guards who were posted on either side of the hallway. There were, she knew, several more guards beneath the balcony and at the stables. The king would allow this one concession to her lady-in-waiting. He would see to it that she did not escape a public trial before the execution.

Moonlight spilled over the woman in the bed. Her skin was as pale as alabaster. Her dark hair was a slash of color on the white pillow. Beside her Rory lay, cradling her in his arms, trying in vain to warm her with his own body in order to stop the chills and trembling that racked her.

As she murmured, at times clearly, at other times incoherently, he held her and listened to the sad, lonely story that poured from her heart. If only he could, he would absorb all her pain, all her sorrow. If only he could.

"No!" She cried out, and he drew her close, pressing his lips to the tangle of her hair. He felt her heart pounding as she struggled against her dream tormentor.

"No!" She stiffened and pushed against him. Her eyes opened. For a moment she seemed stunned to see those blue eyes looking back at her.

"Rory? Oh, Rory, is it really you?" Shyly, tentatively, she touched a finger to his cheek.

He was warm. Flesh and blood. Was he alive? Or had she joined him in death?

"Aye, love. You have been away a long time."

"Away? Where?"

"Somewhere in your mind. There was much pain and suffering there. And I wanted to help you, but I could not reach you."

With his fingertips he traced the arch of her brow, the curve of her cheek. "But you are back now."

"Back." She sighed and studied the beloved face she had feared she might never see again. "Burlingame told me you were near death."

"Burlingame? Nay, my love. He has not been here." Rory studied her, wondering if the king's chief councillor had been the tormentor in her dreams.

"He came to me in Fleet Prison. He told me that Henrietta Maria had turned away from me and that you were near death."

"In prison?" Rory's eyes narrowed. "Lies. All lies meant to break your spirit." He lifted the bedcovers to show her his dressings. "In truth, I was mortally wounded. And had it not been for the kindness of the queen, who had me removed from prison and brought here to be tended, I would not have survived." Drawing the bedcovers around them both, he whispered, "And as for the queen, she loves you."

Courtney could hardly believe the words Rory was speaking. "I confess I believed Burlingame. And when he forced himself on me, I stabbed him with his own dagger. The one I have carried since that night in the forest."

Rory heard this with a sense of outrage and disbelief. "Burlingame claims to have been attacked by one of the French spies in retaliation for having captured you. When I found you on the floor of your cell, dazed and bloodied, your clothes torn, the jailer claimed you must have done this to yourself. I suspected him of attacking you. That was why I persuaded Henrietta Maria to use her influence to have you released."

For the first time, Courtney glanced around the moonlit room. "I am in the palace?"

"Aye. In your own suite of rooms. For two days and nights you have been tormented by dreams. Terrible, black dreams."

She shivered, remembering the terrible visions that had plagued her ever since she had been locked in the dark hold of the English ship. In a trembling voice, she whispered, "I do not blame you for revealing to the king that I am the Mistress of the Seas."

Rory stared at her with a tenderness that said more than words. "I could never betray you, Courtney. It was the captain of the English ship who first recognized you. By now all of England knows of your deeds."

"Oh, Rory. Hold me," she sobbed, suddenly clutching him with a desperation that startled him. "Hold me."

"It's all I've ever wanted to do, my love."

He held her close, stroking her hair. Slowly, haltingly, she began to relate the fragments of her dreams.

By the time dawn's first light streaked the eastern sky, Rory found himself marveling at the things she had endured and at the proud, strong woman she had managed to become.

Chapter Twenty-two

Seated in front of a fire, Rory and Lord Edgecomb spok
in low, muted tones, their heads bent close together.

"The king himself intends to preside at this trial."
Edgecomb carefully folded and unfolded his hands. It wa
the only sign of nerves in his very proper bearing.

"The citizens are crying for her blood. As are th
judges." Rory ran a hand through his hair. "No one wi
listen to what she has to say. They want only a chance t
view this female pirate and to heap ridicule upon her be
fore pronouncing sentence."

"I fear what you say is true." Edgecomb stood and be
gan pacing. "If only they would give me time to prepare
defense. But Charles is adamant. He fears a bloody upris
ing against France unless this thing is finished."

"He has been more than fair. If she were an English sp
caught in France she would have already tasted the hang
man's noose."

Edgecomb nodded. "It is being whispered that Hen
rietta Maria personally trained all her ladies-in-waiting t
spy for France. And, of course, Burlingame is fueling th
fires. Charles is considering sending the queen's entire en
tourage back to France, just to quiet the rumors."

"Lord Edgecomb." Rory stood and placed a hand on th
older man's arm. "Do you see any chance of saving her?"

Edgecomb shook his head sadly. "Burlingame intends to testify that he followed her to the king's park, where he saw her exchange papers with a messenger who spoke French. And he will no doubt relate all that he overheard during that meeting." The older man's frown grew. "If that is not enough, he will have the testimony of the king's own soldier, who not only exchanged information with Courtney but led her to her final rendezvous. I see no chance," he muttered softly, "of saving her."

"You must not grieve. I could not bear it if I caused either of you any further grief."

Both men looked up at the sound of Courtney's voice. She was standing in the doorway of her bedchamber. A night shift of white linen overlaid with pale ecru lace displayed the whiteness of her skin. Though there were dark smudges beneath her eyes, she lifted her head high and met their gazes squarely.

Rory felt his heart lurch at the frailty that he knew lay just beneath her show of strength.

"We will give the people what they want."

"No." Rory started toward her, but she waved him away.

"I will answer their questions, Lord Edgecomb, and I will go to my death," she said quickly, hoping they would not notice the catch in her voice, "knowing that at least the queen's testimony will exonerate Rory from all wrongdoing."

"I cannot let you go into this alone," Rory said fiercely. "I am guilty of keeping certain facts from Lord Edgecomb and King Charles. We will face this together."

"And sully the MacLaren name for all time? Never."

"I am also guilty of keeping facts from the king," Lord Edgecomb said. "I was witness to your reluctance to speak of your past. Yet because of my affection for you I remained silent."

"The only guilt is mine."

Both men watched helplessly as she turned away and sank down heavily on the edge of the bed.

Rory and Edgecomb exchanged worried glances. In her weakened state it was an ordeal for her just to stand. How would she survive an exhausting trial?

"I will plead for more time." Lord Edgecomb crossed the room and knelt before her, taking her cold hands in his. "You must rest, my dear."

"Nay." She shook her head and gently patted his hand. "It is time to face the executioner."

Lord Edgecomb was amazed by the tide of emotions he felt for this young woman. She was so artless, so untouched by the evil that surrounded them. He wished he could shield her from what was to come. Such feelings were dangerous. He cared too deeply about her. His feelings would color his judgment. As the highest-ranking judge of the king's court, it was his duty to uncover only the truth.

He took a deep breath and said softly, "The trial will begin at midday. Whatever you do, speak only the truth. If you lie, it will go much harder on you."

Courtney nodded. He squeezed her hand, then stood and left the room quickly. Courtney noted with sadness that Rory eagerly followed him. She did not blame him. He had every right to wish to be rid of her.

As Edgecomb started down the hallway, Rory's voice stopped him.

"Lord Edgecomb, I would speak with you. In private."

At Parliament's insistence, the English high court was open to the public. The great hall of justice was overflowing with spectators. The king, resplendent in his purple robes, took his seat above the bench. On his left, looking pale and troubled, sat his wife, Henrietta Maria. Because of the delicate nature of this trial, she had chosen a somber gown of purple and black. She wore no jewels or other ornamentation. She was aware of the rumors being whispered about her, and she knew that this trial could damage her already weakened reputation.

On the king's right sat Lord Burlingame, chief councilor to the king and chief accuser of the defendant.

In a semicircle just below the monarchs sat the ten high court judges, all wearing black robes and white wigs. The chief among them, Lord Edgecomb, would speak for the others, and was free to ask as many questions as he chose.

To either side of the bench, a balcony of seats afforded the members of parliament a view of the entire proceeding.

In the first rows reserved for spectators sat members of the royal family, aunts, uncles, cousins and their assorted children. Behind them was seated the elite of London. Viscounts, earls and dukes, accompanied by their ladies, took their seats, while the less impressive members of society watched and waited.

When all were seated, the doors were opened to the ordinary citizens of London, who crowded into every space available. The spectators were eager, expectant.

Outside, lending color to the festive air, vendors hawked their wares to the crowds that could not get inside. This was the day all of London had waited for. This was to be their first glimpse of the infamous pirate, the Mistress of the Seas. From the tales of surviving sailors, legends had sprung up about her. Songs had been written about her.

Rory conferred with Lord Edgecomb, then took a seat at the council table, a rough, scarred table that had been used at the trials of murderers, pickpockets, beggars and aristocrats. Today, the woman who would sit here was accused of spying against the crown. A crime punishable by death.

As the door to the chamber opened, all heads turned. The room became hushed.

Rory looked up with the others, then caught his breath at the stunning sight that greeted him. He had expected Courtney to dress in a modest, somber gown for this occasion. Instead, Courtney was wearing black breeches

tucked into tall black boots. A billowing shirt of scarlet sil
displayed her breasts, and a bright yellow sash defined he
tiny waist. Her thick lush hair flowed past her waist in a rio
of curls.

A thread of excitement rippled through the crowd. A lo
murmur became a babble, and the babble became a roar a
the crowd strained for a better view of the pirate.

Courtney stood ramrod-straight, head held high, an
faced the row of justices.

Lord Edgecomb swallowed back his initial annoyance
Given a choice, he would have suggested something prir
and dark and high necked, to give her an air of innocenc
and repentance. But as he watched her he realized that he
choice was correct. The woman on trial was the Mistress o
the Seas. She was giving all of them a chance to see the leg
end.

"Lady Thornhill, you are accused of using your posi
tion as lady-in-waiting to Queen Henrietta Maria to spy fo
France. What say you?"

The crowd leaned forward to hear her plea.

"It is as you say."

A low murmur of excitement went through the crowd.

"You were a spy for France?"

"For Cardinal Richelieu," she said softly.

"Speak up, woman," Lord Burlingame shouted from hi
position beside the king.

Courtney lifted her head, meeting Burlingame's nar
rowed gaze. "I did not spy for France. I was forced to sp
for Cardinal Richelieu, who threatened harm to my—" She
swallowed, remembering Thornhill's last words. No longer
would she call him "Father." "To the man who raised me."

"Whom would that man be?" Lord Edgecomb sho
Burlingame a look of warning. He would tolerate no out
bursts.

"Captain Thornhill."

"And where did he raise you?" Edgecomb asked gently.

"Aboard his ship, the *Hawk*." Rory heard the little catch in her voice. The place she had called home now lay at the bottom of the English Channel.

"When this pirate ship attacked other ships, did you not take part in the fighting?" Burlingame shouted.

"Aye." Courtney nodded her head while the room buzzed with anticipation.

"And were not many of these ships flying the English flag?"

Courtney nodded. "Aye."

"How many?" Edgecomb could feel the tension of the crowd. It worried him.

"Too many to count."

The room erupted in shouts and jeers.

"One hundred?" Burlingame shouted above the din. 'Two hundred? How many English sailors have died at your hands, Lady Thornhill?"

Edgecomb rapped the table in front of him. When the shouting and jeering continued, he rapped again, then lifted his arms, demanding silence.

"Answer the question," Burlingame shouted.

Edgecomb glanced at the king. Charles nodded slightly. Turning, Edgecomb said sternly, "You may answer the question."

"I do not know," Courtney said. "When we encountered hostile boats, we attacked. I fought alongside the men. I never kept count of the men I killed. Or of how many tried to kill me."

Once more the crowd began to shout. Many stood and waved their fists in defiance. Edgecomb, sensing the surly mood of the crowd, fought a growing feeling of frustration.

"This captain who raised you. What did you call him?"

"I was told to call him 'Father.'"

"Did you?"

She nodded.

"And why did this captain leave the life of a seaman and go to France?"

"He was wounded in battle. While he recovered, he wa. visited by Cardinal Richelieu, who ordered me to spy for him or forfeit my fath—Thornhill's life."

"Could this plan to use you as a spy have originated with Thornhill?"

Courtney looked stunned. How could Lord Edgecomb have guessed that? "Aye. While I thought I was doing thi. evil business to save Thornhill's life, he was laughing at me. He and Richelieu had planned it from the beginning." Courtney's voice carried through the hall of justice, clean and firm.

No one, Rory thought with a fierce welling of pride, would guess what she had been through these last days.

"How did Richelieu approach you?"

Courtney told of her meeting with the cardinal, and of her revulsion at the task he had given her.

"But you agreed?"

"I felt I had no choice."

"Did the queen know what you were doing?"

"Nay." Courtney glanced upward and saw the pale face of her young monarch. "Her Majesty is innocent of any wrongdoing."

At her words, Charles reached over and took his wife's hand. The look he gave her was one of tenderness and regret. At that, a low murmur ran through the crowd. Seeing that sentiment was turning in the queen's favor, Burlingame jumped to his feet.

"The queen is not on trial. Nor is France. It is you, Lady Thornhill, Mistress of the Seas." With a bony finger pointed toward her, he intoned, "I shall prove to this court that the lady did everything in her power to carry out Richelieu's evil plans. I ask that the court hear my testimony and that of a serving wench whom I employed, as well as one of the king's own soldiers, who was witness to the lady's evil scheme.''

"You may be seated, Lady Thornhill," Edgecomb said softly. "We will hear the testimony of the others."

On trembling legs, Courtney walked to the scarred table and took a seat beside Rory. When he glanced at her, she refused to meet his gaze. And when he placed his folded hands on the table, she clutched her own tightly in her lap. She felt cold. So cold. Though Rory was beside her, she felt as though they were oceans apart.

"You should not be here with me," Courtney whispered.

"I vowed to see this through to the end."

The end. She felt a heaviness around her heart. He was here beside her out of some sense of duty. But, though it pained her, she had not the strength to send him away. His presence here brought her comfort. With a sigh, she lifted her head high and faced the stern looks of the judges before her.

For nearly an hour, Lord Burlingame told of the things he had seen and heard on the night he had followed Courtney to her meeting with Richelieu's messenger. He very cleverly avoided any mention of his earlier attack. No one knew about that except the woman who would soon die at the hand of the executioner, and the man beside her. Burlingame exuded confidence. When this was over, he had plans for Rory MacLaren. He would be found dead, the victim of a Frenchman seeking revenge for the death of a loyal spy.

When Burlingame had finished his story, he led the tavern wench and then the soldier through the events of Courtney's last night of freedom. By the time they had finished, the crowd murmured among themselves, convinced that the female pirate was doomed.

Lord Edgecomb, who had been listening intently, stepped forward.

"You said, sir, that you called out a greeting to the lady, and she replied."

The soldier nodded. "That is correct."

"When you gave her the message, did she seem surprised?"

"Yes, my lord. I would say she was surprised."

"Did she say anything to you?"

The soldier thought a moment. "She did say some things. But they meant nothing to me."

"Perhaps they would mean something to this court. Would you repeat what the lady said?"

The soldier glanced at Burlingame for a moment, then away. He was, after all, in the presence of his king. He need not fear the wrath of the king's council.

"She did not wish to go with me. The lady said she would do this no more. After this night, Richelieu would have to find someone else to do his evil deeds."

At this, the mutterings in the crowd grew.

"How did you persuade her to go with you?"

"Lord Burlingame had told me to say anything necessary to convince the lady to go with me. I told her that her father would be aboard the ship in the Channel."

"Did you know that to be true?"

"Nay, my lord. But she had mentioned her father, and I knew that he must be important to her."

Edgecomb paused. "She mentioned her father? What did she say?"

The soldier took a deep breath. "She said that even if Richelieu threatened the safety of her father she could no longer do this thing."

The rumblings of the crowd grew to a roar. Hearing this, Lord Edgecomb pressed his advantage.

"So it is your opinion that the lady was being forced into this business?"

"Aye, my lord. She was most reluctant."

"Thank you."

Edgecomb turned away, feeling for the first time that there was a glimmer of hope. The emotions of the people ran high. But crowds were fickle. Perhaps there was a way to uncover the truth.

"Lady Thornhill. Come forward."

Courtney stood. Forcing her shoulders back and her head high, she approached the bench.

"You have heard the testimony of these people. Is it accurate?"

Courtney nodded. "What has been said about me is true."

Edgecomb watched her a moment, then decided to gamble everything. What Rory had related to him about her tormented dreams and her mysterious memories of the past piqued his curiosity. Since the lady had already been incriminated, there was little to lose.

"You are a puzzle, Lady Thornhill," Edgecomb said in a voice loud enough to carry through the hall. "Raised on a pirate ship by a man not really your father. A French citizen who seems to have no French lineage. A woman who speaks many languages, and has traveled the world, but who has no place she calls home." He fixed her with a piercing look. "Everyone has a place of origin. How did you come to be aboard the *Hawk*?"

Courtney swallowed. How could she explain the bits and pieces of dreams that even she did not understand?

"I am not certain, my lord."

Gently he said, "Tell me what you remember of your early life."

"I remember little before the *Hawk*. Faces from my past are gone. The face of my father has faded. Sometimes..." She paused and glanced at him, then away. "Sometimes I think I remember. But then I realize it is only a dream."

"Tell me about your dreams."

Slowly, without emotion, Courtney told of her early days aboard the *Hawk*. Though at times she paused and at other times felt her eyes brimming, she related everything. The lessons on the stars and navigation. The whippings when she'd disobeyed Thornhill's orders. The time Ian Horn had saved her life and been forced to forfeit his hand.

Though he had known something of her life, Rory found himself spellbound by her story. If it were possible, he loved her even more now that he knew what she had gone through. What a remarkable woman. His first assessment of her, made so long ago aboard the *Hawk*, still held true. She was magnificent.

Glancing around, he realized that the entire crowd shared his fascination with this woman's amazing tale. No one coughed. No one moved.

"This is all very interesting." Lord Burlingame spoke in a loud, sarcastic tone, hoping to break the spell. "But it does not alter the fact that the lady is an admitted spy."

Edgecomb nodded. "Correct, Lord Burlingame. But who among us might not have done the same thing to survive? Lady Thornhill has shown an indomitable will to endure every imaginable hardship."

The crowd murmured their agreement.

"We waste precious time," Burlingame shouted. "Your king asks for a verdict of guilty."

The judges began whispering among themselves.

"Have you told us everything, Lady Thornhill?" Lord Edgecomb felt the last flicker of hope fade and begin to die. Burlingame had won. She would die at the hands of the executioner. And with her something precious would die, as well. A beautiful soul, a free spirit.

Courtney thought a moment. Truth. Lord Edgecomb, her friend, had urged her to tell the truth. She was determined to do that much before facing the executioner.

"I believe that is all, my lord. I have tried to recall my life before the *Hawk*. But it is gone from my memory. I think seeing Lady Montieth lying in a pool of blood was too shocking for a child so young. Not wishing to share her fate, I did whatever I had to do to survive in the company of rough strangers."

She glanced up in time to see Lord Edgecomb dropping to his knees, his face ashen. His hands gripped the edge of the table so hard, that his fingers were white from the effort.

The crowd gasped as Rory raced to Edgecomb's side and caught him just before he slumped to the floor.

"Majesty." Edgecomb's voice was choked with emotion. "I beg you a moment."

"No more mercy," Burlingame shouted. "It is time for justice."

"You mentioned the name Lady Montieth," Edgecomb said as he rose, clutching Rory's arm tightly to keep his knees from buckling.

Seeing his distress, Courtney started toward him. Edgecomb waved her back, staring at her so intently that she was alarmed. Had he, too, turned against her?

"Lady Montieth was the name of my nurse. When our ship was attacked by the *Hawk*, she chose to die rather than reveal where I was hidden."

"I beg you, Majesty," Edgecomb croaked. "Allow me a moment to compose myself. It appears I have just been reunited with my daughter, Anne. A daughter I believed dead all these many years."

Chapter Twenty-three

The hall of justice erupted into chaos. While many, having heard Lord Edgecomb's emotional words, began to shout, others burst into tears.

For a long moment Courtney stood frozen, watching as Rory lowered Edgecomb to the floor and called for water.

Moving as if in a trance, she made her way to the council table and sat down stiffly, unaware of what was happening around her.

This was not possible, she told herself. She felt strangely calm. She had been prepared to die for her crimes against the throne. She had even steeled herself against Rory's cold rejection. But nothing could have prepared her for this.

Edgecomb was merely overwrought, she cautioned herself. He had found the thought of her execution repugnant, and so he had devised a way to hold off, for a few minutes longer, the sentence he knew would be imposed by the judges. She smiled to herself. What an extraordinary man. She had liked him from the moment they had met. But her father?

She watched as the older man got to his feet and consulted with the other judges. When he turned to glance at her, she was surprised by the depth of the emotion in his eyes.

After a few minutes Rory took his seat beside Courtney, staring at her intently. They spoke not a word. It was as if they had lost the power of speech.

Burlingame, beside himself with anger, shouted above the din. "By all that is right and holy, I demand an end to this farce and a verdict of guilty for this French spy."

The king touched Burlingame's arm and spoke quietly. Then, motioning to Edgecomb, Charles asked, "Are you prepared to continue, Lord Edgecomb?"

"I am, Majesty."

Edgecomb motioned to Courtney to approach the bench once more. Reluctantly she did as she was told.

"Is Lady Thornhill your real name?" Edgecomb asked.

"It is the name Cardinal Richelieu gave me when he pressed me into service as the queen's lady-in-waiting."

"By what name were you known before that time?"

"Courtney, my lord."

"Just Courtney? Have you no other name?"

She thought a minute. "When Thornhill discovered me hidden in the wardrobe, he discovered a trunk with some papers as well. On one of them he read my name. He told me that I was named Anne Courtney Elizabeth. And he asked me to choose one."

"You chose Courtney?"

"Aye."

"Why?"

She gave a roguish smile. "To my child's mind, I felt as though I would not be disobeying Lady Montieth's instructions as long as I did not give my real name. In time, Courtney became my real name."

"This is all very interesting, my lord," Burlingame said, "but unless the lady has some proof of what she says, it is simply a lovely story devised to win our sympathy."

Lord Edgecomb said gently, "Do you have the papers that Thornhill took from the trunk?"

"Nay." Courtney felt her heart sink. Why did he continue to lift her hopes, only to dash them?

"If the lady has no proof, I demand that the justices consider the body of evidence against her and return a verdict." Burlingame was nearly beside himself with fury.

Edgecomb studied the beautiful young woman before him. Did she resemble her mother, especially around the eyes? Or was he searching for something that was not there? There was a terrible ache in his heart that had been there for years. For too long now he had kept these feelings buried. Buried as he had known his wife and daughter were buried. But now, if there was even a glimmer of hope that this young woman could be his daughter...

"There is nothing, then? Nothing of your childhood that Thornhill left you?"

Courtney started to shake her head. As she did so, she felt the slight movement of the medallion that rested between her breasts.

"Only this." She lifted the chain from around her neck and handed it to him. "Captain Thornhill took this from me when he found me. I never saw it again until he lay dead on the deck of the *Hawk*. When I bent to him for a last goodbye, I removed it."

Lord Edgecomb took the medallion in his hands, then surprised everyone in the room by crying out and lifting it to his lips.

Climbing the steps to the king's throne, he handed the medallion to Charles and said loudly, "This medallion bears the Edgecomb motto, which reads in Latin, Heart, Hand, Soul, to England Forever."

The king nodded as he read the inscription, then passed it to Burlingame, who sat scowling beside him.

"This medallion was given to me by my dear friend, your father, King James I, when I drove the traitor the duke of Thornlea from English shores. Because of his plea for mercy, King James spared his life, but banished him forever from England. Thornlea swore revenge upon me and my family. And has exacted it in the most cruel, inhuman way."

Once again the crowd erupted into shouts and cries. Most of the crowd could still remember the cruelty of the traitor Thornlea, who had betrayed England and the crown.

For long minutes Courtney could only stare at Edgecomb. Her mind seemed unable to grasp all that was happening. Thornhill was a traitor to England? Thornhill was actually Thornlea, whose name was still cursed on these shores? She thought about all the repressed fury inside him. May God forgive him. He had brought it on himself.

"After the death of my beloved wife, I saw to it that my daughter was always with me," Edgecomb said. "But I feared trouble in Ireland and decided to send her to safety. When I sent my young daughter and her nurse back to England, I placed this medallion about my daughter's neck. Many months later I learned that the English ship, the *Admiralty*, had been attacked by pirates. All aboard were believed dead."

Lord Edgecomb took the medallion from Burlingame's hands. Seeing the look of hatred on the councillor's face, he deliberately turned his back on him and strode to the row of judges.

"I declare that this young woman is my daughter, Anne Courtney Elizabeth. I declare further that my sworn enemy, the duke of Thornlea, took to the waters as a pirate and, out of a sense of revenge, did steal my daughter and raise her in his own image."

"Majesty." Burlingame jumped to his feet and began pacing in an effort to think of some way to regain control of the trial. "Whether or not the woman is Edgecomb's long-lost daughter, she is still an admitted spy for France. We cannot allow sentiment to sway us from our course."

The king studied Burlingame for a long moment, then allowed his gaze to wander to where Edgecomb stood facing the young woman. Though they stood far apart, he could feel their yearning to touch, to embrace.

"Anne Courtney Elizabeth," the king said in a tone of authority. "Do you believe that you are truly the daughter of the Lord Edgecomb?"

She seemed stunned by his question.

"I know not what to think, Majesty."

The king's voice was grave. "It is within my power to offer you freedom in exchange for your oath of loyalty."

Courtney's eyes widened as she realized what was being offered. With tears threatening to spill over, she sank to her knees. Instantly Lord Edgecomb was beside her, lifting her to her feet.

She felt her hand being engulfed in Lord Edgecomb's grasp and closed her fingers around his. In a faltering voice, she said, "I would swear my loyalty, Majesty. Not because it will save my life, though I want now more than anything to live. And not because it will please my father, if he is truly my father, because he is your greatest ally. But because I have found what I most longed for. Here in England, at long last, I have found a home."

Behind them, Rory MacLaren struggled with a warring of emotions. Never could he have imagined this strange turn of events.

"Come forward, Anne Courtney Elizabeth." The king's voice was grave.

On trembling legs, Courtney walked up the steps that led to the throne upon which the king sat. Beside her, Lord Edgecomb walked, his head high, his gaze firmly fixed on her.

"Kneel," the king commanded.

Courtney knelt at his feet. Beside her, Lord Edgecomb placed his hand on her shoulder.

"Do you swear loyalty to England?"

Courtney swallowed the lump in her throat. "I do."

"And do you swear to obey its laws and to defend its shores with your very life?"

Tears welled up in her eyes, and in a blur Courtney lifted her head and glanced at Henrietta Maria, and then at King Charles. "I do."

"Anne Courtney Elizabeth, I accept your oath of loyalty. And in exchange I grant you freedom. May you live a long and happy life as an English citizen."

"Thank you, Majesty."

"And now, child," the king said with a smile, "I suggest you embrace your father. It has been a very long time since he held you."

"Father." With a sob, Courtney stood and threw herself into his arms.

Edgecomb, tears streaming down his face, drew her against him and pressed his lips to her temple.

The king and queen, caught up in the moment, stood and embraced them, as well. The entire crowd began cheering.

"This trial is ended," one of the judges intoned.

As the crowd began filing from the hall of justice, Courtney suddenly gasped and drew a little away from her father. Turning to the king, she cried loudly, "Forgive me, Majesty. My father asked only one thing of me this day. The truth. In the turmoil of discovery, I had forgotten the most important fact of all."

Those who were leaving turned back to hear her. The justices, many of whom were already standing, paused to learn what new thing would be revealed.

Out of the corner of her eye, Courtney saw Burlingame making his way toward an alcove that led to a courtyard.

"While I was in prison, Majesty, Lord Burlingame admitted to me that he was the one who planned to betray you. He is working with Cardinal Richelieu of France."

Loud gasps were heard from the crowd. The king looked thunderstruck.

"This is a most serious accusation, child. Are you prepared to defend it?"

"Aye," she said, meeting his narrowed look.

Before the crowd could react, Rory leapt over the council table and ran toward the alcove. As Burlingame disappeared, Rory drew his sword and followed.

The fire burned low, and still Courtney and Lord Edgecomb sat together, talking in hushed tones. Though he had filled in the gaps in much of her early life, her father knew that she listened with only half a mind. Her mind and heart were in the forest with Rory MacLaren.

Though the king had sent his soldiers to search for the evil Burlingame, the two men would be far ahead of them. The man most likely to find the traitor was Rory. And when he did, there would most certainly be a battle to the death.

"You grow weary, my dear one. Try to rest for a little while. As soon as Rory returns, I will send him to your room."

"I have such strange, troubling feelings." Standing, she paced the room, then paused to wrap her arms around herself, as if to stave off a chill. "Ever since I arrived at the castle I have sensed something about this room. What is it, Father?"

"This was our suite of rooms whenever we visited the palace. You slept in a small trundle beside my bed. You often lay on this very settle with your nurse."

Had she not sensed it? Had she not known this room before ever examining it?

"I cannot remember my mother," Courtney said sadly.

"She died giving you life. She was much like you, my dear. Beautiful, delightful to be with and a bit of a rebel. Her death was a terrible blow to me. But when I lost you, as well, I thought I would never recover from the loss."

"We are together now," she said, touching a hand to his cheek. "And nothing will ever part us again."

He embraced her, then watched as, restless once more, Courtney paced to the alcove to peer out the window. "I remember standing on a trunk and looking out over the grounds."

"Already you are remembering. In time it will all come back to you." Lord Edgecomb noted the way she strained in vain for a glimpse of the soldiers returning. "But for now you must rest. You have been through too much."

Kissing her tenderly on the lips, he turned her toward the bed. "Sleep now. I will send Rory to you as soon as he returns."

She swallowed back the protest that sprang to her lips. Though she feared for Rory's safety, she was too weary to go on. Bidding her father good-night, she shed her clothes and climbed wearily into bed. Within minutes she was sound asleep.

Though she heard not a sound, Courtney awoke and sensed that she was not alone in the room. Lying very still, she peered through the darkness. Red-hot coals from the dying fire bathed the room in an eerie glow. From somewhere below, in the courtyard, she heard the blowing and stamping of a horse. Glancing toward the balcony, she saw a slight movement of the heavy draperies.

Rory. Her heart leaped to her throat, and she tossed aside the bedcovers. At long last Rory had come back to her.

As she swung her legs to the floor, a strong arm came around her throat, cutting off her breath. Before she could cry out, a hand covered her mouth.

"Make not a sound, my lady, or it shall be your last."

Her eyes widened at the sound of the familiar voice. Lord Burlingame.

With his hand still firmly covering her mouth, he began dragging her toward the balcony.

Courtney's heart hammered painfully in her chest.

"It is because of you that I am a hunted man," he hissed in her ear. "It is only right that you buy my safe passage to France. I think, after that tender display with the king, his soldiers will be reluctant to risk your life to kill me."

As they stepped onto the balcony, Courtney pulled away.

"This is madness. You cannot hope to force me to accompany to you all the way to France."

"You have no choice, my lady. You will be my shield against the soldiers' attack, or you will die here. Which will it be?"

"There is a third choice," a voice said from the darkness.

Courtney and Burlingame turned startled faces toward the figure looming in the shadows.

"Rory." Her heart soared at the sight of him.

"Step aside, Courtney. Burlingame and I have a score to settle."

Before she could pull away, Burlingame hauled her against him and brandished his sword. "Put down your weapon, MacLaren, or I will run the lady through."

Rory's voice was chilling. "If you harm her, you will not live to see Fleet Prison."

"I have no intention of ever going to Fleet." Burlingame drew the blade of the sword firmly against Courtney's throat. "I have no qualms about killing the lady."

Rory had no doubt that Burlingame would make good his threat. Slowly, watching him through slitted eyes, Rory handed his sword to Burlingame.

As Burlingame reached for it, Rory yanked Courtney free and threw her roughly aside. Caught by surprise, Burlingame struck out with his sword. Rory ducked, and the blade sang past his shoulder, shattering a looking glass that fell to the floor with a terrible crash. A moment later, as Burlingame lifted his sword for a second attack, Rory brought his hand up in a wide arc. Moonlight glinted on the blade of the dagger in his hand.

"A female pirate taught me to always carry two weapons," Rory said, dancing aside.

From her vantage point beside the fireplace, Courtney watched anxiously.

As Burlingame drove home his blade with a powerful thrust, Rory leaped aside, and the blade embedded itself in the door behind him. Startled, Burlingame pulled his hand away empty and bent to retrieve Rory's sword, which lay at his feet.

With a swift kick, Rory sent the sword flying across the floor.

He faced his opponent with a look of triumph.

Fearfully Burlingame began backing away. With each step he took, Rory took one, as well, until Burlingame found himself backed against the wall.

"You cannot kill me," Burlingame whimpered. "I have no weapon."

"I listened once to your plea for mercy," Rory said through clenched teeth. "And because of that, you caused much pain and suffering. You cannot be allowed to go on with your lies and deception."

"What I did, I did for England," Burlingame cried. "Charles is a weak monarch. He is infatuated with his French-born wife. Under her influence, he will destroy this land."

"And you and the evil Richelieu would strengthen this land?" Rory gave a hollow laugh. "You cannot expect anyone to believe such swill. You are a shallow, vicious man, Burlingame. You tried to force yourself on Courtney as you have with so many fine women who were helpless to stop you in your lust for power. It is the same lust that drove you to betray your king. You covet the throne."

"If I destroy Charles, it will all be mine." Burlingame's eyes glittered. "And if you help me, MacLaren, I will share the spoils with you."

"I have no desire to share your ill-gotten gains. You must die now, Burlingame, as so many have died at your hand."

As Rory stepped closer and lifted the dagger, a voice from the doorway stopped him.

"Hold your weapon, my friend. All of England must be allowed to witness the death of this villain."

Stunned, Courtney turned to see the king framed in the doorway. Behind him stood the queen and Lord Edgecomb.

"I have heard enough to know that everything Lord Burlingame has been accused of is true. The citizens of this good land deserve the right to observe his trial and punishment."

With a feeling of frustration, Rory obediently lowered the dagger. At a command from the king, several soldiers entered and hauled Burlingame away.

As soon as they had gone, Lord Edgecomb hurried to Courtney's side.

"Are you safe, my child?"

She nodded, watching as Rory sheathed his dagger and bent to retrieve his sword. Seeing the direction of her gaze, Edgecomb hurried to Rory's side and extended his hand.

"I am in your debt, Rory MacLaren. Had you not discovered Burlingame in time, he would have surely brought harm to my daughter."

Rory accepted his outstretched hand before turning away, avoiding Courtney's gaze.

"All of England is in your debt, Rory." Charles strode forward and clapped a hand on his friend's shoulder. "Come. We will lift a tankard to our good fortune."

"Aye. A tankard would be most welcome." Rory turned and bowed to Courtney and her father. "I bid you both good-night."

As he left the room, Courtney felt her heart plummet. He had saved her life this night. And yet he had left her certain that he wanted nothing more to do with her.

She stared at the coals, which had burned low until they were little more than ashes. The fire that had been their love had once burned hot and bright, but since her betrayal there was nothing left but ashes. Cold, lifeless ashes.

She turned away to hide the tears that stung her eyes. She had been granted her freedom. She had found the father she had never known. But because of the choices she had made, she had lost the only man she would ever love.

Chapter Twenty-four

Shirtless, Rory leaned a hip against the balcony and stared into the distance. Dawn colored the eastern sky. The sun slowly rose over the horizon, bathing the fields in a hazy pink glow.

During this long, sleepless night he had thought of nothing but Courtney. At long last she had found her home and was discovering herself, as well. She now knew that she was of noble ancestry. What was more important, she had been reunited with her long-lost father. Courtney and Lord Edgecomb deserved a lifetime together to regain all that had been lost to them. After years of hardship and struggle, she could finally put away her painful past and make a place for herself as heir to a life of quality. There could be no place in her life for him now. He would only serve as a painful reminder of all that had come before. A past she would prefer to put to rest. She deserved better. A woman like Courtney deserved to be pampered, to be indulged.

Rory knew he had tarried too long in England. Courtney had been the reason. But now he had to face the truth. As much as he had come to love this green island, he had a terrible yearning for Scotland. His land beckoned. His people needed him. His clan looked to him for leadership, for counsel. It was time to go home.

Home. He could understand Courtney's longing for a
ome. He had no right to deprive her of her hard-won vic-
ory, no right to ask her to give up all that she had found.

Turning from the window, he lifted a tunic from the bed
nd slipped it over his head.

He had prolonged the agony of parting long enough. The
ime had come. Squaring his shoulders, he made his way to
he great hall, where he knew the others would be breaking
heir morning fast.

Courtney sat between Lord Edgecomb and Henrietta
Maria. Around her the conversation was animated as
Charles and Lord Edgecomb discussed the events of the
ast few days. The king was obviously overjoyed at the
ood fortune of his old friend.

Though Courtney had been told by her father that she
ad inherited a fortune in gold and jewelry, as well as a
hare of vast properties throughout England, it meant
othing to her. She gazed around the hall, feeling a terri-
le emptiness. How strange life was. She had spent her
outh yearning for home and family, but now that she had
een granted her wish, it had been proven an empty prom-
se. Because of one man. Rory MacLaren. He had dared to
lo what no other man had. He had dared to touch her. And
er life would never be the same. Home, family, fortune.
All would be empty without him.

The object of her thoughts strode into the great hall. He
was dressed for travel, wearing tight breeches tucked into
is tall black boots. A dark wool cape had been tossed
carelessly over his shoulders. In one hand he held a plumed
at. His shaggy dark hair curled softly around his collar.
The sunlight streaming through the tall windows illumi-
ated the occasional russet strands. Courtney longed to
each out a hand to smooth a wayward lock. Instead, she
urled her hands into fists in her lap.

"So, MacLaren. It looks as though you are leaving us."

"Aye, Majesty. It is time."

Courtney showed no expression when she heard the ex change. If she seemed a trifle pale, it would be blamed o the events of the past week. If her body trembled, it was t be expected after her cruel treatment at the hands of Lor Burlingame.

"You will return from time to time, will you not?"

"Aye, Majesty. Though Scotland holds my heart, I hav a fondness for England." Rory carefully avoided glancin at Courtney, but he was painfully aware of her, pale an silent beside her father.

"How can I ever thank you?" Lord Edgecomb stoo and extended his hand. "If not for you, Rory, I woul never have found my daughter."

"Thanks are not necessary, my friend. I am grateful tha your long grief has ended."

Henrietta Maria stood and placed a hand on Rory' sleeve. As the others pushed away from the table and be gan to gather around him, she said gently, "I know what i is you do, Rory MacLaren. I believe you are a rare and no ble man."

"Not noble, Majesty. Practical." His voice lowered, h spoke for her ears alone. "I have no claim here. I must see my future elsewhere."

With a thoughtful look, the queen turned to stud Courtney.

Rory steeled himself for this final confrontation. As hi gaze met Courtney's he felt the jolt and resisted the im pulse to drag her into his arms and crush her to him.

With studied discipline he bent over her hand and lifte it to his lips.

Courtney felt a rush of heat and drew her hand away a if it had been burned. "Thank you for all you did for me Rory." Her voice trembled, and she prayed no one too notice.

"Do not thank me, my lady. I am grateful you have bee reunited with your father. At last you have your heart' desire. A home."

"Aye." She swallowed back the lump that sprang to her throat. She must not weep here, in public. There would be time for that later. A lifetime of tears, in fact. A lifetime of tears and heartache loomed endlessly before her.

"Do you leave immediately?" Henrietta Maria asked.

"Aye. I see a long, hard journey ahead of me." And a lonely one, he thought. The days would be tolerable. He would keep his mind busy during the long, arduous trip. But the nights... If they were all as pain-filled as this past night, he would almost rather face death.

"Safe journey, Rory MacLaren." Courtney looked away, avoiding his eyes. She could not bear to think about the times those blue eyes had looked at her with love. "May God ride with you."

"I wish—" For a moment he could not go on. What he wished was to kiss her mouth until she cried his name. What he wished was a lifetime to show her how much he loved her. Sometimes love meant turning away from the one you most wanted, for a noble reason. If he truly loved her, he must do what was best for her.

"What do you wish?" Her voice nearly broke.

"I wish you a long and happy life, my lady."

He turned away from her. Bowing to the king and queen, he saluted them smartly and strode from the room.

For a moment, no one spoke, Then, suddenly overcome by emotion, Courtney bolted from the room.

Alone in her bedchamber, she threw herself across the bed and wept the scalding tears she had so carefully held back until now. Rory had gone out of her life. Forever. As abruptly as he had entered. Because of him, everything about her had changed. Because of him, she had been touched in a special way. And nothing would ever again be the same.

She felt the bed sag. A soft hand touched her shoulder.

Henrietta Maria watched in silence as her young friend struggled to stem the flow of tears.

"Why?" Courtney wiped her eyes and sat up. "Why did he leave me?"

"Because he loves you."

"Love?" Courtney began to weep once more, more softly now, with a feeling of despair.

"Yes, love. Rory MacLaren is a noble man who thinks only of placing another's needs before his own."

"Noble." Courtney sprang to her feet and began to prowl the room. Stopping before the balcony, she peered at the feverish activity in the courtyard below. Wagons and pack horses were being loaded with trunks, while more horses were saddled and weapons readied. "Is it noble to refuse to forgive me my sins against England?"

"Is that what you think?" Henrietta Maria watched as Courtney continued to prowl the room.

"Aye. I lied to him. He cannot forgive my deception. Also, he is a man of action. He grows tired of the soft life here at court. He returns to his own country to find a woman worthy of the MacLaren name."

"If you believe that, you are a fool. Anyone can see that the man is obsessed with you. His heart near breaks each time he looks your way."

"Nay. If that were true, he would take me with him."

"And deny you the chance to treasure your newfound home and father? Never. A man like Rory would choose another path."

Courtney went very still. Could this be true? Was Rory leaving because he loved her? She turned and stared for a long moment at the queen. Thoughtfully she whispered, "I thank you, Majesty. But now I must be alone."

Henrietta Maria embraced her young friend and hurried from the room. A frown furrowed her brow. Perhaps she should not have meddled. But she understood only too well the tender, uncertain feelings of young love. Her own marriage to Charles had withstood terrible tensions. But they had overcome the first obstacles to happiness. And, hopefully, they would grow stronger in their love.

Love. Henrietta Maria shook her head as she hurried to rejoin her husband. It was strange and terrible. And wonderful.

Rory moved among the men and horses, checking the supplies. It would be good to begin the journey. Once started, there would be no turning back. The worst would be over.

"All is in readiness," the captain of the guards reported.

"Aye. Order the men to mount."

As Rory pulled himself into the saddle, a blur of color caught his eye. Glancing toward the balcony of Courtney's room, he blinked and looked again. His eyes had not deceived him. It was Courtney.

She wore tight breeches tucked into tall black boots, her crimson blouse and a bright yellow sash. Her hair streamed down her back in a cloud of tangled curls. She was as he had first seen her aboard the *Hawk*, a fearless pirate. She lowered herself to the ground on a rope, a sword hanging in a scabbard at her side.

At the sight of her, all activity in the courtyard came to an abrupt halt. Men who were pulling themselves into the saddle froze. Soldiers who were carrying supplies stopped in midstride.

"So, MacLaren." She stood and drew her sword, feet apart as if to do battle. "You would leave me here while you return to Scotland?"

"Aye, my lady."

"You would have me wed to some ailing old count?"

Inwardly he winced. Outwardly he showed no expression. "If that is what you wish."

"Ah. My wishes are to be considered, then?"

He shot her a puzzled look. What was she up to? "Aye, my lady. Your wishes are always uppermost in my mind."

Courtney strode across the courtyard until she was standing directly in front of his mount. Every man watched

her with a mixture of surprise and admiration. The lad
was the most extraordinary woman any of them had eve
seen.

"Have you forgiven me for drugging you, my lord?"

"Forgiven? It is in the past."

"And my spying. Is that also forgiven?"

"Can I do less than the king himself? It is truly for
given, my lady. You did what was necessary to survive."

Courtney took a deep breath. This had been a terribl
gamble. She could only hope that Henrietta Maria wa
correct.

"Why, then, do you leave me, Rory MacLaren?"

Rory looked away. Damn her. How much longer coul
he endure her beauty without giving in to the need to touc
her? "I leave you here to enjoy your home and father."

"I am most grateful for your noble offer. I would like
one day, to visit my properties. To walk the paths m
mother walked. I love my father," she added softly, "an
I wish to know him better." Her voice then rose. "But
yearn to see this land of yours, Rory MacLaren. This Scot
land of which you spoke so lovingly. I wish to travel th
rugged forests you described, to swim in the clear cryst
lakes. I desire to call your clan my people."

"This cannot be."

For a moment she was taken aback. He was rejecting her
Her offer of love. Then, clutching her sword tighter fo
courage, she took a deep breath. "You are ashamed to a
low a pirate to share the MacLaren name?"

"Ashamed?" His eyes narrowed in hot anger. "How
could the man who loves you ever be ashamed of you?"

She lifted her sword in a battle stance. "You speak o
love when you are leaving me?"

"Love. Aye, love," he said when she opened her mouth
to make further protest. "I love you, Courtney. And hav
from the first moment I saw you. But I would be selfish t
deny you this chance to get to know the father you have al
ways sought, the home your heart has yearned for."

"You are the home my heart desires, Rory MacLaren."

He sat, unmoving, as her words washed over him. When at last he found his voice he said, "Your father..."

"...will come to visit. Scotland is not so very far away, after all."

For a long moment Rory absorbed what she had just said. "You would give up all this for my land? My people?"

"Our land. Our people." She tossed aside the sword. "I had intended to force you, if need be, to take me with you. I had no doubt that I could best you in a duel."

Hearing this, Rory threw back his head and roared. "Modesty has never been one of your virtues, my lady."

"Nor shyness one of yours. Why do you hold back from me now?"

"Why, indeed? Come here, Courtney."

As he leaned from the saddle, she threw herself into his outstretched arms. He drew her to his chest and held her in a fierce embrace.

"MacLaren."

At the sound of the king's voice, Rory and Courtney looked up to see the king and queen, along with Lord Edgecomb and half the palace staff, watching from the windows, doorways and balconies of the palace.

"I would seek your permission, Lord Edgecomb, to wed your daughter."

"I give it gladly. From the looks of her, I would say she was prepared to go to the ends of the earth with you. You both have my blessing, Rory MacLaren. I know you will treasure Courtney as I do. And I wish you courage and patience. If she is anything like her mother, you will need both."

Rory laughed before turning to the king. "And you, Majesty. Have I your blessing?"

Charles placed an arm around his wife's shoulders. Both of them smiled down at the couple below. "Aye, MacLaren. It was always my fondest wish that you would wed an Englishwoman, so you would be induced to visit our fair land often."

"And you, Majesty, must visit Scotland. We would ask you and the queen to be godparents to our firstborn."

"Indeed we shall. I would like Henrietta Maria to see the land of my ancestors. This will give us a reason to visit as often as time will permit."

"Forgive me, Father," Courtney called from the safety of Rory's arms, "for this abrupt departure."

"I understand, my dear. Love has a strange way of altering all our plans."

"Rory, my friend," the king called, "in the name of the Crown, I pronounce you wed. Though I suspect that the clan MacLaren will demand a fine big wedding for their leader."

"Aye. And they shall have it."

As Rory wheeled his mount, Courtney turned for a final wave. "Farewell, Father."

As they led the parade of mounted men through the courtyard, Courtney waved to the cheering household staff before snuggling close against Rory's chest.

"How many days before we reach Scotland?"

His breath was warm against her cheek as he brought his lips to her ear. "We will be a long time on this journey." He grazed her cheek and felt the heat spread through his limbs. "A very long time. We stop at yonder forest."

"So soon?"

"Aye. I can wait no longer than that, my love, to lie with you again. We may have to postpone our journey many days, in fact."

She smiled and drew his head down. Their lips met in a slow, lingering kiss. Instantly the fire spread.

"I love you, Rory MacLaren," she murmured against his lips.

"And I you, my beloved Mistress of the Seas."

His lips covered hers in a savage kiss that bordered on desperation.

At his signal, the long line of men and horses halted. All eyes watched as Rory's mount sped toward the forest. But the man and woman locked in a tender embrace had eyes only for each other.

Epilogue

Rory sat before the fire and watched as his wife descended the wide stone stairs. Since their arrival in Scotland, Castle MacLaren had become a place of warmth. Of love. The MacLaren clan had taken her to their hearts as one born among them. They would die for her if need be.

"You grow more beautiful with each day." He drew her into his arms and pressed his lips to her temple.

"And fatter." She touched a hand to her swollen stomach, and he tenderly placed his hand over hers.

"How many more days?"

She smiled. It was a secret smile, a woman's smile. "Soon. Very soon you shall have your son."

"And how would you know it is to be a boy?"

"I know. We will call him Malcolm, for the brother you lost."

Overcome by emotion, he drew her closer. "Charles and Henrietta Maria are accompanying your father for the christening. They arrive within a fortnight."

"It will be so good to see them."

For a moment he looked worried. "Do you miss them very much?"

"Rory, my love." Touching a finger to his lips, she traced their fullness before brushing her own over them. "This time spent alone with you has been the happiest of my life."

"And mine, my love."

He drew a settle close to the fire and sat, pulling her onto his lap.

As she stared into the flames, she thought about the strange events that had brought her to this beautiful land. The journey from lonely pirate to contented wife had been a long one. But in the end she had so much more than she had ever dreamed. Home, husband, child and love. After a lifetime of danger and intrigue, this was the greatest adventure. Love. Enough love to fill her life forever.

There was no hope in that time and place
But there would be another lifetime...

The warrior died at her feet, his blood running out of the cave entrance and mingling with the waterfall. With his last breath he cursed the woman. Told her that her spirit would remain chained in the cave forever until a child was created and born there.

So goes the ancient legend of the Chained Lady and the curse that bound her throughout the ages—until destiny brought Diana Prentice and Colby Savagar together under the influence of forces beyond their understanding. Suddenly each was haunted by dreams that linked past and present, while their waking hours were fraught with danger. Only when Colby, Diana's modern-day warrior, learned to love could those dark forces be vanquished. Only then could Diana set the Chained Lady free....

Next month, Harlequin Temptation and the intrepid Jayne Ann Krentz bring you Harlequin's first true sequel—

DREAMS, Parts 1 and 2

Look for this two-part epic tale, the

Temptation

"Editors' Choice."

Spot-1A

Harlequin Temptation dares to be different!

Once in a while, we Temptation editors spot a romance that's truly innovative. To make sure *you* don't miss any one of these outstanding selections, we'll mark them for you.

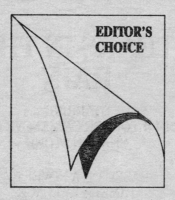

EDITOR'S CHOICE

When the "Editors' Choice" fold-back appears on a Temptation cover, you'll know we've found that extra-special page-turner!

THE *Temptation* EDITORS

Harlequin Romance Movie ™

TEARS IN THE RAIN

STARRING
CHRISTOPHER CAVZENOVE AND
SHARON STONE

BASED ON A NOVEL BY
PAMELA WALLACE

PREMIERING IN NOVEMBER

TITR-1

Exclusively on

SHOWTIME ®